THE SHACKLETONS

— of —

COATES LANE

LORNA HUNTING

Published by Goldcrest Books International Ltd
www.goldcrestbooks.com
publish@goldcrestbooks.com

ISBN: 978-1-913719-99-9

This book is dedicated to Rosanna with whom I shared many a trek to The Temple folly and back at school when rain stopped play.

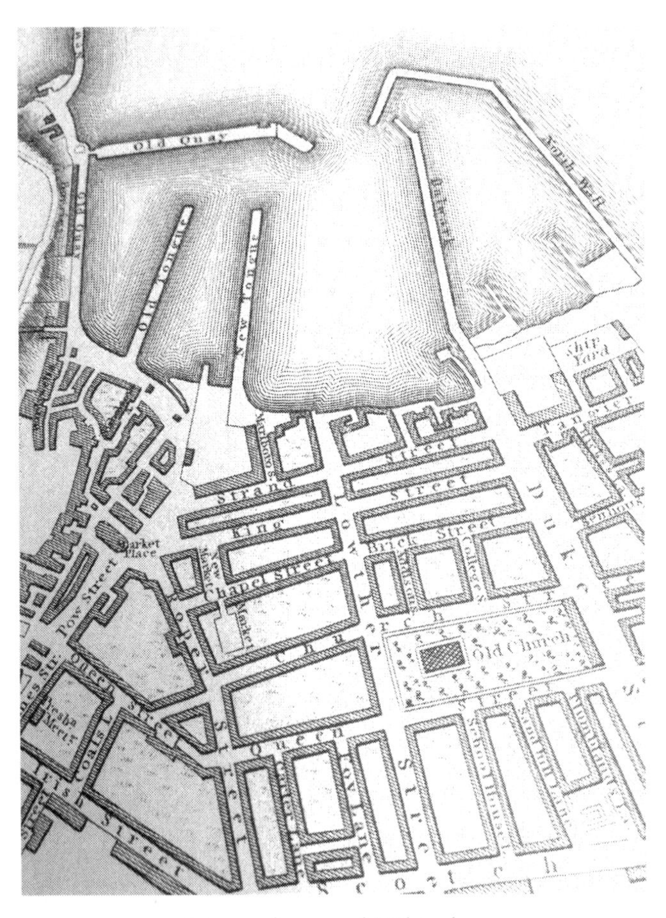

Map of central Whitehaven

CHAPTER ONE

Whitehaven February 20th 1861

On his way to the Gentlemen's Club at the Lonsdale Hotel, Fergus stopped, brushed his fringe from his forehead and checked his watch. He had just time to take the long route and cut down Roper Street for a stroll along the harbour front. With his parents absent, he was overseeing not just the business of his own shipping line, but also his father's, and with Shackleton & Company having three ships loading, he could scan them and check progress along the way. Normally he would drop by the Indian King when passing this way and see his fiancée Becky, but however delightful the thought he knew it would delay him, so he satisfied himself with glancing up at the building. The windows were wide open, which meant the upstairs guest rooms had been serviced and air was being drawn in to freshen them. Dolly, Becky's mother, was obsessed with her overnight rooms not being 'sticky'.

On reaching the harbour, Fergus saw that the quayside was bustling with men and boys loading cargo and supplies yet there seemed to be fewer ships. He was forced to keep sidestepping to avoid tripping over casks and ropes. An impatient wind was blowing in off the sea and Fergus could taste its salt on his lips. Gulls ducked and dived, searching for discarded fish scraps. Of his father's ships, two were close to finishing loading and the third was casting off its ropes. Several of the crew recognised him and raised their caps.

Fergus's own ship, the Sophie Alice, the second ship in his Louisa Line, was also in the harbour. Fergus stopped to speak to the first mate. 'Good to see all progressing, Sven.'

The tall, sturdily built Norwegian transferred a weather-beaten canvas bag from his left shoulder to his right. 'It's much easier now we don't have so many big ships to manoeuvre around. More room in the harbour and fewer men getting in our way on the quay.'

They chatted for a few minutes about the new harbour master, then Fergus continued on his way along the quay. With Sven's comment about the big ships ringing in his ears, he saw a less advantageous side to the changing situation. There were fewer ships because the bigger ones were moving to Liverpool permanently. Whilst that did mean less crowding in the harbour, the loss of these ships also signalled a drop of trade for the town. This would affect not just the shipbuilders and repairers, but also the chandlers supplying the ships. In addition, there would be fewer tying up fees to maintain the harbour's fabric. Whitehaven would continue to be an important harbour, Fergus felt sure, but there was no doubt things were changing. As he entered the Lonsdale Hotel, a steward was cleaning the 'Gentlemen Only' plaque outside the club rooms. The acrid smell of brass polish caught the back of Fergus's nose and he thought for a moment he was going to sneeze.

The steward stepped forward. 'Good morning, Mr Shackleton, sir,' he said, opening the door.

Fergus acknowledged his greeting and, after handing him his topcoat and hat, proceeded to scan the room for Bill McRae, his Louisa Line business partner and friend. He found him sitting in a bay window, a pot of coffee on the table in front of him. Fergus made his way over, greeted his friend, and ordered coffee with wafers, before taking two sheets of folded paper from his pocket, one of which he gave to Bill.

'There's much we need to attend to,' Fergus said. 'I've made a list for us both with the main topics. You'll see straight away that you have free range on all matters at sea with the Sophie Alice, as does Captain Jessop on the *Eleanor Bell.*'

Bill unfolded the paper. 'I'm happy with that. You're continuing to oversee the business administration? Are you finding it a bit of a struggle running two companies?'

'I can't deny it would be easier not to have to oversee Shackleton & Company, but Father has put his trust in me.'

'Will he take up management again when he returns?'

'I doubt Mother will let him; he's hinted he's going to make more shares in the business over to me, which indicates he was serious last year about stepping back. I've made enquiries about employing a bookkeeper at the

Chapel Street warehouse in the meantime, someone to keep our books in order. It's a waste of my time when I could be drumming up business.'

'Good idea.'

'I approached Mr Rudd and he says he's enough with Shackletons' accounting. Trouble is he's known me since I was a boy, and still calls me by my Christian name. So, I felt it necessary to send a memorandum to the office staff instructing them that as I'm now running the business in Father's absence it's no longer appropriate that they refer to me simply as Fergus.'

'What did you suggest they call you?'

'It's a slight change, but in my opinion an important one. From now on they are to refer to me at all times as "Mr Fergus".'

'Appropriate while you are in charge.'

'I hesitated to do it, but staff continuing to refer to me as "Fergus" smacks of inappropriate overfamiliarity. Anyway, Mr Rudd says he's enough to see to with Shackletons's accounting and that a fledgling company needs a young man. He's suggested his sister's grandson, Dicken Birkett. He says he has a sound basic knowledge and we can train him up. He's coming for interview this afternoon.'

'Good, but before we work through this list, we've something else important to discuss.'

Bill was biting on his thumbnail. 'You seem out of sorts,' Fergus said. 'What is it you have to say?'

'When Sven and I were in Glasgow this trip, Campbells' Textiles mentioned how convenient it is becoming to send cloth by rail to Carlisle, and then transport it direct to haberdashers throughout Northern England and the Borders. He didn't say it out loud, but what he implied was they could pass us by completely.'

'Are we going to lose them? Campbells are our strongest textile customer. We make a lot of money from their business.'

'The high cost of rail freight is a major factor at the moment, but with charges falling to more affordable levels all the time, I think we will lose them, and sooner rather than later.'

'This is bad news.' *Adding to the loss of the big ships.* Fergus felt a grip of apprehension. First the loss of the bigger ships to the town, and now the encroaching rail business. How were they to survive?

Bill continued. 'Mr Campbell took great pains to point out the physical barrier of the fells between Durham and Yorkshire. Another thing he mentioned in favour of trains is that they run to timetables, and although he didn't touch on it, he was probably thinking there's less risk. No chance of losing a cargo in a storm if it's carted on dry land.'

Fergus sucked in his cheeks. 'We have to accept Whitehaven will soon no longer be the coastal gateway to the north it is today. What do you think Campbells will do?'

'It would not surprise me if, when our contract expires in two months, they don't renew it. It was as if he was preparing me.'

'That soon?'

Bill nodded.

'Can we send our agent to negotiate and offer more competitive terms? A reduced profit is better than no business at all.'

'My understanding, as he put it to me, is that it's more about convenience and direct access to markets. So no, I don't think we can compete.'

'Whitehaven is still strong on the three staples – iron ore, coal and grain. Perhaps we can carry more liquor. I'll write to our Glasgow agent and you can hand the letter to him in person for debate on the next trip.'

Bill picked up the topic list. 'Future plans.' He signalled to the steward for more coffee.

Fergus spread his fingers and put his hands palm down on the table. 'The nub of it is we're back to the usual problem. Sail or steam?'

'I'm still wary of the mechanics of steamships,' Bill told him. 'I'm thinking their engines need more refinement to be as reliable as we need them to be.'

'I'll make enquiries, talk to some of my contacts.' Fergus pulled out his pocket watch and checked the hour. 'Becky and I are visiting our Coates Lane house to check on the work there. Then I've this bookkeeper to interview at the warehouse. Do you want to sit in?'

'If you want me to, but I won't have much of value to add. Administration is your department and you're a decent judge of men.'

On the short walk to the Indian King, Fergus thought through the morning's events and news. He chastised himself over the pending loss of Campbells; he'd been guilty of complacency. If he'd given it more thought, he would have realised the inevitable shift to the railways was not in the future, but already upon them. To the big ships' withdrawal to Liverpool and the increasing reliability of steamships must now be added the threat of the railway.

CHAPTER TWO

In the kitchen of the Indian King, Becky Moss was trying not to laugh at Rory Rooke who was looking at her, head on one side, while his dog Charlie, his ever-present best friend, sniffed the aroma of freshly baked beef pies, his head tilted at the same angle. Fergus, who had just arrived and was sitting at the table, was also smiling at the mirrored expressions.

Becky wiped her floury fingers on her apron. 'You've been ages,' she told Rory. 'I've had time to start a second batch of pies. There must have been a host of folk waiting to see the doctor.'

'Aye, and what's more 'twas a new one,' Rory said.

'Not Dr Lennagon?' She leaned forward to straighten the boy's jacket collar.

Rory shook his head. 'Nay, and this one took forever asking all kinds of questions.'

'What's he called?' asked Fergus. The previous year, Fergus had sought help for the boy after he'd injured his leg in a street accident. 'There's been nothing said at the club about a new doctor.'

Rory scratched his head. 'I forget, but he's really old. He's been at sea, and he likes dogs. I told him about Charlie and how I take him for walks. You should have let me take him with me.'

Becky was surprised. Dr Lennagon had a reputation for being rather abrupt, not wasting time on social niceties, whereas this one sounded quite different. Perhaps even engaging. 'How do you know he likes dogs?'

'When I went in, there was a dog curled up in a tight ball in a basket by the fire. The doctor told me he was poorly, but that I could stroke him if I was gentle.'

'And did you?' asked Fergus.

'Aye. I think he smelt Charlie on me, as he kept sniffing my sleeve and nuzzling it.'

Becky turned her attention to Rory's shirt, checking the cuffs for fraying. 'That's more than likely, but what did the doctor say about your boils?'

'Did he examine your neck?' Fergus added.

Rory stared at his feet, as if the answer to Fergus's question was inscribed on the floor.

'Well?' Becky stepped back to inspect him.

The boy grimaced. 'Aye, and he says they'll go away if I eat more greens.' Then, as if to steer Becky and Fergus away from the idea of loading all future dishes with overcooked cabbage, he added, 'He asked me why I walked funny. I told him about the barrel landing on my leg and that I go to sea and work for you, Mr Shackleton, and that's when he said he'd been at sea a long time.'

'What did he say about your leg?' asked Fergus.

'He said from the sound of the accident I was lucky it

wasn't more twisted. If I get any sores on it, or it starts to hurt for no reason, I'm to see him straight away.'

Becky lifted a boiling kettle from the range. 'He sounds thorough. I hadn't heard we were getting a new doctor. I hope Dr Lennagon's not ill.'

'I don't think so. I saw him coming in when I left. Do you think the new doctor chopped sailors' legs and arms off at sea?'

Out of the corner of her eye Becky could see Fergus was trying to suppress a smile. She was minded to reprimand Rory for such bloody thoughts, then stopped herself; it was probably quite normal for eleven-year-old lads to bandy about such expressions. 'I suppose he's done that sort of thing as a ship's surgeon,' she said. 'But I wouldn't dwell on the details if I were you.'

Fergus stood. 'Becky and I are going to Coates Lane to see how the renovation is going. Are you and Charlie coming with us?'

By way of answer, Rory picked up his cap and took Charlie's lead from his pocket. He grinned. 'It'll be good when you're wed. Charlie and I will have somewhere new to visit.'

At Coates Lane, only one workman was to be found in the house. He was mixing plaster in a metal bucket. He doffed his cap when he saw Fergus and Becky. Seeing the mess, Becky insisted Charlie be tied up outside and, after a couple of whimpers, he settled down with his head on his paws.

The air inside was full of plaster dust, and it wasn't long before Becky could taste it, even though she hadn't put her hands near her mouth. The table the workman was using for his tools was covered in a thick layer of it. Rory made straight for it and started drawing the outline of a ship with his finger.

'Where are the other workmen?' asked Fergus.

The plasterer wiped his hands on the back of his breeches. 'One's got real bad toothache and t'other's mammy's sorely sick, and he's left for Cockerm'uth.'

Becky didn't believe the man for one instant. He was obviously lying, since he was failing to hold their gaze. More likely the missing men had spent the previous night in the Three Tuns, or a similar ale house, and were sleeping it off.

Fergus was cross. 'If this happens again, I will be forced to have words with your contractor.'

With his father away, Fergus was too busy to waste time on unnecessary confrontation, but Becky knew it wasn't an idle threat.

'I don't want to have to tell my friends and family our wedding may have to be postponed because a few workmen have failed to keep to time,' he went on. 'I'll be keeping a more watchful eye on progress from now on.'

Despite the workmen, Becky was excited. Their own house. It was small: two bedrooms, a box room, a tiny dressing room for washing and bathing, a parlour, dining room, kitchen and scullery. No more than a cottage, but it would be theirs, and she would be Mrs Shackleton living there. Although it was a mess, all that was needed was the plastering, some attention to the stairs and painting right through.

Rory interrupted her thoughts. 'I've remembered the name of that doctor.'

'What is it?' asked Becky.

'Fincham.'

Fergus, who was checking the sills on what would be their parlour window, turned round.

Becky thought she hadn't heard correctly. 'Fincham? F-I-N-C-H-A-M?'

'Fincham with an "F".' Rory drew a large 'F' in the dust, next to the ship. 'He's not lived in Whitehaven for a long while.'

From Fergus's stunned look, Becky could see he was thinking the exact same thing. *Is it Aunt Louisa's Dr Fincham? Has he returned to Whitehaven?*

CHAPTER THREE

Dicken Birkett appeared to have a sound head on his shoulders. He was softly spoken, which Fergus regarded as an asset. He smelt strongly of soap, his nails were clean and even in length, and he was of good personal appearance. He'd chalked up several marks in his favour when he'd beamed on being shown their box of unfiled papers and bills, and so Fergus had no reservations in hiring him to start the following Monday.

Fergus had been invited to supper at the Indian King. After closing the warehouse, he had time to call at his parents' house in Queen Street, where he was living until the Coates Lane property was ready. He was hardly through the door when Samuel, his parents' butler, appeared with a letter on a silver tray.

'It's from Paris, sir.'

Fergus read the letter standing in the hall. 'My parents are returning,' he told Samuel. 'We can expect them here on the afternoon of Monday April 8th.'

'I will inform the staff, sir.'

After reminding Samuel he was dining out, Fergus retired to his room, washed, shaved and changed his clothes. There was plaster dust on his jacket and breeches, as well as in his hair. It wasn't obvious, but he could feel its dryness on his fingers. He picked up his parents' letter and put it in his pocket.

On the short walk to the Indian King, as the daylight was beginning to fade, he mulled over the consequences of his parents' return. They had parted amicably and he had missed them. He wondered if the bridges they had so recently mended and forged before their separation were holding fast, or whether his father would fall back into his old petulant ways. A new thought popped into his head. *What if it really is Aunt Louisa's Dr Fincham? How will Father feel coming face to face with him, after thirty years or more?*

It was Monday, which meant the Indian King was quiet, and less smoky than it might have been. Sergeant Adams, in his green coat with the brass buttons, and his dog Molly, both having partaken of Dolly's pies, were dozing in their usual place by the door. A few men were playing dominoes, while others were reading the *Whitehaven News*. As always, the brasses in the room gleamed, and the tables had been freshly polished. In one corner, where a group of pipe smokers liked to sit, clean sawdust had been laid on the floor. This was a task Becky told Fergus she thought of as her 'end-of-the-day job'.

In the kitchen, the table was laid for supper and Fergus saw straight away that, like him, Becky had changed. She was wearing a green skirt with matching bodice, replacing the blue one she had been wearing earlier. A lace fichu collar had been added around her shoulders and tied in a loose knot at the front.

'You are breathtakingly stunning,' Fergus said.

'That's overgenerous of you. Aye, well, I was covered in plaster dust, and we were only there no more than ten minutes.'

'As was I. With me keeping a sharper watch, they'll soon be finished with the walls and then on with the painting, and we can start thinking about furnishings.'

'Ma'll be through in a few minutes. She's watching over the new barman changing the barrels. Rory's upstairs. I've set him four pages to read and then he's to tell me about it in his own words.'

Fergus drew out his parents' letter from his coat pocket and passed it to Becky.

'I thought they'd be gone longer,' Becky said, reading it.

'They'll have been away four months. Frankly, I'm surprised Mother's been able to keep Father away from the business for this long.'

'I wonder if he's still a changed man?'

'We'll soon see,' said Fergus.

'All will be right enough, don't worry.'

'I'm not,' he said. It was a partial untruth. He was going to have to tell his father that both Shackleton & Company and the Louisa Line were probably going to lose their Campbell accounts. His father wouldn't like that. In the old days, he would definitely have blamed Fergus for the loss. Fergus wondered if he'd still react in the same way. Whilst he was looking forward to seeing his parents, he knew there would be tensions on some level.

Becky reached up to take plates from the warming rack above the range. 'What about this Dr Fincham?'

'It may not be the same Dr Fincham, of course. A cousin perhaps, or even a brother. We don't know much about this new doctor, and Rory could have made a mistake. If we knew his first name, we'd know for sure.'

'What was your Aunt Louisa's Dr Fincham called?'

'Nicholas,' said Fergus.

'Aye, of course, but thinking on it, how many Dr Finchams can there be? And a ship's surgeon, too. It's got to be him. How old is he?'

'Rory described him as "really old", which a man in his fifties would seem to him.'

Dolly came in from the bar. 'Ee, I thought I'd never get finished and you'd have to start without me,' she said, taking off her working apron and putting it in a basket near the scullery door. While she washed her hands, they told her about Coates Lane and the name of the new doctor.

'Sounds to me as if it's him. I'd lay brass down on it,' she said, drying her hands. 'I wonder if he knows Louisa has passed away?'

'I've been wondering that too, but I'm sure Dr Lennagon would have told him how she died.'

'You'll not rest, Fergus, until you find out,' said Dolly. 'Go and see him for yourself.'

'Make an appointment?'

'Aye. Better in private than in front of the whole Gentlemen's Club, where it could be embarrassing for both of you.'

'But there's nothing wrong with me.'

Becky frowned. 'You could ask him about your headaches.'

'They're nothing.'

'Not when you're in the clutches of one, they're not,' Dolly said. 'I've seen you rubbing your forehead to ease the pain in your eyes. Do that – consult him about your headaches.'

'Perhaps I should go and mention them,' Fergus conceded. He'd experienced some bad headaches recently that couldn't be put down to too much port.

'Aye,' said Becky. 'And he'll probably realise you're Aunt Louisa's nephew from your name. There'll be a clue. He'll say something, or you can ask him straight out if he knew her, if he's as approachable as Rory says.'

Dolly took a pie from the central oven and put it on the range rack. 'That's settled, then. Make an appointment, and if that irritable housekeeper of his opens the door and says you're registered with Dr Lennagon, stand your ground.'

'Oh, yes, the dreaded Constance.' Fergus groaned in mock horror. He remembered how rude she'd been the day of Rory's accident and how she'd tried to turn him away from the doctor's door because the boy was only a pit lad.

* * *

Three days later, Fergus was sitting in the doctors' waiting room. Constance, as dour as ever, had admitted him with no comment, other than to tell him Dr Fincham was running a little late. Left to his own devices, Fergus wondered what to expect from the meeting. Did he want it to be Aunt Louisa's Dr Fincham, or not? He wasn't sure, but he needed to settle the matter and find out. If it *was* the Dr Fincham who had loved his beloved Aunt Louisa, then what? It must have been thirty years since the engagement was broken off. Then it occurred to him that perhaps Dr Fincham had found romance elsewhere – that in the intervening years he'd married and had a wife, or perhaps was a widower. Did he have children? Confronted with the reality of the moment, these thoughts raced through Fergus's mind. He was on the point of talking himself into abandoning the consultation when Constance called him through.

The man sitting behind the desk stood when Fergus entered, leaned over his papers and held out his hand. Noting the firmness of his grasp, Fergus recognised a man who must have spent a great deal of time outdoors. His complexion was ruddy; if he was in his mid-fifties, he was prematurely wrinkled. Probably from too much sun, Fergus thought. The man was sturdily built, without appearing fat. Fergus remembered his mother saying Aunt Louisa's Dr Fincham had held himself proudly on a horse. He could imagine the confident, mature man in front of him at ease on horseback. His hair was combed to one side, although somewhat sparse at the crown, and he had a moustache that was slightly yellow at the sides, which Fergus put down to smoking cigars or drawing on a pipe. He greeted Fergus in an educated accent and gave him a welcoming smile, the sort it was impossible not to respond to in similar fashion.

'Mr Shackleton, please take a seat. What can I do for you?'

'I've been suffering from severe headaches.'

'Is this new to you or are they long-standing?'

'I think you would call them recent. I've had them a few months now.'

'Have there been any changes in your circumstances? Anything that would cause anxiety?'

Fergus gave a wry laugh. 'In the last six months I've gone from working for my father at Shackleton & Company as a lowly employee, to running his business whilst at the same time managing my own company, the Louisa Line.' The doctor didn't react at the mention of the name Louisa, but then why would he? This was a medical consultation, and Fergus could see the man was nothing if not professional.

Dr Fincham asked more questions, then inspected Fergus's eyes and ears, before listening to his chest. 'You appear a fit and healthy young man to me. From what you've told me, I would suggest these headaches are due to the added responsibilities of leadership and administration, which have caused unwelcome anxieties and tension. The tension results in venous contraction, which instigates pain as blood is forced through a narrower passage than usual. It is most likely unhelpful of me to suggest you take life at a slower pace, but perhaps you could aim to avoid situations that are certain to bring anxiety in their wake.'

Fergus thought back to his father's notorious irrational outbursts and hoped, not for the first time, that they didn't pass down the family blood line.

'Crises seem to arrive with little warning,' he said.

'I understand, like the sudden onset of a storm at sea. I

recommend one of my linctus tonics. Used sparingly, it will bring a feeling of well-being without the light-headedness and drowsiness some calming linctus medications can cause. It's perfect for the early stages of a venous headache. Hopefully, with time, this situation will pass as you become used to your new responsibilities, and we can withdraw the linctus. Take no more than a dessertspoonful at a time and limit the dosage to thrice daily.'

While the doctor was writing out an apothecary's note, Fergus inspected the room. A dog was curled up in a basket by the fire, and on a table next to it was an ivory chess set, the pieces lined up ready for play. Fergus guessed it to be an imported Indian set, because the kings were seated on elephants with long tusks.

Dr Fincham put down his pen and blotted his writing.

'I see you play chess,' said Fergus. 'My Aunt Louisa played chess and she taught me.'

There was a long pause before Dr Fincham spoke, and when he did there was a slight catch in his voice. 'That's good to hear, because it was I who taught your aunt.'

Fergus felt a rush of relief course through his body. It *was* him and Fergus liked him. It was an unexpected fresh link with his beloved aunt. He hadn't realised until then that that was what he had been seeking and hoping for. 'You are Nicholas Fincham?'

The doctor smiled. 'Yes, I cannot deny it. And you, as Fergus Shackleton, must be Louisa's nephew. I wondered when I saw your name on today's patient list, and then as soon as you entered, I saw the resemblance.'

'Was it the eyes? People have often commented on the likeness.'

Dr Fincham laughed. 'Indeed it was and I have never forgotten hers. The hazel eyes with the gold flecks. Your aunt and I were friends years ago, before you were born, yet you recognise my name. How is that? Did she speak of me?'

Fergus had no idea what Dr Fincham wanted him to say. Should he say his aunt had spoken of her lost love? Would that please him? Or would it be better to say she'd never uttered his name? What would he think of that? Would he be hurt? With the thought that the truth will always out, Fergus decided he could not lie.

'She didn't speak of you directly.' He thought of the letter that the man sitting in front of him had written to his Aunt Louisa all those years ago, professing his undying love for her. 'She left some personal papers. To me.'

'Dr Lennagon told me she'd left the bulk of her estate to you. I was saddened to learn of her death, and how unexpected it was. It may not seem it to you, but at not yet sixty, she died young. A tragedy.'

'It was a difficult time for all of us; she is often in our thoughts. Her Seamen's Haven work is still carried on, and my fiancée, Becky, and I are going to live in one of the cottages she left me.'

'You are engaged to be married? Congratulations. I was not at all surprised to hear about Louisa setting up the Seamen's Haven. She would often talk of the miserable plight of sailors coming back from long voyages, landing on the quay with no plans, far from their families, just when they needed support and a warm bed.'

Their conversation was cut short by Constance opening the door and putting her head round.

'You're running late, Dr Fincham, and your next two patients are waiting.'

Fergus left the surgery feeling elated. He'd felt at ease with Dr Fincham, and he now had someone who'd known his aunt when she was young. Perhaps, when they got to know each other better, the doctor would tell Fergus what she'd been like as a young woman. It was as if a door to the past had been unlocked for him – one he had thought forever securely bolted.

That afternoon, Becky had two bottles of ginger wine to deliver to one of their housebound customers near Chapel Street and, being anxious to hear about Fergus's consultation, she took the opportunity to call at the Louisa Line's warehouse.

As she drew near, she could see several carts drawn up outside. One of the drivers was talking to Rory, who was holding a sheaf of papers in one hand and a pencil in the other. Another man was standing by, as if awaiting instruction. The man who delivered cheese to the Indian King passed by with his wife and two children, and raised his hat to Becky.

The warehouse doors were wide open and, stepping aside for a man carrying three boxes piled on top of each other, Becky ventured inside. There were voices coming from the partially glassed-in office to her right and she realised Fergus was taken up with a visitor who had his back to her. She went upstairs to pass the time. When Becky had ventured there soon after Fergus acquired the warehouse, there had been nothing to see but an empty, dusty void. Reaching the top step, and pausing for breath, she found the area on the left had new shelving, which was now crammed with crates and boxes. There was a different odour, too, from which she could make out liquor, jute, machinery oil, new wood – and was it cinnamon? Fergus had not been jesting when he'd told her he thought they might soon need a second warehouse for more storage.

A separate area had been reorganised to house different-sized casks, which were stacked on top of each other. They must have used the new hoist to raise them from the street. Each cask was labelled with its contents. Becky recognised Rory's squiggly writing and smiled. He was becoming as much at home in the warehouse as she'd been told he was at sea.

Only two days previously, Fergus had said, 'I want Rory to learn all aspects of the business and, as much as I can, I will treat him as able-bodied.'

Remembering these words, Becky reminded herself to caution Rory again about keeping away from the warehouse doors when loading. They opened outwards, and were twelve feet above the street on the first floor, and at least twenty-four feet or more above it on the second.

Hearing the visitor leave, Becky made her way downstairs, holding tightly to the stair-rail. Fergus put his arms out and wrapped them around her waist.

'I heard you come in and saw your bonnet pass by. I'm sorry you had to wait, I needed to sign off some papers for the harbour master's office.'

'How was Doctor Fincham? Is he who we think he is?' Becky so hoped it was. It would be so romantic.

'Yes, it's him. Aunt Louisa's lost love.' Fergus told Becky about the consultation and the chess set.

'I can't wait to meet him.'

'You'll like him. I'm wondering if you'd like to invite him for luncheon? He's like family, even if he doesn't yet realise it.'

Becky hadn't been thinking of such a formal meeting. Obviously, this couldn't happen at the Indian King, because they didn't do formal sit-down meals – only pies and sausages – and besides, it would be too lively.'

'No. What about Queen Street? With Mother and Father away, we could entertain him there. You wouldn't have to do anything. The staff will take care of it, you can instruct them.'

Becky hesitated.

'Don't you want to?' asked Fergus.

Becky guessed Fergus was interpreting her hesitation as being unwilling to instruct the staff in her future mother-in-law's home, but that wasn't the problem uppermost in her mind. 'Aye, I do, but don't you think it could be painful for Dr Fincham?'

'Painful?'

Just like a man not to see. 'I'm wondering if the last time he was in the Shackletons' Queen Street house was when he learned Louisa was more or less forbidden to marry him. I mean, it could bring back all sorts of distant memories for him.'

'My darling Becky, how thoughtful of you. Your empathy is one of the traits I most love about you. However, it was thirty years ago, and the fact he's decided to come back to Whitehaven to pass his remaining years indicates to me he's prepared to confront whatever ghosts reside here for him. Allow me to invite him for next Sunday. I can speak with Samuel this evening, and you can call tomorrow and discuss the arrangements.'

Discuss the arrangements? Becky felt a burst of anxiety in the pit of her stomach. She'd expected such a task to fall on her shoulders in due course, but she'd thought it would be after they were married and in their house on Coates Lane, not the big house in Queen Street, with all the rigmarole of instructing staff. Her mind returned to the disastrous afternoon tea when Fergus's mother, Elizabeth, had questioned her social competence, a requirement of a Shackleton wife. She pulled herself together, drew in a deep breath and held it for a few seconds before letting it out slowly. *Becky Moss from the Indian King of Roper Street, you can do this,* she told herself. *You can do it and do it acceptably, and it will mean so much to Fergus.*

On the day Fergus confirmed Dr Fincham had accepted their invitation, Becky found herself standing outside the Shackleton residence, waiting for Samuel to answer the door. The only indication that Hector and Elizabeth were away was that the carriage entrance doors were locked. She remembered Fergus telling her the horses had been put out to livery at Cleator Moor. When he decided to leave his rented accommodation to take up temporary residence, he had instructed the household that his wants would be frugal and that the sheeting and covers in the main rooms were to remain, unless they were advised otherwise. Several of the maids were let go, but all had been found suitable replacement positions. Those remaining had been set to sorting and spring cleaning, and Fergus told her the house always smelt fresh and cared for as a result.

Samuel answered the door and stood to one side to allow Becky to pass. As she stepped onto the black and white tiles in the hall, the sound her boots had made when she'd walked upon them on previous occasions came back to her, along with the waxy aroma of expensive beeswax polish. The staff were certainly not letting standards slip while their master and mistress were abroad.

Samuel took her coat and placed it on a stand. 'I must apologise for the house being closed whilst the master and mistress are away, although I understand from young Mr Shackleton we are to have guests this Sunday.'

Becky smiled to herself at Fergus being described as 'young Mr Shackleton'. Not that it was wrong, because he *was* young – she'd just never heard him described that way before.

'Only the one guest,' said Becky. 'Dr Nicholas Fincham, so there will be three of us.' She hoped she sounded more confident than she felt. She'd gone over everything she might need to say with her mother the previous evening. 'May I see the dining room?'

'Please follow me.' Samuel led the way, apologising again for the fact that the furniture was under covers. Once inside, he pulled a large sheet from the table to reveal an expanse of polished mahogany.

'About the seating arrangements. With you seated here,

Miss Moss,' he pointed to the end of the table nearest the door, 'young Mr Shackleton could be seated here.' He pointed to the other end of the table. 'Would you like Dr Fincham seated on your right or your left?'

'Is this how Mrs Shackleton seats her guests?'

'We rarely had three for luncheon, usually four or six, but when Miss Louisa was alive, and she and the master and mistress dined together, we adopted this arrangement. He pointed to his right. 'Miss Louisa always sat in the centre on this side.'

Becky was silent for a moment. *Samuel must be thinking I'm out of my depth, yet he's treating me kindly. There's a lot he can teach me and I need him on my side.* 'Samuel, you're far more experienced in this sort of thing than I am. May I ask your advice?'

Samuel moved over to the door and put his head round it, as if checking for eavesdroppers. Then he stepped back and closed it. 'By all means,' he told her.

'Do I have to do follow Mrs Shackleton's ways? I mean, this is her house, I am aware that the situation is unusual.'

'Young Mr Shackleton told me this morning that I was to follow your instructions. You are free to make your own arrangements and we shall be happy to carry them out.'

'In that case I would like the three of us to be seated together at one end of the table. I think it will be less formal and much friendlier. Besides, what if Dr Fincham is hard of hearing?' Lots of the older men who came into the Indian King were hard of hearing, although in their case it was probably a legacy from working underground.

'Will you be seating young Mr Shackleton at the head?'

'Yes, and Doctor Fincham and I shall be seated opposite each other.'

'And the menu?'

'Oh, aye, the menu.'

'You need to discuss that with Mrs. Harvey, our cook. I'll call her.'

After Samuel had disappeared, Becky walked up to a large, bulky piece of covered furniture. She went to peep under the sheet but, as if anxious to reveal the furniture's magnificence after several months providing cover, the whole thing came away and trailed on the floor. She found herself in front of an ornate sideboard that matched the table in wood and shine. There were three drawers in the centre. She opened one and found it full of silver cutlery: knives, spoons, forks, all on their sides, nestling into one another. From the smell rising from the drawers, and the way each piece shone, she could tell it was not long since they'd been polished.

She opened the left-hand cupboard to find silver serving dishes of various sizes. Beside a gravy boat and ladle lay an ornate pair of scissors. They, too, were silver and the arms were decorated with a silver-leaf filigree. She picked them up, and was opening and shutting them when she heard a cough. She turned round. A small stout woman with a white mob cap perched on her head was standing in the doorway.

'I'm Mrs Harvey, the Shackletons' cook. In charge of the kitchen and all meals and entertaining.' She glanced at the scissors Becky was still clutching. 'We'll be having grapes then, I take it?'

'I'm sorry?'

'You're holding the grape scissors.' Mrs Harvey approached her, and was soon so close, Becky got a strong whiff of fresh garlic. She put the scissors back where she'd found them, as if they were red hot. She felt as if she'd been caught with an open till.

'Yes, grapes,' she said, feeling herself begin to colour up. *How stupid I am. The filigree leaves are vines.*

The cook frowned. 'I thought we were having a luncheon for the new doctor?'

Becky nodded. 'Aye, we are.'

'Oh. You see when the mistress is entertaining, we only serve grapes with dinner, and then only if we offer cheese.'

Becky was about to riposte with, 'But we're having dinner', when she remembered 'dinner', for the well-to-do, was the evening meal, whereas for people like her and her ma 'dinner' was the midday meal. *What do I do now? Insist on my own way, or back down? Either way, the cook realises I didn't know what the scissors were for.*

Mrs Harvey was pursing her lips and scrutinising Becky, her head on one side. There was not an ounce of friendliness in her demeanour.

Becky gave a tight smile and moved away from the sideboard. 'Let us discuss the menu and then we can decide. I was thinking that, as it will be a Sunday, we could have the usual Sunday lunch.'

'The usual?'

She's not going to give an inch.

'Soup, a roast, and a pudding.'

'What kind of soup were you thinking of?'

I'll not let this woman get the better of me. 'Mrs Harvey, are you telling me that you and your staff are incapable of providing a traditional Sunday luncheon?'

Mrs Harvey's jaw dropped.

Becky, now spurred on and feeling courageous, continued, 'We shall have pea broth followed by beef on the bone, Yorkshire pudding, vegetables, roast potatoes and gravy. I take it you and your staff can provide such a meal, given enough notice?' Becky knew her neck and cheeks were now bright red, indicating discomfort in their verbal exchange, but she didn't care. She turned slightly, moving away from the cook as if about to dismiss her.

'Of course we can,' said Mrs Harvey, in a put-out sort of voice. 'My staff are correctly trained.'

'And let us have one of Mr Fergus's favourite puddings.' Becky had no idea what that might be, but surely the family cook must know, and if Becky herself didn't, she wasn't going to admit it.

'The lemon syllabub with almond biscuits?'

'Excellent choice,' said a male voice. 'And I'm sure Mr Fergus will want to choose the wines himself.'

Becky, with her back to the door, hadn't realised Samuel had returned.

'And the usual Sunday table linen?' asked Mrs Harvey, her mouth set in a long thin line.

'The usual Sunday linen will be most suitable.'

On her way home, Becky wondered if she had spoken too directly. No matter. She had taken courage from Samuel's welcome and support. She had wondered if he would be stand-offish, but she needn't have worried. The cook, however, had found the lass who came from a pub an irritation. *I must remember the next time she tries to undermine me that I can probably cook as well as she can – and I'll wager she knows it.*

CHAPTER FOUR

On the day of the luncheon, Dr Fincham arrived with a generous bunch of daffodils. Taking Becky's hand, he said, 'Miss Moss, it is a great pleasure to meet you.'

'And for me too. You're most welcome.'

After Samuel had taken the doctor's hat and coat, Becky led the way upstairs.

He was as Fergus had described – gentlemanly, with an approachable demeanour, and smartly dressed. Becky warmed to him straight away. If he was experiencing any unease about being in the Shackleton drawing room, he wasn't showing it. The reverse was true of Becky. She had spent a restless night tossing under the blankets, worrying that the staff would take their cue from Mrs Harvey and make life difficult for her. She wanted the meeting to be agreeable for both men's sakes, because despite being from different generations, they shared a love for Louisa.

To her surprise once they were settled in the drawing room, after covering the expected greetings and enquiries regarding health and commenting on the weather, Fergus leapt straight in with, 'You must have been in this room before?'

'Indeed, in my youth, many times.' Dr Fincham's gaze swept the room, lingering on the bookshelves before moving to settle on the ornate fireplace.

Becky wondered if much had changed. She studied him. Was it his final visit all those years ago that was foremost in his mind? Surely, after the engagement was called off, he would not have entered the house again? Perhaps he'd left this room with a joyful heart, thinking he was to marry Louisa, only to have all hopes dashed later by a letter or a summons to the Shackleton offices. Or had this room been where he was told he would not be marrying Louisa, because her duty lay with caring for her widowed father?

Becky reprimanded herself. *I'm getting carried away; he doesn't appear in the least bit sad.*

Fergus must have been holding similar thoughts. 'Are there ghosts in here for you?' he asked.

Dr Fincham gave a half-smile. 'How perceptive of you to ask that.' He pointed to an oak chair. 'I remember your grandfather, Norman, sitting in that chair. It used to be on the other side of the fireplace. There was a small table beside it on which there was usually a fine cut-glass whiskey noggin. Always half-full, if I remember correctly.'

'That's Father's chair now,' Fergus told him.

'One day it will most likely be yours, then,' said the doctor, smiling.

Becky had a vision of a grey-haired Fergus sitting in the chair, holding a leather-bound book, while she sat on the chaise-longue, sewing. Hopefully they were going to grow old together. It was a comfortable scene, but not one she envisaged becoming reality for several decades. She was more than happy with their Coates Lane home. As far as Becky was concerned, as long as Elizabeth was alive it would always be her mother-in-law's home. She couldn't see herself sharing a roof with Elizabeth – neither of them would flourish under those circumstances.

'What was he like, my grandfather?' asked Fergus.

Dr Fincham drew in breath to speak, then paused. When he did speak, he blew out his cheeks and spoke slowly. 'He was a man who didn't suffer fools gladly. He had an excellent business brain. His manner was gruff, but he loved his children, and no doubt you, too.'

'But do you think he loved Louisa too much to let her marry and have a life of her own?'

Dr Fincham bit his bottom lip. 'I see you are aware of the history between Louisa and myself. Suffice to say it was a long time ago and attitudes were different. Another day perhaps we can discuss it.'

Becky was aware that her role as hostess at this point was to put their guest at ease, which meant leaping in and channelling the conversation onto something light. She rose to the occasion. 'Talking of old times, do tell us about your travels.'

At that moment Samuel arrived to announce their meal was ready, and ask would they care to adjourn to the dining room. Becky had inspected it before their guest arrived and, realising there were no flowers she'd summoned the housekeeper, who apologised for the oversight. Entering the room now she found a small arrangement of spring flowers had been placed in the centre of the table and a more elaborate one on the sideboard.

Samuel showed them to their places, where they stood to attention behind their chairs, like military men on parade, while Fergus said grace. Becky sat down and examined the array of cutlery set out for each place. She had been too busy noticing the lack of flowers to pay much attention earlier to the table settings. She could hear her mother's voice: 'You start at the outside and work in, and you wait until all've been served before you begin. As hostess you must lead the way.' The first course was easy – the spoon was obviously for the soup. Becky was surprised at how heavy it was. She took a few mouthfuls, then noticed that the men were lifting their spoons to their mouths and tipping them slightly, to take the liquid from the side of the spoon rather than the end, as she was doing. It seemed affected and a bit showy to her, but this must be the way they did things at these formal luncheons, so she copied them. Dr Fincham finished his soup first; he tipped the bowl away from his body towards the centre of the table, scooped up half a spoonful, finished that, and only then did he put his spoon down.

As the soup was being cleared away, the conversation turned to the menu, and in particular the source of the beef and the wine importer. Becky, fearing a lull in the conversation that Fergus might fill again with the subject of Louisa, said, 'Dr Fincham, you were about to tell us of your travels.'

'Call me Nicholas, please, both of you. I prefer informality on social occasions with friends, although I am always "Dr Fincham" when on duty.'

'Nicholas it will be,' said Fergus, 'and we are honoured to be regarded as friends.'

'Aye, that we are,' said Becky, meaning it.

In between mouthfuls, Dr Fincham told them about his life. 'I was a ship's surgeon for many years, but I don't think regaling those tales is suitable for the luncheon table. Instead, allow me to tell you about my last port of call, Mauritius.'

'Mauritius?' asked Becky. 'Where's that?'

'An island off the coast of Africa,' said Fergus. 'East of Madagascar in the Indian Ocean.'

Becky was still not much wiser, but she wasn't going to admit it.

'That's right,' said Fincham. 'I spent some years in India, and then my wandering spirit took hold again, and the tales I'd heard of Mauritius from Indian traders tempted me to visit. When I landed at Port Louis, the island's capital, I was not disappointed. Mauritius had been under French rule, and then British; I found the mix of the two cultures fascinating.'

'How long did you stay there?' asked Becky, wondering, not for the first time, if she would ever visit any of the places the mariners always referred to so casually, despite their being thousands of miles away.

'After three months I decided I liked it enough to live there, and I stayed for five years. I set up a private medical practice for the planters and their families.'

'It's a different world, no doubt,' said Fergus.

The vegetables being brought through from the kitchen, Fergus motioned to Samuel to begin carving the beef. Dr Fincham was twirling his empty wine glass.

'You'll have another glass of the claret?' Fergus asked him, raising his own glass for a refill.

Samuel stopped carving and stepped forward to see to both their glasses.

Dr Fincham inclined his head towards Fergus. 'Thank you. I rarely partake of more than a single glass during the day, but this wine is exceptionally fine.'

When everyone had been served, and Samuel had retired, Becky picked up the large knife and fork. Again the cutlery felt heavy, but when she thought about it, it was the first time she'd held a solid silver knife and fork. To her relief, the meat was tender and the gravy delicious. The cook might have been offhand with her personally, but she had done the Queen Street kitchen proud.

Dr Fincham took up his life story. 'Mauritius was a happy time for me. The European residents were badly in need of professional medical services, and I was immediately embraced by society, both French and British. The tea- and sugar-planters' mansions all had spacious verandas on the ground and upper floors. We would go out onto them to relax and smoke cigars.'

'You say planters. Were there slaves?'

'Oh, no, slavery was abolished in 1833. The government paid generously for the freed slaves to set up in their own businesses, to give them a good start in their new lives.'

'Was it hot?' asked Becky.

'Yes, sometimes exceedingly so, but in the evenings,

there was usually a light breeze. We would sit on cane chairs and admire the manicured lawns and gardens.'

Becky could not imagine herself ever having the time to engage in such a pastime as sitting on a veranda, although she had no doubt she would enjoy it. 'What were the rooms like?'

'The plantation houses were full of imported French and English furniture. The English style is what I'd call heavy wooden furniture of substance – large mahogany desks, ornately carved wardrobes, that kind of thing. The French houses were filled with delicate pieces that were far more decorative than the English, and they papered their walls with floral patterns. As you would expect, the best room was the drawing room, where all the dances were held.'

'Dances?' said Becky, imagining the excitement.

'These were the main social events and were held several times a week. They commenced at eight when the evening was cooling. We knew each other, so time was never wasted on introductions. We would dance, and then refreshments were served.'

'What kind of refreshments?' That was the specific detail Becky's mother, as a public house landlady, would want her to glean.

'My personal favourite was a rum-based punch, but there were French wines and many other cool drinks. Lemonade cordial was particularly popular amongst the ladies.'

'It sounds wonderful,' said Becky picturing it in her mind's eye – all the women in silk evening dresses, kid gloves up to their elbows, the men in smart velvet jackets. 'Was there much dancing?'

'A great deal. As a single gentleman I was much in demand to make up numbers and dance with the daughters of the grand plantation houses. In fact, I once heard myself described as a "safe pair of hands".'

The three of them laughed, although Becky was thinking of Louisa spending her whole life in Queen Street, and how she might have loved such a life, given the opportunity.

Dr Fincham paused to drain his glass. Was he, too, thinking of how it might have been with Louisa? Or perhaps he had other ladies he had enjoyed dancing with.

Fergus stood and, without ringing for Samuel, lifted the claret decanter from the sideboard.

Dr Fincham motioned towards his glass. 'Only a splash for me or I shall sleep the afternoon away.'

'It all sounds wonderful,' said Becky. 'Do go on.'

'If I'm honest, it wasn't wonderful all the time. As a doctor, there were occasions when I was called to a godown – what you would call a warehouse – because a cask had rolled off a shelf and caught someone, or a worker had become trapped in machinery.'

Becky shivered.

'My apologies, my dear,' said Dr Fincham. 'I did not mean to alarm you. I hope I haven't put you off this magnificent luncheon?'

'The same things happen here,' said Fergus. 'In fact, I've been thinking of putting lockable grills over some of our warehouse shelving to combat pilfering, and such a barrier will also prevent the kind of accidents you describe. Items appear safely stacked, but if someone is careless and shifts or removes something, causing a firkin to roll, then the whole load becomes unstable.'

'Aye, I worry about Rory in the warehouse,' Becky said.

'Rory?' asked Dr Fincham.

'You probably don't remember seeing a young lad with a twisted leg. He came to you about boils. I worry about him tripping and falling out of the loading doors.'

'Oh, but I do remember him. He told me he has a little dog.'

'Aye, he does. Charlie. Goes everywhere with him.'

'How is he connected with you?'

'It was Fergus who witnessed his accident and had him seen by Dr Lennagon.'

Fergus nodded. 'Yes, I did and it was a nasty accident, with the result he had to give up his job in the pit.'

'So, it's you he works for. He told me he went to sea with Shackletons.'

'Fergus and I take a special interest in him,' said Becky. 'He's an orphan and a lovely lad. He's happy working for the Louisa Line, isn't he?'

'Yes, I think so,' said Fergus.

'Ma says he's in good spirits when he's at the Indian King. He lives there with us when he's not at sea.'

'You could teach him to play chess,' said Dr Fincham.

'I intend to, but I'd like to do much more for him. Perhaps we could ask your advice?'

'Certainly. How can I help? Do you have plans for the boy?'

'I have no worries about his life at present; it's the future I'm thinking of. We need to afford him some protection. Becky and I are of like mind.'

'We'd like to care for him, and although Ma says she's happy for him to stop with her if he wants to, he can come and live with us when we're married.'

'Have you considered taking legal advice on this?'

'You mean take out legal papers?'

'Yes. There's a legality called "guardianship", whereby a minor can be given security by someone they're not blood-related to.'

'Why don't you ask your solicitor, Fergus? I'll come with you if you want.'

'That's what I'm thinking. Thank you, Nicholas.'

The presentation of the lemon syllabub was a triumph. Fergus's face lit up when it was brought in and he licked his lips.

'My favourite. Dr Fincham, you must try this; it's one of our cook's specialities and only she knows the recipe. I've always threatened I am going to sneak down in the middle of the night and scour her recipe books.'

It was so delicious, Becky forgave the cook for their stand-off earlier in the week. She had toyed with the idea of sending for grapes and cheese with their coffee to make a point, but she couldn't possibly do that now. In any case, it would have been provocative and would only have made things worse between her and the cook.

After coffee was served, Dr Fincham asked Becky, as their hostess, if she would mind if he 'put his medical hat on'.

'Not at all,' she said, wondering what was coming.

'How are your headaches, Fergus?'

'They are much better, thank you. I'm finding the linctus most helpful when I feel one starting. If I wake up with one, it's more of a problem, but luckily that's rare.'

'Good. If the ones on waking become more frequent, come and see me again. I'm finding picking up the reins of general practice most varied and rewarding.'

'What's brought you back to Whitehaven?' asked Becky.

'It's quite simple. Mauritius has the most beautiful sunsets, the climate is delightful, my friends pleasantly amenable, but I am in my mid-fifties and I have endured one nasty mosquito bite too many. Whilst age brings with it a certain amount of welcome respect from others, particularly in *my* profession, the price that has to be paid is a waning tolerance of heat, and a growing fear of the chaos caused by cyclones. At the risk of sounding over-romantic, it could be said that home was calling me. I found myself more and more thinking of the quay at Whitehaven, the fresh breezes coming in over the water, the saltiness of the sea – even the cawing of the seagulls.'

'You never married?' asked Fergus.

'No.' The speed and abruptness with which Nicholas replied indicated quite clearly he had no wish to provide further information.

A question too far, thought Becky. She kicked Fergus under the table. He could be insensitive sometimes.

The way Nicholas had spoken, it passed through Becky's mind he might be ill and had returned home to die, but he appeared the picture of health. Time would tell on that one.

Fergus picked up the conversation. 'All the things we, living here, take for granted – are these the things you missed?'

'Indeed. I called on my old friend Dr Lennagon after I arrived, and finding him wishing to work fewer hours, and myself with time to spare, it seemed God's will we should work together. We have known each other a long time. We met in Edinburgh as surgeon-apothecaries in 1827, and after seven years graduated together.'

'Fate,' said Becky.

'Yes. And there was much to catch up on with my having been away for thirty years.'

Thirty years. Becky couldn't imagine not seeing someone for so long. It was more than a complete lifetime for some people.

The next hour was filled with pleasant discourse and much laughter, until their guest declared he had to leave, and that he was sure he must have outstayed his welcome.

While Fergus was outside talking to Nicholas, Becky approached Samuel, who was standing in the hall.

'Please ask Cook to speak with me in the dining room.'

He left and came back alone, saying, 'Cook begs your pardon, but would you mind calling into the kitchen to see her rather than her come upstairs?' Becky's surprise at his words must have shown, for he continued, 'I can guarantee no disrespect intended. It's that she's up to her elbows in soapy water. With the master away we let some of the servants go, and she's begun the washing-up. It'll take her several minutes to dry off and change her apron, and she doesn't want to keep you waiting.'

It hadn't occurred to Becky that the cook would have had to set to herself and carry out some of the menial tasks associated with their lavish luncheon. No one had pointed that out to her, and it wouldn't have occurred to Fergus. They'd put the reduced staff to a lot more trouble than she'd realised. She wondered how she would have felt in the cook's place. Annoyed? Put out that a young lass from the Indian King was telling her what to do in *her* kitchen, when they were short-staffed?

'That will not be necessary. Kindly tell Cook I would like to thank her and her staff for a delicious luncheon, which was enjoyed by all. Especially the lemon syllabub.'

Samuel nodded. 'She'll be pleased to hear that. Shall I thank the housekeeper for the flowers?'

He's guiding me again. 'Aye, please do.'

Samuel was halfway across the hall when he paused. 'I may be overstepping myself by making this comment, but I would like to say I thought your luncheon went well, Miss.'

'Thank you, Samuel. Thank you – so did I.'

CHAPTER FIVE

At Cartwright, Lockhart & Company, Solicitors, in the town of Whitehaven, the old days of being kept waiting at the reception desk before being admitted to Mr Needham's office were over, and Fergus and Becky were ushered into his presence as soon as they arrived.

Fergus was proud to introduce Becky; he thought her particularly pretty in her new bonnet, with its narrower curved sides that showed off her pretty profile.

After they'd settled themselves, Fergus opened the conversation. 'We're here to talk about Rory Rooke.'

'The pit boy you saw struck by the barrel in the street?'

'Yes. I employ him as a cook's apprentice on the *Eleanor Bell* and the *Sophie Alice*.'

'How old is he now?'

'He's eleven…' Fergus hesitated; he had forgotten the boy's birthday month. 'Becky, when is his birthday?'

'He'll be twelve in November, on the 8th.'

Mr Needham raised his eyebrows. 'That's young to be at sea. It's a tough life.'

'His mother asked me to take him on,' Fergus went on. 'She died while he was on his first voyage, so he's an orphan. I feel a responsibility for him.'

'We both do,' said Becky. 'He boards with me and Ma at the Indian King when he's not at sea.'

Fergus thought, from Mr Needham's quizzical expression, that he was likely struggling to understand why a wealthy Shackleton would want to take on an impoverished orphaned pit boy. 'It sounds strange,' he explained, 'but I feel we have a bond, because I was there when the barrel fell on his leg. I'm sure the boy can make something of his life, despite his disability, and I want to help and support him.'

This appeared to satisfy Mr Needham, for he dipped his pen, made some notes, then blotted his writing.

'I assume your intention is to protect the boy and provide for him financially.' He glanced at Fergus, then at Becky.

'Rory can take care of himself day to day,' Becky said. 'Especially as Ma keeps an eye on him and the company he keeps. But what's to say his leg won't worsen? And as it is, his work opportunities are limited. Although he can draw well enough; he outlines ships on slates and sells them to other mariners.'

'Mr Shackleton, couldn't you, in that case, take him into your shore-based operations? A desk position, perhaps?'

'He sometimes works in the offices. My plan is to have him learn all aspects of the Louisa Line. However, what if something happens to me, or Becky?'

Becky leaned forward. 'We think it would be cruel to educate him and bring him into the business for it all to be taken away and him be cast onto the streets.'

'I've been told we can apply for guardianship,' said Fergus. 'But I don't know what that actually entails.'

Mr Needham clasped his hands together. 'There *are* ways to afford the boy protection. The usual term is "Ward in Chancery", but that is for orphaned children with inheritances, and I'm assuming, as a former pit boy, Rory has no wealth or income of his own, apart from the wages he receives from you.'

Fergus shook his head.

'In any case,' Mr Needham continued, 'both of you, being under twenty-five years of age, are too young, and I'm afraid with reference to women, only mothers and grandmothers are eligible. Similarly, Rory could be made a "Ward of Court", but that's rare.'

'What about signing him up with an indenture?' asked Becky.

Fergus shook his head again. 'I can't do that yet. He's not old enough – he has to be fifteen.'

'That is correct,' said Mr Needham. 'But my thoughts are that, there being no funds belonging to him, we do not need to involve the Chancery in any way, other than filing the paperwork with the Justice of the Peace. We can execute a straightforward document making him your ward, outlining any financial provision you wish to make for him.'

'And I don't have to be twenty-five for that?'

'As long as you have achieved the age of majority,

twenty-one, then a straightforward wardship should be sufficient. If I recall correctly, Fergus, you are twenty-two.'

Fergus nodded. 'You say "should" be sufficient?'

'My meaning here is your application would have a much more secure standing were you to be married and –'

'We're betrothed,' Becky cut in.

Mr Needham smiled, 'I am aware of that, or I would not have suggested it at this meeting. If you haven't set a date yet, April is a good time. Mrs Needham and I were wed in April.'

'My parents are home in three weeks.'

Mr Needham studied the brass calendar on his desk. 'Today is March 14th, giving you time for the banns to be read and your parents to settle at home.'

Fergus could see out of the corner of his eye that Becky was blushing, which he always found most attractive. 'Let's discuss this with your mother this evening,' he told her. 'In the meantime, Mr Needham, can you begin drawing up a wardship document ready for, say, the end of the month?'

'You will need to drop in a note regarding the financial considerations,' he replied, tidying his papers. 'There's one more item. I will need to sign an affidavit stating that I have interviewed Rory and ascertained his orphaned state, and he will have to sign a proxy naming you.'

'I can bring him,' said Becky. 'He can sign his own name.'

'It would seem at the moment, Miss Moss, that your mother...Her name is?'

'Dolly, er, I mean, Dorothy Moss.'

'That Mrs Moss is acting as his *de facto* parent, since

he is living with you both in her household, and we require an adult to confirm his details. Are you twenty-one?'

Becky shook her head. 'I'm nineteen.'

'Then, in that case, would your mother be prepared to attend in such a capacity and to sign that his statement is correct? You would also be welcome.'

'I'm sure she would agree to that.'

'That's settled, then.'

'Rory's leaving on the *Sophie Alice* the day after tomorrow. It's a Shamrock run to Cardiff and Dublin.'

'When will he be back?'

'During the first week in April. I can't be more exact. Winds and tides.'

They agreed an appointment on Friday April 5th.

With the meeting at a close, Mr Needham rose from his desk. 'I wouldn't mention anything to the boy yet; it will keep until he's back.'

'We won't,' said Fergus, trying not to show his disappointment. He had thought taking care of Rory would amount to signing a few papers. But then nothing to do with solicitors was ever straightforward.

* * *

Back at the Indian King, Dolly put up a convincing pretence of not having the time to attend solicitors' offices and sign documents, but Becky could see she was secretly pleased to be involved. Rory was becoming a proxy grandson. As Becky had often thought before, the lad had been most fortunate to have Fergus walking by at the time of the accident that crippled him, although his disability was proving a high price to pay for the benefits.

Dolly poured tea for herself and Becky in the kitchen. 'That solicitor suggesting you get wed next month is not such a bad idea, with Fergus's ma and da coming back earlier than expected. The cottage in Coates Lane should be ready too, come the back end of April.'

'We need to send out the invitations, but who will the Shackletons want to invite? It's their son's wedding, after all, and they've no other children.'

'You keep saying you want a quiet wedding. Well, this is your chance. If it's all arranged before they get back, it'll be too late for his ma to fill the church with long-lost relatives. Give her an inch and she'll be setting up a big society wedding at St Nicholas's. Apart from anything else, we can't afford that sort of do.'

Becky sighed. 'I've always wanted to get married at St James's. It's where you, Nan and Granddad were wed, and where I was christened. Besides, it's such a beautiful building on the inside, with the gallery.'

'And the wedding breakfast? What about that?'

'For my future mother-in-law, nothing but the Lonsdale Hotel will do, but I'm thinking the Waverley. I've been to nice do's there.'

'Aye, they put on a good spread, that's for sure. What does Fergus say?'

'He's coming in half an hour. You can ask him for yourself.'

'There's nowt you can plan without a date.'

'We thought maybe the 20th. It's a Saturday. What do you think?'

'I need to check there's no racing that day.'

Becky chuckled. 'Is that the first thing you can think of for my wedding? Whether there's racing or not?'

'We can make a lot of brass on a good race day and with a wedding coming up we'll be able to make use of the extra.' Dolly rummaged through an untidy stack of papers on the kitchen table until she found a calendar.

'You should put that up on the wall, Ma.'

'And let our domestics see all our business? Nay, I don't think so.' She ran her fingers along the entries until she came to April 20th. 'There's no racing that week. I wouldn't want to miss my pie stand. Even people who've backed losers have to eat, and we're getting a reputation with folk from out of town.'

Becky had always thought manning a stand at the races was a tough way to fill their coffers. It was all right when the weather was fine, but up on Harras Moor, where there was no protection from the wind and rain, it could be a nightmare. On days like that, it never seemed worth the reward.

Fergus arrived dripping wet just as Rory came down from upstairs, with Charlie bouncing around his heels.

'You're soaked,' said Becky, putting an arm out for his coat.

'I checked the clouds when I left the warehouse and thought I'd risk it. Then, half way here, the heavens opened.'

'I was going to take Charlie out,' said Rory, turning his nose up at Fergus's wet hair.

Dolly tutted. 'You should have taken him out when I suggested it earlier. I told you I smelt Irish rain coming in off the sea.'

'Irish rain?' Fergus helped himself to a biscuit from a plate in the middle of the table.

'Aye, rain from the west. Rain that's passed over Dublin on its way here.'

'There's no such thing, really,' said Rory bending down to pat Charlie. 'It's just rain.'

'Sometimes if the wind is in the right direction, it's Belfast rain,' said Dolly, laughing.

'A good joke.' Fergus rolled his eyes good-naturedly. 'And what have you two been gossiping about today?'

'Ma and I were talking about the wedding, and where to have the reception. What do you think?'

'The Lonsdale?'

'We were wondering about the Waverley? They've a good reputation.'

Fergus shrugged. 'The Lonsdale, the Waverley – which ever you think. Or why not here at the Indian King?'

'Certainly not,' said Dolly. 'No publican has their only daughter's wedding party on their own premises.'

'Why not?' asked Fergus.

'Because it would be regarded as cheap. People will talk – say I can't afford a decent do. I've brass put by a long time for our Becky's wedding. I've the one daughter and she's getting wed in style.'

'Oh, Ma.' Becky gave her mother a hug.

'Anyway, it's what Da would have wanted for you. A good send-off for his favourite daughter.'

'Only daughter and only child.'

'Aye, so perfect we knew we'd never better you, so we stopped there.'

'Very funny.'

Dolly tapped Fergus's arm. 'Mind you, I'm expecting you to dip into your own pocket for the flowers and the honeymoon.'

'Where are you going on honeymoon?' asked Rory. 'Can I come?'

'No, you can't, I'm afraid,' Fergus told him. 'It's a secret from Becky, but we'll be going on a train. That much I can tell you.'

'Can I wave you off at the station, then?'

'I'm expecting more than *you* to wave us off at the station,' said Becky. She could see it in her mind's eye: their friends and relations on the platform, all wishing them well. Would they be heading north to Carlisle or south to Barrow? Wherever it was, Becky knew she would lose him one afternoon for a few hours to a bookshop, whence he would return with the latest publications.

CHAPTER SIX

Bill was on the Shamrock Run in the *Sophie Alice,* having taken Rory with him, and without his business partner Fergus was having to spend more time than he wished training up their new bookkeeper, Dicken.

When shown the small exercise books they'd been using, Dicken had grimaced.

'Mr Shackleton, the Louisa Line's books are more than account records, wage- and day-books; they are destined to be historic documents. Future generations will pore over them for guidance. Apart from presenting the correct formal appearance, they need to be sturdy. Take the minute-book, for instance. It may still be in use in twenty or even thirty years' time. Also, remember, if you buy cheap, buy twice.'

To begin with Fergus was not convinced by his argument, but when he thought about it, Shackleton & Company did have sturdy record books – the expensive kind, with marble-edgings and heavy card covers – and perhaps it was a false economy not to invest in similar for the Louisa Line.

'For a bookkeeper, you certainly seem to understand how to spend money rather than count it.'

Dicken laughed. 'My aim is to begin as we mean to carry on.' He pointed to the receipts and scraps of paper that had fallen out of the accounts box Fergus had given him. 'You can't expect me not to serve you professionally. Croxall's Bookshop and Stationer's on Lowther Street will have all we need.'

Dicken held out an upturned palm, which Fergus interpreted as a request for money. He sighed. 'You know where the petty cash box is to be found?'

'Yes, in the bottom right-hand drawer over there.' He pointed to an old chest-of-drawers with blackened metal hinges. 'Although, thinking about it, I would suggest we open a credit account with Croxall's. That way we don't have to pay until they send out their invoices, and stationers are notoriously lazy about doing that. We might be able to tweak two – or even three – months' credit.'

This young man's got brains. 'Good idea,' Fergus said, handing Dicken one of their business address slips. 'Take this. If you need authorisation, I can call on them tomorrow.'

'Regarding the petty cash, I think I ought to purchase a proper box with a solid lock.'

Fergus was dubious. 'If you say so.'

'Then as the business expands, which I am sure it will, we can incorporate a strongroom with an iron door. Like they have in banks.'

Fergus thought his new bookkeeper was getting carried away, but then again, he obviously had good ideas, and he didn't want to dampen his enthusiasm. He took out his watch. 'It's locking-up time and I have a business meeting. I suggest you go and place the stationery order now and we can take delivery next week.'

Dicken raised his brows. 'Are you sure? Delivery incurs a charge. I'll call for the items myself on Monday morning, since I'll be passing their door.'

Fergus had an inkling that the reason Dicken was so insistent on calling personally was the presence of Mr Croxall's seventeen-year-old daughter, the beautiful Evangelina. As he shooed the young man out of the door, he found himself anticipating when he could leave him to get on with things. Accounts and paperwork bored him these days, although he acknowledged they were the backbone of any business.

Fergus had stretched a point when he'd told Dicken he had a business meeting. Becky was engaged in doling out mariner wages at the Indian King, as she did each Friday. Some of the shipping companies traditionally arranged for their crews to be paid by the inns and ale houses of the town, knowing they had plenty of small change. It was a custom many disapproved of, since it meant many of the men went straight to the bar. For Fergus, delegating the payment of wages provided him with the opportunity for a quick brandy in the Gentlemen's Club and a glance at the Liverpool newspapers.

* * *

The Gentlemen's Club was always busy as Friday drew to a close. It was the end of the week for the professional offices – the solicitors, bankers and accountants. As Fergus hesitated at the door, wondering whether to go straight to the newspaper table or take out the book he had brought with him, an arm shot up.

'Fergus, come, join me. I could do with a young man's company.'

Fergus was surprised to see Nicholas Fincham, who was smoking a cigar and nursing what looked like Irish whiskey. Fergus had been approached by the club steward earlier in the week to complete membership forms for him. Usually, it took at least a month for someone to be elected; his fellow members must have seen the benefits of admitting an experienced doctor to their rarefied ranks, and hadn't wasted time in doing so.

Fergus made his way over. The smell of the cigar smoke in the room might have been offensive had it not been fresh. It always reminded him of his grandfather, and he closed his mouth and breathed in deeply through his nose for the full effect.

'What will you have, Fergus? An Irish whiskey? A brandy? Or perhaps some Madeira? Now my membership has come through I am able to entertain others, rather than rely on their charity for my refreshment.'

Fergus decided on a French brandy and eased himself into a commodious brown leather armchair, which gave out an audible sigh as he sank into it.

Dr Fincham was in good spirits. 'I'm pleased to see you. How has your week been? And how is the delightful Miss Moss?'

'My week has been busy and Becky is in good health, thank you.'

'And your business? How goes that?

Had anyone else asked him how his business was going, Fergus would have batted the question away with a perfunctory reply. If you said business was anything other than barely satisfactory, people thought twice about paying their bills on time, thinking you didn't need the money. However, already he regarded Nicholas Fincham as family. He had always trusted Aunt Louisa's judgement and if *she* had thought him a suitable person to spend the rest of her life with, then he had no qualms about Nicholas Fincham's character.

Fergus lowered his voice. 'I don't usually discuss business in the club, partly because it is frowned upon, but also because I don't want people to overhear.'

'Forgive me. Club rules and competitors. I am out of practice with gentlemen's clubs. It is a while since I was in India, and the same rules applied there.'

'This week I have been exasperated by the slack management of the Board of Trade.'

'What's that?'

'The Whitehaven Town and Harbour Board of Trustees. They are blatantly inefficient and their priorities are all wrong. I sat in on their meeting as an interested party.'

'Why are they inefficient?'

'They keep the harbour clear of debris, maintain its fabric, that sort of thing, but you know what it's like with committees – there are always groups with opposing views. Take the wet dock, for instance. The shippers and mariners know Whitehaven must have one if it is to thrive – survive, even – especially with all the steamships coming in these days. The professional, non-maritime people of the town don't understand this and can't see the need, while Lord Lowther, despite all his wealth and position as "lord of the manor", doesn't want to be involved with the time and expense of building it.'

'I hadn't realised there was still no wet dock.'

'You've seen ships sitting in mud, waiting for the tide to come in and raise them? Workington has the advantage over us in this matter. They've a fine wet dock, and tugs can operate any hour of the day or night. They are stealing our business, and I can see Whitehaven's trade dwindling as a result. What with that and the shifting of the bigger ships to Liverpool, there's a lot of change going on, and not much of it for the better.'

'That must be a frustration. I suppose you can't transfer your business operations?'

'I'm aiming to improve things here. For a start, Shackleton & Company have strong roots in Whitehaven, and then there's Becky. She'll not want to move elsewhere. We are planning a future here.'

'I assume there are no plans for a wet dock?'

'The trustees go round in circles. The trouble is, this sort of thing can't be rectified overnight. Committees must be established; Lord Lowther has to have his say, and then, even if they should reach agreement, there are the plans to draw up and the time it takes to build a wet dock.'

'Have you considered sitting on the committee yourself, to shake things up a bit?'

Fergus shook his head. 'This will sound weak, but I

don't have the time. I've the Louisa Line, my new business, to build up, as well as Shackleton & Company to oversee. Having said that, we've got tried and trusted managers for Shackletons who save me a lot of day-to-day work. I wouldn't say it can run itself, but it doesn't need nursing like my own company.'

'Have you considered sending your ships further afield?'

'Somewhere like America or Canada? Bill, my partner and the master of the *Sophie Alice,* has worked the west coast of South America, but I'm not sure I want to take on the financial and personal risks of going round the Horn on a regular basis.'

'What about going the other way?'

'To Africa? No, although I hear from our Liverpool agents the African Steamship Company are making wholesome profits in West Africa, since they picked up a colonial government ten-year mail contract.' Fergus glanced over at the club's newspaper table. 'I read the Liverpool papers in here for the comings and goings.'

Dr Fincham swirled the whiskey in his glass, a thoughtful look on his face. 'In Mauritius I often used to dine with the sugar- and tea-plantation owners and brokers. Exactly as you have a continual problem with the Board of Trade, so they have their own ongoing source of vexation.'

Fergus leaned forward. 'Which is?'

Before speaking Nicholas looked around the room and leaned forward with his hands resting on his knees. 'Shipping carriers such as yourself are not prepared to ship the parts for their machinery.'

'Why?

'It's somewhere new, far afield and they don't see opportunity. They can't see the advantage of taking out machine parts and returning with unusual luxury items. Perhaps it would be truer to say they are unaware of the goods they could bring back. For example, my ivory chess set, and exotic textiles, which would sell well amongst the factory and mill owners in Liverpool, Carlisle and the North of England.'

Fergus dropped his voice to little more than a whisper. 'I can see there could be a market for the exotic goods you speak of, but a shipper would have to be sure of a tightly packed outgoing ship, commanding high carriage rates, and a full hold coming back.'

'I'll wager if you ask the shippers and carriers in here this evening where they can buy Indian ivory and gold jewellery, they'll all say India. They don't realise that kind of merchandise can also be purchased in Mauritius, giving a significant saving in voyage time, cost and manpower.'

'And you think there is a real opportunity in such business?'

'You are perfectly placed geographically to pick up the baton I am holding out to you. I'm thinking of Macintosh & Warrilow, engineers in Glasgow who specialise in machinery for sugar production. I was introduced to Macintosh senior in Mauritius. He was thinking of setting up a parts warehouse on the island, but then he changed his mind. Were he still alive, I think he would sorely regret that now. Condensing-plant and evaporators are like gold dust in Mauritius.'

'You're suggesting I think seriously about transporting these spare parts from Glasgow and bringing back exotic goods?'

'You and Bill could easily visit Macintosh & Warrilow to sound them out – your ships go regularly to Glasgow. My thoughts are they will welcome you with open arms. I can provide Bill with letters of introduction for purchasing agents in the capital Port Louis. Think about it, but keep the idea close to your chest. You don't want a competitor leaping in front of you.'

'We'd need a steamship.'

'I thought you were thinking of purchasing one?'

'Yes, but...'

'But what?'

'It would be a huge risk.'

'True, but the rewards could be great. If you do decide to go ahead, I'd be prepared to invest.'

CHAPTER SEVEN

By the spring in his step and the width of his grin, Becky could see Fergus was elated about something when he called at the Indian King that evening. After she'd finished the mariner's wages, he sat in her da's chair by the range while she washed and dried some pots.

'You seem as if you've had a good day. How's Dicken settling in?'

'He's got his head screwed on the right way, and it's good to have someone else carry the chore of keeping the books up to date. Despite insisting we need proper accounting books, I think he'll save me time and the company a great deal of money.'

'And that's put you in such a joyful mood? There's more, I can tell. A newfound freedom from totting up columns of figures and chasing invoices isn't enough to give you the broad smile you've been sporting since you arrived.'

Fergus hesitated, and for a moment Becky wondered if he wasn't going to share his thoughts. 'I spoke with

Nicholas earlier at the club and he made a business proposition. One he would be prepared to invest in himself.'

'What's that?'

'That the Louisa Line take machinery to Mauritius and bring back exotic goods.'

Becky put down her drying cloth. It was such an unexpected suggestion she thought at first she hadn't heard him properly. 'Go to Mauritius? All that way?'

'Yes.' Fergus went into further detail and, as he talked, Becky drew up a chair and sat down opposite him.

'Of course, we'd have to buy a steamship. This is probably the push we need. Bill and I have talked for a while about getting one.'

'Can the company afford one? Are they reliable enough for you now?'

'This time I'll take out a loan. I'll not make the mistake I made last year of using all my own money and not having enough to run the ship. As for reliability, seeing what comes and goes in the harbour my fears are somewhat less than they have been.'

Becky could see Fergus was ignited by the idea; Nicholas had lit a fire that was not going to be easily doused.

'Do you think Bill will want to go?' she asked. 'What about Mary? She hates it when he's away, and with her expecting the bairn.'

'There are lots of things to consider. I think we can say if Bill won't go, then we can't do it. I wouldn't trust anyone else with such a voyage.'

'You'll not go yourself?' Becky would fight tooth and nail against such an idea.

'I've far too much to see to here.'

'And Rory? What about him?'

Fergus shook his head. 'He's not old enough, but if it becomes a regular route, then it would be unkind not to give him the opportunity as an indentured hand. But you rush on. I'm mentioning it as something suggested to me to mull over and discuss with Bill when he's back.'

'But you're excited by the idea, aren't you?'

'I'll not deny it has its attractions. It could set our business up.'

Becky wasn't so sure, but she didn't want to waste breath over something if it might not come to fruition. The idea of a loan was worrying, and when the exotic goods came back, had Fergus given thought to how they were going to sell them?

'We'll not say anything to anyone,' Fergus said. 'I don't want Bill learning of our plans prematurely.'

'And does that mean not saying anything to Ma?'

'I know you share most things with her, but let's keep this to ourselves for now.'

Later that evening, when she was getting ready for bed and brushing her hair, Becky had further misgivings – not so much about the voyage itself, but more about Fergus's impulsiveness. He wasn't one for thinking things through. He'd left home after an argument and paid too much at auction for the *Eleanor Bell*, landing himself in unexpected debt. What if he did the same and lost his inheritance from Aunt Louisa? He would never forgive himself for that. The disgrace to her memory would shatter him.

* * *

The next morning, Fergus called for Becky at half past nine, for their appointment with Rector Longrigg, at St James's at ten.

It was a steep climb up to the church and Fergus soon strode out, leaving Becky to call out, 'Wait for me! What time is it?'

He paused and took out his pocket watch. 'Ten minutes to ten.'

'Exactly, we don't want to be early or late. This rector runs to a strict timetable and he may have others to see. We should enter exactly as the clock strikes ten – show him we can be on time and that we won't keep him waiting on the day.'

Fergus put out his arm for her to take. 'If you wish, although I thought the bride was always late.'

Rector Longrigg was waiting for them at the church door. The interior was familiar to Becky, who attended most Sundays with her ma, but for Fergus it was a surprise. His jaw dropped.

'I had no idea the church was so magnificent,' he said, taking in the decorated pillars and the gallery running all the way round, from the north-facing wall, along the west side over the entrance door, and to the south.

'The gallery is always crowded on Sundays,' said Becky.

When they were in the vestry, Rector Longrigg said, 'The church is over one hundred years old. The exterior, with its box-like shape, does little to prepare the newcomer for what is truly a gem in the town. From your expression, this must be your first visit?'

Fergus nodded. Then, because he didn't want the rector

to think he was a heathen, he said, 'The Shackletons have worshipped at St Nicholas's since my grandfather's day.'

'In that case, it is there you will need to have your marriage banns read. Are you personally a regular attender?'

The rector was studying him and Fergus was glad he was able to reply truthfully, for he was sure he would immediately see through a lie.

'Indeed,' he said.

Rector Longrigg indicated they should sit at a small table. The four chairs around it were the kind with a slot in the back to hold a hymn book for the people sitting behind. Becky and Fergus sat facing him. Fergus searched for Becky's hand underneath the table where the rector could not see, and squeezed it. She squeezed him back.

After taking their details, they were asked why they wanted to marry in St James's.

Becky answered first. 'I was christened here, and you know Ma and I are regular worshippers.'

'Isn't it the custom that a marriage always takes place in the bride's parish?' Fergus asked.

'It is the usual practice, but not essential.' Rector Longrigg placed his hands palm down on the table. 'There are couples who want to marry here solely because of the beauty of this place of worship, not because it's God's house.' He paused, then, in the manner of a judge delivering a sentence, added, 'However, I detect you have both risen above such small-mindedness. I have decided I am prepared to marry you here. Let us discuss a date.'

It had never occurred to Fergus the rector would – or

could, for that matter – refuse to marry them. He was shocked.

'We are thinking of April 20th,' said Becky.

'So soon?'

The enquiring glance he threw at Becky was quick, and had Fergus not, still in shock, been focused on the rector, he would have missed it. *He thinks we're in a hurry because she's expecting.*

Fergus cleared his throat. 'My parents are abroad and will be home again at the beginning of next month. They are only here for a short while before possibly being away again for several months.' *No need to mention Mr Needham's advice that they marry to aid Rory's wardship application.*

'Your parents must be Hector and Elizabeth Shackleton,' said the rector.

'Yes,' said Fergus, bracing himself for further comment.

'I heard your father had retired and gone abroad.'

Fergus knew what Becky would be thinking – that his father would never use the word 'retired' in relation to himself. As far as *he* was concerned, he was only stepping back. He would die in harness.

'I know your father,' said the rector.

Oh, no, someone else Father has upset.

'I approached him for a donation for the church repair fund a few years ago.'

Fergus sent up a small prayer and mentally crossed his fingers.

'I have to say Shackleton & Company were generous.'

Relief flooded Fergus's veins. Had Rector Longrigg

caught his father on one of his 'difficult' days he might have received a less generous response. He made a mental note to ask Mr Rudd to set aside £10 in Christmas week as an annual donation for St James's.

On their way back, they were halfway down the hill when Becky burst out laughing. 'Did you see his expression when we gave him the wedding date?'

'Yes,' said Fergus, chuckling, 'and I saw him look you over again when you stood up.'

'He thought I might be expecting.'

'I know, and I bet he won't be the only one thinks that.'

'Folk'll be eyeing me sideways for a few months, especially the lasses.'

'And the rector.'

'Folk being what they are, they'll be disappointed.'

They sauntered on in silence, each concentrating on the uneven cobbles beneath their feet, until they reached the bottom of the hill. Their conversation, although in jest, had prompted thought. Fergus was not without experience of the physical side of male and female union, and he understood why a lesser man, similarly betrothed, might try and hasten things before the wedding, but he regarded their relationship as too precious to threaten with unacceptable advances. Becky would want their wedding night to be special, and so did he. He would not give his beloved Becky Moss reason to be embarrassed walking down the aisle on her wedding day.

* * *

Dolly, wearing her cross face, was holding a long-handled cobweb brush while standing on the second rung of a small stepladder, dusting off Queen Victoria's portrait. Her Majesty reigned down on them all from the wall behind the bar and was the silent recipient of many drunken toasts throughout the year. She stepped down when Becky came through the door.

'I'm fretting over the Easter weekend work shifts. I thought folk'd want to work Easter Saturday when I'm paying extra. We'll be crowded, and as yet I'm still short on help.'

Becky was keen to change the subject. After she'd said goodbye to Fergus, a problem about the wedding had come to mind as she'd crossed over Duke Street.

'You've a week yet, Ma. There's plenty of time. Anyway, I need to talk with you.'

''Appen, you're right, but I like the work shifts to be settled in advance. What's up?'

'Who's going to give me away?'

'You mean who's going to walk you down the aisle?'

'Aye. Who can I ask? There's no one I can think of now Da's passed on.'

'I'm sure someone from church will step up. I'll speak with the rector.'

As her mother broke off to serve a regular customer, Becky felt an unfamiliar sadness sweep over her. She'd always missed her da, but this was the first time she'd given much thought to what *he* was missing. Every father wants to be the one giving his daughter away to the man she loves. Her father wasn't a particularly God-fearing man;

she couldn't think of anyone connected with the church he'd have been happy to bless on taking his place. She considered the men in the half-full room – men playing cards, chatting, arguing good-naturedly over nothings. Working behind the bar at the Indian King, she probably knew far more men than most girls of her age, but they were customers, not friends, and if she did single one out there would be others who would probably quite rightly feel slighted. The only one she felt any real fondness for was Sergeant Adams, who had been with the Cumberland Regiment and came in daily to sit by the door with his one-eyed dog, Molly. He'd been wearing the same brown coat with brass buttons all the years Becky had known him. Were he twenty years younger, she would have no hesitation in asking him, and she didn't doubt he'd be splendid in his dress uniform. However the occasion, not to mention the walk, would be far too much for him.

Becky's thoughts turned to the other problem that had been waking her in the early hours. She waited for her mother to finish serving a customer his ale, then continued, 'And my dress? I've been having thoughts about that, too. There's so little time and so much to do.'

'What about Christina Burns, the dressmaker on George Street? She's always got pretty frocks in her window.'

'It's not a pretty frock I'm wanting, Ma. Nothing too fancy, but it's got to be special.'

'Aye, lass, you're right, and you want to feel perfect in it. It's *your* day, after all. What about Drake's on King Street?'

'They're drapers, not dressmakers, and they're famous

for mourning dress. Black's hardly suitable; it's a wedding, not a wake.'

'Thinking on it, you're right, they specialise in common clothing. Isabella Little on Church Street – she might be able to do it.'

Becky took a deep breath through her mouth and let the air out slowly through her nose. What she was about to suggest was something her ma might disagree with. 'If you help me, I can make my own.'

Dolly, cloth in hand, cleaning up drip spills on the bar counter, paused mid-wipe. 'Given more hours in a day we could make a dress. We can both sew, but there's Easter coming up, then the race meetings and…Have we the time?'

Although she knew it had nothing to do with the cost, since they only ever bought what they could afford, Becky said, 'It would save a bob or two.'

'Aye, there's truth in that, but –'

'We could work out what cloth we'd need tomorrow and price it all up on Monday. I've seen what I'd like in an *Englishwoman's Domestic Magazine*. It's upstairs, I can show you.' Becky could see her mother was thinking her suggestion through. 'If I wasn't working for you in the pub and could choose my job, I'd want to be working for a smart dressmaker. You know I can sew well enough.' She pointed to her bodice. 'See.'

'It's not right you making your own wedding dress.'

'Let me at least show you the pattern.'

'I've a break in half an hour. We can talk some more then.'

Becky rushed upstairs. The half-hour wait for Dolly

to appear at the kitchen door seemed forever. When her mother came back, Becky was sitting at the kitchen table with the magazine open. Without waiting for Dolly to sit down, Becky launched into describing the dress.

'It's white taffeta. I'm thinking a wide skirt, with three flounces edged in lace. I've seen some lovely French lace in Christina Burns's window, so delicate. We could use it afterwards to edge a christening gown, so we'd get good use of it. See, the corset-shaped bodice is modest, covering the whole of the bosom, with more French lace round the neck. Then matching cuffs for the full sleeves. What do you think?'

Becky held her breath. Dolly didn't answer immediately, and Becky fiddled with a button on her sleeve.

'Would you consider two flounces rather than three?' her mother asked.

Becky put her arms around her ma's neck and hugged her. 'Can we do it?'

'Seeing as how it's not over-fussy, I think so. You'll have to do most of the sewing, but I can cut the pattern and do the fittings. I may be able to find someone to help us. The main question is whether we can get hold of the material at the right price.'

'What about a veil?'

'That's easy. Plain gauze, and we won't have trouble getting that.'

'I'd like flowers in my hair, rather than a bouncy bonnet.'

After they'd discussed further details, and Dolly had been called back to the bar, Becky sat down to make a list of what they would need. Putting pencil to paper made everything fall into place – but what if Elizabeth and Hector took a dislike to the arrangements they were making in their absence? Then what?

CHAPTER EIGHT

When Fergus arrived at the warehouse, Dicken, surrounded by neat piles of paper, was writing in one of the new ledgers. Fergus saw at first glance there were areas of the office now free of clutter. The new record books were lined up against the wall, their spines all clearly labelled in black ink: 'INVOICES', 'CREDIT NOTES', 'CORRESPONDENCE', 'SHIPS', 'HARBOUR TOLLS', 'WAGES'.

Dicken put his pen down and stood to hand Fergus a bundle of papers. 'These came. Mostly advertising.'

Fergus settled down at his desk to go through the bundle. Apart from one sheet, which he put to one side, he ripped the rest in half and tossed them in the wastepaper basket. The item holding his interest concerned a Mr James Harland, general manager of a small Belfast shipyard, who, with his partner Gustav Wolff, had taken the business over from his employer. The new company would be replacing the standard wooden decks with iron ones.

He called out to Dicken, 'Do we have a spare filing box?'

Dicken went over to a wall cupboard upon which, the previous day, a sign had been fixed reading 'STATIONERY'. He took out a grey-and-red-flecked rectangular box.

'How shall I label the box?' he asked, looking at the sheet Fergus was holding out for filing.

Fergus thought for a moment, then said, 'THE FUTURE'.

Dicken gave him a funny look. 'Are you sure?'

'Yes, quite certain.'

Fergus watched him write a label, wet the back of it with a small round sponge, then press it firmly to one side of the box. After putting the sheet inside, he made to put the box back in the cupboard.

Fergus stopped him. 'Wait, I want you to put it in plain sight. This is the path the Louisa Line is going to take. We must be able to see where we're going at all times.'

'How will I decide what documents to file in it?' Dicken was still holding the box.

'Think steam, iron and...' Fergus paused; he wasn't sure himself where the company was going.

'Growth?' offered Dicken, finding a space for the box beside some rolled-up sea charts.

'Yes, steam, iron and growth. The two former will bring about the latter.' He took a sheet of paper and wrote 'MAURITIUS' on it, then folded it and put it in an envelope, which he sealed and handed to Dicken.

Dicken pointed to the front of the envelope. 'You've not put what's inside.'

'I know. That's because the future is never known to us.'

Dicken gave him a look that told Fergus his bookkeeper thought he was peculiar, then put the envelope in the box with the Harland and Wolff document.

'I'll be out of the office now,' Fergus said. 'I'm going to Gudgeon's, the chandler's. The *Eleanor Bell* will need restocking on her return.'

Fergus wanted to check the state of Mr Gudgeon's shelves. As the prominent chandler in Whitehaven, it was his business that would be feeling the effects of the big ships decamping to Liverpool.

When Fergus arrived at Gudgeon's, despite, as always, the acrid smell of rancid oil and newly twisted rope invading his nostrils, it was immediately apparent things were different from his previous visit. For a start, everything was much more orderly than usual. It was as if Dicken had been engaged to tidy up for them. Secondly, Mr Gudgeon, usually to be found out and about issuing instructions to his harassed staff, was sitting behind his counter surrounded by what seemed to be piles of invoices.

Wanting to scout around unnoticed, Fergus made his way to the back of the shop, where the heavier items could be carried in and out more easily through a goods door. There seemed to be plenty of stock on display. The shelves weren't empty, but neither were they full to bursting, as he'd previously seen them. The door to the stock room was ajar, which wasn't unusual, since it was often kept propped open with a doorstop. However, this time some of the shelving was bare, and in other areas goods were spread out, instead of being tightly packed together.

He was about to retrace his steps when he heard angry voices coming from the front of the shop.

'I tell you, we took delivery before we left for Lancaster, with two full sacks of potatoes, and we were only out of port three days for Madeira when cook saw half the potatoes were rotten. So rotten he smelt the stink when he opened the sack, and digging down there was a layer of slime. That's on top of the weevils in the flour last month.'

Fergus heard Mr Gudgeon say, 'Our produce leaves here in the freshest of states. How do I know one of your crew didn't slip in some rotten ones to blacken our name?'

'How do I know one of your staff didn't put a layer of rotten potatoes halfway down the sack?'

'Are you accusing me of malpractice?'

'I'm accusing you of selling goods not fit for purpose. I expect a refund.'

'We don't give refunds.'

'Then you'll not be seeing us again. If you're selling rotten produce, what's to say you're not short weighing other items and selling cheap goods? There's other chandlers, you know.'

'It's your choice.'

'I'll make sure word gets round, sure I will.'

The shop door banged.

Mr Gudgeon appeared embarrassed when Fergus appeared, as if he'd forgotten he was in the shop and able to hear the disgruntled customer.

'Mr Shackleton, kindly take no notice. I've no doubt one of their crew sabotaged my potatoes.'

And the flour? And for what gain?

'I'll be back when the *Eleanor Bell* docks,' said Fergus.

His visit hadn't allayed his fears for the chandlers of the town. He would discuss the situation with Bill and make sure all Gudgeon's stores were carefully checked and signed off for freshness before being loaded. Or, as the previous customer had said, there were other chandlers. He wondered if the big ships leaving were a causative factor in Gudgeon's declining stock and standards.

That evening in the drawing room at Queen Street, as he savoured one of Samuel's generous brandies, Fergus thought about Becky and her wedding dress. He knew it would offend both her and Dolly if he offered to fund it. He could perhaps pay for them both to spend time in Carlisle choosing material, but Dolly would say she was too busy, and he didn't think Becky would take to the idea. He surveyed the room until his eyes came to rest on the tallboy, and he remembered the shawl he had brought back for Aunt Louisa from Dublin – the one with the new synthetic purple dye that Padraig Conran, the agent who had fallen out with his father, had introduced them to. After his aunt's death, his mother had stored the shawl in the tallboy. From there it was a small leap to remembering Conran and his trade token – 'Importer of Wholesale & Retail French & English Cloth'. There had been a deal of trouble on that trip to Dublin.

Fergus swirled the brandy round in its glass and spoke out loud. 'Of course, Padraig Conran. He owes me a favour.'

By seven o'clock the next morning Fergus was at the warehouse, and by a quarter past he had written a letter on Louisa Line notepaper addressed to Padraig Conran in Dublin. By half past seven he had written to Macintosh & Warrilow in Glasgow, to introduce the Louisa Line as a potential carrier of sugar-manufacturing spare parts to Mauritius. At eight o'clock he was back in his office, having personally handed both letters to the captain of the post steamer, with instructions that the deliverer of the Dublin letter was to wait for a reply. The same was to be relayed back by the first available steamer. How he wished Whitehaven had a telegraph office; it would make things so much easier and quicker.

His errand completed, he went to check on the progress of their cottage in Coates Lane. He was relieved to hear singing and whistling as he approached. The smell of plaster dust had been replaced by the chemical odour of paint.

The foreman greeted him. 'We're making good progress, Mr Shackleton, sir.'

'And how is the sick mother in Cockerm'uth? Is your toothache better?'

The foreman scratched his head. 'Sick mammy? Toothache?'

'Oh, never mind.' Fergus didn't want to get into a confrontation over missed working days – he was only too thankful the three men were there, getting on with things.

CHAPTER NINE

Apart from a quick visit to Coates Lane to measure the windows for curtains, Dolly kept Becky too busy preparing for the Easter trade at the pub for her to venture out. It wasn't until Maundy Thursday that her ma sent her to Croxall's Bookshop and Stationer's for paper for dressmaking patterns.

'Once Easter has passed, and things are quiet because folk are short of brass, we'll get cracking,' Dolly said. 'Tomorrow, Good Friday, we'll draw up the pattern after church and I'll set about fitting it on you. Then we'll see precisely what we need. You can run up an underslip on Sunday after the reading of your banns. Folks'll want to talk to you after the service, so we'll be home a bit later than usual. No matter, you'll still have time enough.'

'It feels odd making a dress without having all the material.'

'That's as may be, but remember Nan telling us over and over again – preparation is the most important part of dressmaking. She used to make a tidy sum on the side making outfits for people and doing alterations. If the measurements and the pattern are the right fit, then, cut to true, the dress'll be perfect. Remember all the trouble we went to with the silk-mix material Fergus brought back from Dublin? And that turned out well.'

Becky did remember, and the dress, reserved for special occasions, was in her wardrobe to prove it.

'A shame it isn't white or we could have used that.'

Dolly laughed. 'Aye, a purple wedding dress would raise some eyebrows. You'll get to wear it on your honeymoon. Has Fergus said where you're going yet?'

'It's still a surprise.'

'So, come Tuesday we'll go get the material?'

'Aye, don't worry. If needs be we can always buy from the market on Wednesday.'

'Then we've two and a half weeks to make the dress? Is that enough?' Becky wasn't sure it would be, what with the pub to run too.

'I've come round to the idea. Wedding dresses have been made in less time. "Dinna fash thasen," as Nan would say. Things'll come right. Anyway, I've a notion you'd walk down the aisle in any old thing to marry this love of your life.'

How true, thought Becky. *How true*.

* * *

If he hadn't had the return of the *Sophie Alice* to occupy his mind, the painters at Coates Lane to oversee, what he was going to say to Bill about Mauritius to think about, and the imminent arrival of his parents to prepare for, Fergus would have spent more time thinking about whether he was going to hear from Padraig Conran in Dublin. As it was, with the letter despatched, he put the matter to the back of his mind.

He was fully aware that he and Bill also had to firm up plans for the Louisa Line's future. Over the last two months they had had several serious discussions, but never actually reached workable decisions. There always seemed to be new considerations. This time there was Mauritius to discuss, and if they decided to take that path their hands would be forced, because they would need a steamship.

When Fergus arrived at the warehouse, as soon as Dicken saw him he pointed to some envelopes.

'I've gone through the post,' he said. 'There's an order for collection from the Isle of Man, more advertising material, and a young lad wanting work.'

Fergus was uncomfortable with his newly appointed bookkeeper opening the office post, especially as he was expecting a reply from Macintosh & Warrilow. He was about to say so, when Dicken carried on, 'I've organised an "In and Out" system. The "In" section is for post, orders, messages and the like. The correct ledgers are there.' He pointed to the appropriate area. 'And this area here is for work completed. Paid invoices, credits, reports, that sort of thing.' Dicken's eyes were shining.

'Thank you,' Fergus said. 'I can see you've put in a lot of thought and work. Things are much improved. In future there is no need for you to open the post, it is not your job. If you leave it on my desk, I will see to it myself.'

With the expression of a severely scolded child, Dicken turned his attention back to writing in his ledger, his head down.

Fergus wasn't sure what to think. The young man was obviously organised, but if he was going to go into a sulk when he received instruction, that was going to be a nuisance. For a brief moment he wondered if he had made a mistake employing him, but he had to admit the office was in much better shape. The books and papers were organised, neat and tidy, and he'd grown used to the smell of soap that emanated from his bookkeeper.

Upstairs, checking the first-floor shelving recently packed with casks, trunks and other merchandise awaiting carriage, Fergus was pleased. Their business was growing. He'd already decided he would introduce his father to this centre of the Louisa Line's operations. It would be akin to showing a grandchild to a grandparent. The top floor was empty, but there was no need to show his father that. Besides, he would grumble at having to climb the steep stairs.

Then Fergus pulled himself up sharp, startled to realise he still needed his father's endorsement. Old habits die hard. He wondered if it was going to be the same old petulant, short-tempered Hector who stepped down from the carriage at Queen Street, or whether he really had been delivered of his demons. Surely his mother would have kept reminding his father that his renowned cantankerousness was the root of his ill health? In whatever mood his father returned, they would soon all know.

* * *

It was Good Friday morning and, dressed in their Sunday best, Dolly and Becky were beginning the Queen Street climb up to St James's Church when Becky stopped.

'What is it, love?' asked Dolly. 'Forgotten something? You're wearing your gloves.'

'Are you going to speak with the rector about who will walk me down the aisle?'

'I think today is a good time to do so. We can wait behind after the service and catch him. Don't you want me to?'

'I've been thinking. There's only one person I can think of who Da would have wanted to take his place.'

"And?'

Becky wasn't sure how her ma was going to take her suggestion and now she was hesitant to voice it.

'Am I expected to guess, lass?'

'Why don't *you* give me away?'

'Me? There's a thought. Come on, lass, we'll be late.'

She didn't get cross, thought Becky, taken by surprise.

It was only later, after people had expressed their pleasure at hearing her banns read, and Dolly had carried straight on outside without holding back, that Becky realised they were not going to be having a word with the rector. She held her tongue until they'd crossed George Street.

'You didn't speak with the rector,' she said.

'I used the sermon to think about what you said, and I think you're right. Your da would want me to take his place.'

'And you will?'

'Aye, though there's folks'll think it queer.'

'We've never been worried o'er much about what other folk might think.'

'We won't say anything. They'll hardly turn me away from the door with you on my arm, both of us all dressed up. Will they?'

Becky put her arms around her mother and hugged her. 'Thanks, Ma. Da will be happy.'

They had only been home a few minutes when there was a loud knocking on the door.

Dolly, still in her best bonnet said, 'Tell whoever it is we'll be ready for business in half an hour.'

Becky opened up to find one of their regulars, the carpenter from further up Roper Street. He'd been doing some work for them at Coates Lane and she didn't think he would be working on Good Friday. However, he hadn't come about the house.

'Seeing as how you were locked up, I took in some parcels for you. Came on last night's late boat, apparently.'

'Ma, we're not expecting any parcels, are we?'

Dolly shook her head and came to the door. 'What kind of parcels?'

'Three. They're heavy, which is why I haven't brought them with me. I'll send the boys down with them. We're working today – we've coffins to get ready for the Robertson twins.'

Becky flinched. 'I'm grieved to learn that. Mr Robertson only lost his wife in January.'

'Aye, and now the twins. When the mammy dies in childbirth, it's hard to keep twins. We get a lot of this.'

After he'd left, Becky and Dolly talked briefly about the Robertsons and the bad luck they'd suffered, then racked their brains, but still couldn't think of anything they were expecting.

'What's to say after all this palaver the parcels aren't for us?' asked Dolly.

'They're here.'

Two tall lads came in, each carrying a package. The stockier one said, 'Here y'are, missus. Where you wanting 'em?'

Dolly examined the address label. 'They're for you – Miss Becky Moss.'

'Where from?' asked Becky, coming forward to check the label for herself.

'Dublin. And there's another one to fetch.' Dolly opened the door to the kitchen. 'Put them in here, on the table.'

The third parcel was heavier than the others. After the lads had left, with the tuppence Dolly had given them for their trouble, the two women stood and stared at the delivery.

'You'd better open one,' said Dolly, giving Becky a pair of scissors. 'Take care, though. Whatever it is, you don't want to damage it.'

Becky made a small cut at one end then gingerly tore away some of the outer covering. 'There's sailcloth, loads of it. That's why the parcels are so heavy.'

'That'll be to protect whatever's inside,' said Dolly, coming in closer.

As more of the outer covering came away, Becky came across a white envelope. She pulled gently to release it.

'This'll tell us where it's come from,' said Dolly.

The envelope seal broke easily and Becky took out a white card. At the top was a printed heading in swirly lettering: *Padraig Conran, Importer of Wholesale & Retail French & English Cloth, Dublin.* Underneath this, in what Becky would later describe to Fergus as 'fancy writing', were the words:

'*To dear Becky,*
My wedding present to you and Fergus.
Yours, Padraig.'

Becky's head shot up. 'I think it's material for my dress.'

'I never!' said Dolly. 'And in time, too. No guessing who put him up to this.'

After the parcels had been opened, accompanied by much excitement and laughter, only a small box remained. Dolly spread two clean cloths on the table to protect the material. They stood and stared in awe at the feast of fabric laid out before them.

'I can't believe it,' said Becky. 'Don't cry, Ma, we should be happy.'

'Don't be such a ninny. I'm crying because I'm happy.'

'Can I accept it?' asked Becky.

'I don't see why not. It's a wedding present.'

'Some of this is properly expensive. We'd never've been able to afford anything like this. There's pure silk and taffeta.'

'Aye, and there'll be enough left over for six christening gowns, I'd say. What's in the box?'

The top was firmly fixed so Becky, with difficulty, eased it off. Once removed, the contents came spilling out.

'Ribbons,' she said. 'Lots of silk ribbons. Different widths, too.'

Dolly tipped the box upside down and a packet fell out. 'There's more.'

Both of them held their breath as Becky unwrapped the tissue from the final parcel. 'It is…it's French lace.'

Dolly touched it.

Becky picked up a length and danced around the room, waving it above her head, while her ma watched and laughed.

'Now I can have as many flounces as I want.'

'Aye, you can, and with the brass we're going to save, we can afford someone to help us.'

When Fergus called later that afternoon, Becky couldn't thank him enough.

'Not only the material, but see all this.' She opened the box and all the ribbons and lace fell out.

'I didn't expect him to respond so generously.'

'He does owe you, after the whiskey customs fiasco last year.'

'Isn't it bad luck to see a bride's dress before the wedding?'

'I don't think it counts when it's not made up. At least, I hope not.' She began to pack up the parcels. 'Did they read your banns at St Nicholas's?'

'Yes, and it caused quite a stir. Several people came up to me afterwards.'

I'll wager they were surprised, thought Becky. *A Shackleton marrying a Moss, and none of them knowing me. I'll be a curiosity.*

CHAPTER TEN

It was gone two o'clock. In Fergus's pocket was a letter from Macintosh & Warrilow he had yet to open. He was authorising some invoicing with Dicken at the warehouse when he heard a familiar voice.

'Mr Shackleton! Mr Shackleton!'

'Someone's come in the front,' said Dicken. 'Sounds like a young lad.'

'It's Rory, and it means the *Sophie Alice* has returned. I've been expecting her. Brocklebank's *Veronica* overtook her at dawn and reported she was on her way.'

Rory burst into the office, with Charlie at his heels. When he saw Fergus, the young dog started barking and leaping with excitement, before running between everyone's legs, chasing his tail. The noise was deafening and Dicken covered his ears. Fergus saw him edge back, in the way people do who are afraid of dogs, or who dislike them.

After Rory had rounded up Charlie and settled him with a biscuit, he told Fergus, 'We're tied up, Mr Shackleton. All hands returned safe and sound. Captain McRae said to tell you all's shipshape and he'll be in to see you by four, after he and Mr Sven have signed off.'

'That is welcome news, Rory,' Fergus took the boy by the shoulders and turned him towards Dicken. 'This is Mr Birkett. He is our new bookkeeper. Do you understand what that means?'

'He reads a lot?'

Fergus laughed. 'Sort of. He takes care of the money.'

Rory put out his hand. Dicken held back for a moment before accepting it, then, after they had shaken, he rubbed his own hand down the side of his trousers.

To Dicken, Fergus said, 'And this is Rory Rooke, Cook's assistant on the *Sophie Alice,* previously on the *Eleanor Bell.* He makes a flavoursome sultana duff, even when the oven's doused for a storm.'

'Aye, that I do.' Rory pulled a small flax bag from his pocket and tipped some shells into his hand. 'Here's more shells for my mammy's bowl.'

'I thought your mammy had passed away,' said Dicken.

'Aye, but she had a blue-and-white bowl that I said I'd fill with shells for her. When she died, she left a note saying she wanted Miss Becky to have it, and so now I'm collecting shells for Miss Becky.'

Fergus patted Rory's head. 'Away right this minute to see Mrs Dolly and report home. She and Miss Becky have missed you. I've no barley sugar for you here, but I'm sure you'll find some waiting at the Indian King.'

After Rory had left, Fergus asked Dicken to buy a tin of barley sugars and a bag of dog biscuits for the stationery cupboard, the next time he passed the confectionary shop.

Dicken raised his brows. 'With the petty cash?'

'Yes,' said Fergus. 'Mark them in the books as "customer refreshments".'

'I don't think –' Dicken began.

'No, put "client refreshments". That sounds better.'

* * *

At a quarter to four, Fergus sent Dicken to deliver an invoice to the far end of Lowther Street, telling him that after that he could go home. This gave him time to read Macintosh & Warrilow's reply and ensured he would be alone when Bill arrived.

He sat at his deck and picked up his letter opener, then paused and turned the letter over. The contents could change everything or nothing. He slit it open and read:

'*April 1st 1861*

Dear Mr Shackleton, Sir,

We are in receipt of your letter of the 26th ult, and reply herewith. The partners suggest a meeting at our offices where we may discuss the matter further, perhaps when you are next in Glasgow.

Kindly convey our best wishes to Dr Fincham. Our agent in Mauritius has mentioned him in his reports on occasion as having treated some of the residents there with good effect.

Yours Truly,
Guthrie Macintosh,
Macintosh & Warrilow,
Weston Works, Cook St,
Glasgow'

Fergus had dithered over mentioning Dr Fincham when he'd written, but was now glad he'd done so. His thoughts were racing. All they needed now was for Bill to come aboard and for the Company to purchase a steamship. Aware of his tendency to be impulsive, Fergus told himself he must not thrust the idea on Bill the moment he entered the door. It would be difficult, but he must work up to it.

It was a quarter past four when Bill arrived with the *Sophie Alice*'s papers under his arm. They exchanged pleasantries and Fergus made ready to update him with the local business gossip.

'A good voyage?' he asked.

'Profitable,' said Bill, handing over his papers. 'Here are the sale and commission notes.'

'And the conditions?'

'Mostly the wind was fair for this time of year, but we've suffered heavy rain and blow since we left Dublin. Nothing like the big Atlantic swells, but she plunged until we were far past the Isle of Man.'

'That's to be expected. I knew she was a bit of a plunger when I bought her.'

'You didn't make a mistake. With a sound, foot-sure crew a bit of plunging is of little bother.'

The term 'foot-sure' reminded Fergus of Rory and he asked how he coped on board.

'He's a few bruises to show for his efforts chasing Charlie up and down the deck, but he's sensible. After a minor crack on the head, which he admitted afterwards was because he was going too fast for his twisted leg, he learned his lesson. He's a useful lad to have on board.

Spent his spare time painting his slate ships and reading. Sven taught him to play whist, as only a first mate can. Only complaint is, we had the devil of a job getting him to wash. In the end, after more than a few comments, Sven picked him up and dunked him in a barrel on deck.'

Fergus grinned. 'Feet first, I hope.'

'Indeed, but he told him if he didn't keep himself clean it'd be head first next time.'

Fergus laughed. 'No young boy likes washing, but that should do the trick.' He toyed with the letter on his desk. 'I know you're anxious to see Mary. How long until she makes a father of you?'

'Late May. The crew have been placing bets on it being a boy.'

'We'll know soon enough, but right now we need to speak. I've Father and Mother returning tomorrow and they will command my attention for a while.'

Bill took the seat opposite Fergus. 'That will liven things up a bit.'

'Let's hope Father returns as the new Hector and not the old cantankerous one. Becky and I are to be married on the 20th while they're here.'

'That's been decided quickly.'

'It's partly to do with making Rory my ward, since being married strengthens my application. Incidentally, Rory doesn't know anything about it yet. You'll be my best man, I hope?'

'Gladly. A lot has transpired while I've been away.'

'More than you realise.' Fergus took a deep breath. 'I'd like to talk to you about the new doctor and Mauritius.'

'That's a combination I didn't expect and don't understand.'

Released from the strain of not being able to discuss the idea of Mauritius with anyone except Becky, Fergus launched right in with an account of the doctor's suggestion that they ship machinery there and bring back exotic goods. Bill sat quietly taking it all in. Occasionally he nodded. At one point Fergus stood and paced around the office, as if speaking were not enough to relieve him of the tensions he was experiencing. When he'd finished, he took his seat again.

'I realise you haven't had time to dwell on the idea,' he said, 'but what are your first thoughts?'

Bill didn't hesitate. 'That we'll need a steamship and that, while Mauritius is an exciting prospect, it *is a* distance. Assuming I'd be master, I'd be gone over six months, leaving Mary with a new baby, and she'll not like that. But for the Louisa Line, it sounds possible. Even advantageous.'

'Dr Fincham is happy to come in with us as an investor. You must meet him. He's a sound fellow.'

Fergus knew it was too much to expect a rushed, unconsidered opinion from Bill, especially when he'd sprung it on him within hours of his arriving back. However, he had to know whether the proposition held any sparks for his partner and if so, whether he was willing to begin planning right away.

'There's a lot to ponder, I know,' he said, 'but I've planted the seed with you. Now, I can tell you I've already gone ahead and written to Macintosh & Warrilow and they've replied showing interest.' Fergus gave Bill the letter. 'We can both visit them on the next Glasgow run.'

'I'm not opposed to such a long voyage, but with the best will in the world, Fergus, we need to think this through. You can be impulsive sometimes.'

'I like to think of myself as spontaneously enthusiastic.' He stood up. 'This is where *your* caution comes in. Between the two of us we make a formidable alliance. Are we decided on that much?'

'I'll certainly drink with you to that, but I must away. Let's talk further.'

Bill had got as far as the door when Fergus said, 'Not a word to Father when he returns.'

Bill chuckled. 'And be the cause of another near-fatal attack?'

'Or to Mary, although I've discussed it with Becky.'

'What did she say?'

'Her concerns were for you and Mary and, like you, she thinks it's a long way. Now, away to your wife.'

Whilst Bill had succeeded in keeping his immediate thoughts to himself, Fergus noted there had been no instant condemnation. He was sure, when Bill thought things through, that he would be on board. What ship's master wouldn't leap at the chance of a trip from Cumberland to the Indian Ocean? New places and fresh faces. Bill was more than capable of captaining a steamship on such a voyage. And regarding Mary, surely most married mariners had, at some time, left a wife with a newborn baby? It was almost part of their job.

* * *

Fergus stood on the front steps at Queen Street, watching his parents alight from the carriage. He saw immediately how his father was strained and appeared older. To what extent his aged appearance was due solely to journey fatigue, it was impossible at that moment to say. His mother, however, appeared rejuvenated. She rushed to him with open arms.

'Fergus, how wonderful to see you.'

'And you, Mother.'

A peacock feather making an escape bid from her bonnet brushed across Fergus's forehead as she embraced him.

His father came forward with an outstretched hand. It's skin was thin and veiny, and Fergus noticed he was walking with a stick. Elizabeth followed his glance.

'I'm afraid your father had an accident in the capital. He moved to avoid a flower-seller's basket and stepped right into the path of a handcart. The front wheel caught his ankle.'

'Yes, I fell straight down, landing on my elbow and hip. I was fortunate not to fare worse. It drew quite a crowd, too. A pleasant young man helped me up.'

'Have you seen a doctor?' Fergus took his father's arm to lead him up the steps into their front hall.

'I saw a London quack, if that's what you mean.'

Elizabeth corrected him. 'No, Hector, you saw a well-regarded physician.'

He thrust out his right foot. 'So well regarded, his bandage is falling off after only two days. It needs strapping up good and tight. I'll consult Lennagon. He's no horse doctor, he'll put me right.'

Fergus could see through the gaps in the bandage that his father's ankle was badly bruised and swollen. He had a moment of foreboding. His father would demand a house call and that might mean Dr Fincham arriving. His plan had been to introduce Nicholas's return gently, over a cigar and a large brandy, when his father's feelings would be mellow. He was sure he wouldn't greet the news of Nicholas Fincham's return with much joy. And although it had been Fergus's grandfather who had forbidden his Aunt Louisa to marry, his father had been her brother, and of age at the time, and Fergus suspected Nicholas held him partly responsible. However, it was more a feeling than a truth because whenever his father was mentioned, Nicholas always changed the subject.

With Samuel's help, Hector was guided upstairs and settled in his favourite chair, his leg supported on a stool. Elizabeth excused herself, saying she was needed in the kitchen to instruct the staff and check the stores.

Fergus followed the butler downstairs. 'Samuel, when you send for the doctor, ask specifically for Dr Lennagon.'

'Certainly, sir. By that you mean not the new Dr Fincham?'

'My father and Dr Fincham have history from a long time ago and there could be a certain awkwardness between them. Especially as my father is in pain.'

Having satisfied himself Samuel understood his instructions, and knowing he could rely on him to do his best to carry them out, Fergus returned to the drawing room.

When the three of them were reassembled, they chatted about the journey for a while, and the people who'd shared their carriage. Then Fergus broached the subject of the wedding. His parents met the date of April 20th with surprise, but when Fergus explained about Rory's wardship, and pointed out that Coates Lane was almost ready, they seemed more accepting. The same could not be said for the venue.

'St James's?' Elizabeth's expression was one of dismay. 'But the Shackletons have always married at St Nicholas's Church. The carriages have always drawn up outside it. St James's is way up on the hill.'

'Your mother's right,' said Hector, his brow furrowed.

'It's traditional for the wedding to take place at the bride's church,' said Fergus.

He watched his mother mull over his words. 'You mean Shackleton men must always have married other St Nicholas's worshippers?'

'That must be so,' said Hector.

Elizabeth did not appear mollified.

Fergus continued, 'Our banns are being read in both churches.'

This seemed to placate her a little. 'And the wedding breakfast? At the Lonsdale?'

Fergus shook his head.

'The Indian King?' asked Hector.

'No,' said Fergus, noting a flash of relief pass over his mother's face.

'Then where?'

'The Waverley.'

'Oh,' said Elizabeth, in a tone that implied 'oh, no.'

There was a silence.

'Not the Lonsdale, then?' repeated Hector.

'No.'

'I see,' said Elizabeth, although her manner indicated she wasn't happy.

Fergus changed the subject. 'You must tell me about your travels.'

His mother launched into an account of the trouble they'd endured in Paris due to all the rebuilding work, and how difficult it was for the carriages to get around, even though the streets were now so much wider. She was in full flow when Samuel announced Dr Lennagon.

Fergus's relief was short-lived.

The doctor bounced in. 'Elizabeth, and my dear friend Hector, how wonderful to see you. You must tell me all about your trip over a whiskey. I am far too comfortable at home to undergo such foreign travels, so I am forced to survive on second-hand accounts.' He put his bag on the floor, knelt down and raised Hector's foot, ignoring his wince. He unwound the bandage and, when the foot was visible, ran his hands over the injury.

'Ooh, this is unpleasant, Hector, but it will mend.'

'I do not need you to tell me it's damnably unpleasant.' Hector winced again as the doctor pressed the centre of the swelling.

'Apologies, I don't mean to hurt you. All part of the examination.'

Hector managed a tight smile.

Dr Lennagon continued, 'I don't want to belittle your pain, but it's not that bad a sprain. There'll be a lot more bruising and you'll have to rest it. You're lucky nothing is broken.' He closed his bag. 'Speaking of travelling, I expect Fergus has told you Nicholas Fincham has returned to Whitehaven to see out his days.'

Oh no, this couldn't come at a worse moment. Father tired and in pain. What a time for the cat to leap out of the bag.

Hector's head shot up. He peered at Elizabeth, then back at the doctor, who was getting up from the floor. 'Nicholas Fincham? The doctor?'

'Yes, he's joined the practice. A useful addition, especially for pit accidents. Being a ship's surgeon, he's carried out a lot of amputations. Not so experienced in childbirth, though, he's not had many of those. But if you enjoy travellers' tales of fresh horizons at sea and on land – in India and that island off Africa, Mauritius – then he's your man. You do remember him, don't you?'

Hector responded with a long slow nod. 'You know I do, you scoundrel.'

'I thought for a moment you'd forgotten. After all, it's thirty years ago, and more than that since he and I were surgeon-apothecary students together.'

Fergus stole a glance at his mother. She was staring at Hector, her lips tightly sealed.

'I expect you'll run into him at the club.' Dr Lennagon turned to Fergus. 'I see you acted as one of his membership sponsors, Fergus.'

'Yes, the secretary asked me to.' *It's all out in the open now.* Fergus wondered briefly if he could make his exit while the doctor was still there, but he knew he'd have to face the music. He might as well stay and get it over with.

The post-examination whiskey delayed things and the doctor could have been only halfway down the stairs when Hector said, 'You didn't tell us Nicholas Fincham had returned.'

'It was not my first thought to impart the news when I saw you. Your health, your trip, the date of my marriage and our home seemed of greater importance. I'm sure you will agree?'

Elizabeth stood up. 'We understand. Your father is surprised, aren't you, Hector?'

'Surprised? That's an understatement. I'm astonished. I never thought we'd see him here again. In fact, when I gave him any thought, it was to imagine we would be learning he'd gone down with all hands in some remote foreign place, or been knocked overboard by a main boom and drowned.'

'Does he have family?' asked Elizabeth.

'If you're asking me if he's accompanied by a wife, the answer is no. He never married.'

'And you've seen and spoken with him?'

'Yes, several times, at the club. He's an interesting fellow.' *I'm going to have to tell them.* 'And we entertained him here for luncheon.'

Hector frowned. 'I thought the house was closed socially while we were away.'

'You don't mind, do you?' asked Fergus, knowing his parents probably did mind.

Elizabeth was the first to speak. 'I'm surprised you would entertain him here – in our home, when we were abroad?'

'Where else could we show hospitality?'

'I suppose the Indian King was not an option?'

'No,' said Fergus. 'I wanted to hear about Mauritius, and a working public house is noisy. Anyway, it gave the staff of the house something to do, and Becky was a delightful hostess. All earlier concerns you had regarding her social skills are unfounded.'

Elizabeth shrugged. 'It's done. It is your happiness we seek, Fergus, but I repeat, I am surprised you opened the house, and for Nicholas Fincham of all men.'

Fergus's father appeared about to say something, until a glance passed between his mother and him, and seeing perhaps what was a reprimand in her expression, he changed his mind. Fergus had no doubt his parents were annoyed. There was also something else. Could it be guilt? Did his father now accept they should have let Aunt Louisa marry Nicholas?

He decided it would be a good idea to make his escape, before more was said. 'I'll leave you both to rest. I have two businesses to run.'

'How are they doing?' asked Hector.

I can't tell him about losing the Campbell account after the Fincham news.

'All in good time, Father. When your ankle is healed, we'll have a business meeting at Shackletons' office.' Fergus held his breath. Was his father going to attempt to assume command again, or was he going to keep his word and sit back?

Elizabeth was scrutinising Hector as if she, too, knew this was a critical moment in his return.

'Don't make me wait too long. I've handed over the reins, but it's my carriage you're driving, and I want to know what's been going on in my absence.'

CHAPTER ELEVEN

It was not long before Fergus's father insisted his injury was no problem, and a meeting was duly arranged. Waiting for his father at the Shackleton & Company offices, Fergus was nervous. Would his father blame him for the expected termination of the Campbell account?

When Hector entered the building, the staff rose as one and clapped. This spontaneous welcome appeared to take him by surprise. He ran his fingers through his hair, seeming momentarily embarrassed. Then he smiled and began greeting several of the staff by name, waving his stick at others in a show of greeting. After the applause had died away, he made his way slowly up the stairs to his old office. He paused at the door.

'You lead the way, son. I expect these days you're used to sitting in my chair.' He gave a wry grin.

Fergus knew it had taken a lot for his father to make that comment, but although it warmed his heart, it didn't check his nervousness. He waited until Hector was settled, then took up his position behind his father's desk. He'd prepared some paperwork, including the minutes from the monthly board meetings. Hector listened intently to the figures Fergus presented. They'd talked for fifteen minutes about Shackleton & Company's general business before Fergus raised the matter of the Campbell account.

'I'm afraid not all is going as we might hope.'

Hector raised an eyebrow. 'And?'

'We are subject to changing times.'

'I know that,' said Hector. 'Nothing is as it was. At times I feel I am not living in the same country I was born into.'

'The railways are carrying more and more freight.'

'You're beating round the bush. Out with it.' There was a hint of the old grumpiness in Hector's voice.

'It seems we're going to lose the Campbell account to the railways.'

'The Campbell account? We've had that for ten years or more. I know old man Campbell.' He rapped his knuckles on the desk. 'I'll write to him.'

'You can't. He died a year ago and his nephew's taken over.'

'I didn't know that. No one told *me*. That explains it, then. Old Mr Campbell would never have let us down.' He paused and then, as if a new thought had occurred to him, he said, 'We must have upset them. Who goes there these days?'

'Bill and the *Sophie Alice*. We have not upset them. They, along with others, have discovered they can now access the Yorkshire and Lancashire mill towns directly, by train.'

'So this affects our competitors as well as ourselves?'

'Yes. All carriers. We cannot compete with the carriers of goods that are easily transportable. The trains run on time, there's no risk of loss at sea and, in due course, they are bound to become cheaper and more profitable. Success will bring success.'

Hector made one of his 'humph' sounds and Fergus braced himself. In the past this had always been the preface to a loss of temper and much shouting.

'Father, please don't vex yourself. It's a sign of the times. We're being buffeted by the seas of change.'

'My doctor tells me I must not become angry over things I cannot change. Are you sure there is nothing *I* can do?'

'Were old Mr Campbell still alive, I don't think it would make any difference. Campbells are making a sound economic decision.'

His father put his lips together as if about to hum. The knuckle-tapping became faster and louder.

Fergus leaned across the desk and put his hand over his father's to steady it. 'The loss of this account is unfortunate, but it's certainly not going to break Shackletons. Let me tell you about the Louisa Line. Will you take a cigar?' He opened a desk drawer.

Hector frowned. 'I can't. Your mother will smell it on me, and I am now only allowed them on special occasions.'

Fergus closed the drawer. 'The Louisa Line has two ships now – Captain Jessop with the *Eleanor Bell* and Bill with the *Sophie Alice*. We're still doing the Shamrock Run with limestone to Cardiff and coal to Dublin. I see these as cargos we won't lose to the railways, since trains cannot cross the sea.'

'So, you've two crews to keep afloat?'

'Yes, and the Chapel Street warehouse to run. We're picking up good storage business.'

'Making a profit?'

'A small one. Our aim is to secure carriage routes and customers.' Fergus had already decided not to mention Mauritius. He knew his father would regard the contract as far too risky, or the stuff of dreams. Better to present him with a *fait accompli* should they choose to go ahead.

'You own two ships outright,' Hector said. 'Have you thought about issuing shares for them? Or perhaps for a third one? There's greater responsibility if you do, because you're answerable for other people's money, but effectively they're giving you an almost interest-free loan. Your grandfather did that when he started out with the post-boats.'

Fergus recognised the validity of his father's observations. The Louisa Line shouldn't go on buying ships outright; it was bad business if they could take out cheap loans instead. 'Bill and I have talked about it. What is your advice?'

Hector leaned forward. 'It is common for masters to buy shares in other mariners' ships, to offset the possibility of a total loss in their own ships. Also, should all hands be lost, then widows still have a source of livelihood. While I'm in the mood for giving advice, and you seem interested in listening to it, I have a couple of other suggestions I'd like to put forward, and I'd like to view the warehouse.

Although I'm conscious your mother has given me specific instructions I am to advise, not to order.'

Fergus smiled. It was clear his mother was doing her best to keep the relationship between father and son on an even keel since their falling out. Now that the Campbell account had been dealt with, Fergus was enjoying discussing the two businesses with Hector. It was a sharing of minds they could never have achieved previously. Although it was a dreadful thing to think, he was almost thankful his father had had his death fright and changed his ways.

'Tell me, son, are you keeping a firm eye on your competitors?' Hector asked.

Fergus was surprised by the question. 'I know who they are.'

'That's not enough. You need to know exactly what they are up to.'

'Spy on them?'

'The best way is to put an ear to the ground outside Whitehaven. In Glasgow, Edinburgh, Dublin, Carlisle and especially, these days, Liverpool. You don't need to do it yourself. Speak with your agents – they're the ones who are privy to what is going on, because they're rubbing shoulders with each other. Next time you're in Edinburgh, call and see Shackleton & Company's agent, Mr Cameron. You've met him before. He may have gossip he's prepared to share with you, or might even take on your interests.'

Fergus had been dithering over whether to organise the honeymoon for Edinburgh, Carlisle or Lancaster. His father's comment cemented his decision. Edinburgh it would be, and he could call on Cameron at the same time. He would write to him and make an appointment.

'Who are your allies?' his father continued.

Fergus thought for a moment. 'Bill McRae. Apart from being a valued friend, he has a financial interest in the business.' Fergus wanted to say Becky, but he didn't want to get into an argument with his father over a woman's place in business. He knew his father disapproved, and whilst he had mellowed in some areas, Fergus didn't think his attitude would have changed much on that score.

'What about your chandler? Isn't Gudgeon getting on in years?'

Fergus could see where Hector's mind was going with the question. 'I was there the other day and, yes, it's clear they are having problems. Whether Gudgeon is too old to care about the business or whether they're simply losing customers it's too soon to tell, but I have my eye on them. As my father's son I'm more than aware that a chandler keeps a ship afloat. Do you have any further advice?'

'Retain the goodwill of those providing the bulk of your cargoes. Be ruthless and restless. Complacency is your enemy in the shipping business.'

Fergus thought this somewhat strange advice from a man who'd consistently refused even to consider making enquiries about steamships. He couldn't hold back from commenting, 'And steamships, Father? What is your view on those these days?'

A slight red flush appear on his father's cheeks. 'I will admit, thanks to my continental tour, that I have partly revised my view of steamships. They have their place, but my own preference will always be for sail.'

'You'll come and visit the Louisa Line warehouse tomorrow, will you? If your ankle can stand it.'

'I'd like that. Now I'm properly strapped up, I can get about. I tell you that London doctor had no right to be practising medicine. Didn't know a whit. Give me a good country doctor anytime – one used to hunting and proper accidents.'

Fergus glanced up at the oversized clock on the office wall then pulled out his pocket watch to double-check the time. 'I must away, Father. With my wedding I have a lot to attend to. You'll be wanting to catch up with the staff downstairs. I'll call Mr Craggs to attend you, but before I do I need to ask you something.'

'What's that?'

'It's about Nicholas Fincham.'

Hector's features changed and for a moment Fergus was reminded of the old Hector, the crabby Hector so quick to find fault. 'I have to say we have decided he won't be passing the threshold when your mother and I are in residence,' he said, clamping his jaw. 'Too many things were said by both sides that cannot be unsaid. I have neither forgiven nor forgotten, and I doubt Fincham will have done so, either.'

'Father, we all loved Aunt Louisa. She was your sister. I realise there may be bad blood between the two of you, so I'm not asking you to be friends. My request is that you allow Becky and me to enjoy his company, without interference or derogatory comment.'

'I'm not sure what your mother will have to say about it all.'

'Mother will understand. This last year she has been instrumental in bringing you and me together, and in welcoming Becky into our lives. Without her, you and I would still be at loggerheads. She was unkind to Becky, but upon reflection she recognised my love for her and accepted our relationship. As for the luncheon with Nicholas, I know mother doesn't like it, but she has kept her counsel on it.'

'Hmm. It's "Nicholas" now, is it? No longer "Dr Fincham"?'

'We have a wedding at which you and Nicholas will rub shoulders. Can I rely on you to forget old animosities? Even if only for one day? If I may be so bold, Nicholas has more reason to be angry with Grandfather and yourself than you with him.'

'There is much you do not understand. We did not force Louisa to break her engagement.'

'Not physically, but it's obvious from the letters she left that it was deemed morally desirable for her to forsake her own happiness to care for Grandfather.'

Hector sighed. 'It was the right thing.'

'At the time perhaps, or so it seemed. Things have moved on. I'm not asking you to apologise to him, or fawn over him, just to be civil. At the club for instance. There may initially be some embarrassment on both sides, but –'

'All right,' said Hector. 'I hear you. You're saying I am to acknowledge him, but I do not have to stand him a brandy.'

Fergus laughed and stood up. 'You've put it perfectly. I

should have said that, instead of going round the houses.' *I can see I'm going to have to force an introduction before the wedding. I can't have a meeting between my father and Nicholas to worry about on my wedding day.*

'Before you leave,' Hector said, 'your mother and I have opened an account with Whittles and placed £40 in it as your wedding gift from us. I think your mother has certain items of furniture she is going to offer you now Coates Lane is ready, but I've told her you young people these days like to choose your own things.'

Fergus embraced his father, something he had rarely done. He was halfway down the stairs when his father's voice boomed out, exactly as it used to when he was issuing instructions to the staff. 'And don't go cashing any of it in for one of those expensive illustrated books you like to buy!'

'Illuminated, Father, illuminated. And they're manuscripts, not books.'

As soon as he'd returned to the warehouse, Fergus wrote a note to Dr Fincham inviting him to meet at the Seamen's Haven the next day at four o'clock. Thinking it only fair that he should know, he added a postscript: '*My father will be accompanying me.*'

* * *

'Keep still, lad, while I button you up,' said Becky, taking a firm grasp of Rory's arm.

'I'm not used to a waistcoat like this that does up so tight.' He wriggled his shoulders.

Becky sighed. 'You'll have to get used to it. To start

with, I spent a lot of time making it while you were at sea, and second, we're going to see an important gentleman in a solicitor's office and you need to be smartly dressed. I've told you all about it, and Mrs Dolly is coming with us.'

'The man about my future?'

'Yes. He's going to ask you questions and you're going to answer truthfully. And Charlie stays here.'

'But Charlie always comes with me everywhere.'

'Not to see a solicitor, he doesn't.'

Dolly, putting on her bonnet, said, 'We'll stop by the butcher's and bring Charlie something special after we've called at Coates Lane.'

'A lamb's kidney?'

'If you behave yourself.'

At the solicitors' offices, Mr Needham was waiting to escort them to his room. He settled them in front of his desk, with its impressive inkstand, and Rory scanned the shelves.

'What's in those boxes?' he asked, pointing. 'The ones with the names on?'

Mr Needham glanced at the metal boxes lining the walls 'They're deed boxes. People leave important papers with us to keep them safe.'

'Oh, that's disappointing. I thought they might be full of treasure.'

'They are in a way, but paper ones, not gold and jewels. Do you understand why you are here, Rory?'

'Aye, it's about my future and you're going to ask me all sorts of questions that I must answer truthfully.'

Mr Needham turned to Becky. 'I see he is well prepared.'

'I've done my best.'

'How old are you, Rory?'

'I'm eleven. Twelve in November. The 8th.'

Mr Needham made a note. 'And your surname is Rooke?'

'Aye, like the bird, but with an "e" on the back end.'

'Where were you were born?'

Rory frowned and looked to one side. 'It wasn't here. Mammy would've known, but you can't ask her.'

'Sadly, your mother passed away. Is that correct?'

'Aye, when I was at sea last year.'

'And your father?'

'My da's dead. I never saw him and Mammy didn't talk about him.'

'Do you have any other relatives?'

'There was Nan, but she died a long time ago. She came from Carlisle, I think.'

'What was her name?'

'Nan Rooke.' He pulled his shirt collar away from his neck. 'It's warm in here.'

'Is Nan Rooke your father's mother?'

'Nay, my mammy's mammy.'

Mr Needham picked up his pen and made a note. 'So, your mother was a Rooke and your grandmother too.'

'Aye, that's reet.'

'And there's no one else?'

'I'm what folks call "orphaned". There's lots of those in the workhouse. One of the mariners told me that means I have to make my own way in the world.'

Mr Needham made another note. 'You know Miss Moss and Mr Shackleton are to be married?'

'Aye, I do. There's bits of wedding dress all over the place at home.'

Mr Needham gave a little chuckle.

Becky laughed. 'What he means is we're making the dress and it's still in pieces.'

'Ah, I understand. Tell me. Rory, would you like to live with Miss Moss and Mr Shackleton when they are married?'

'In their house?'

'That is correct.'

'I would but...' He turned to Dolly. 'Will you mind, Mrs Dolly? Will you miss me?'

'You'll be round the corner, so I'll be able to see you all the time when you're not at sea. I'll do my best to manage without you.'

'And Charlie? Will you miss him too?'

'Charlie? Is there a brother?' enquired Mr Needham.

'It's his dog,' explained Becky.

Dolly nodded. 'Aye, I'll miss him too,' she told Rory.

'Rory, I need you to listen carefully,' said Mr Needham, adopting a deeper, more serious tone than he had used so far. 'Mr Shackleton is offering to make you his ward. This means he is going to sign papers that mean he can take care of you until you are twenty-one.'

'Like a da?'

'Much like that. Would you like that?'

'So, I'd be his lad?'

'Not quite, but, as I say, much like that.'

Rory clapped his hands. 'That would be reet grand. That's what the men say on the ship all the time when something is good. *Reet grand.*' In his excitement, he swung his legs back and forth, tapping his toes against the desk. Becky leant forward and placed a hand across his knees to stop him.

Mr Needham put his pen down and sorted through his papers. 'I can see you are getting restless, Rory. I just need you to sign some documents. I've already drawn them up.'

Becky was fanning herself. She was beginning to feel warm too. The room was stuffy.

'I should be able to produce the necessary papers for the end of the month. Then we can set the papers before the Justice of the Peace. I don't anticipate any problems. I will write to Mr Shackleton to that effect.'

They all signed the necessary papers. Rory looked towards the door. Dolly thanked Mr Needham for his time and he wished Becky good fortune for her upcoming nuptials.

'I'm glad that's over,' said Rory, when they were outside. 'It's hard being well behaved.'

While Rory was walking ahead to the butcher's, Becky said to her mother, 'Do you really think Rory's da is dead?'

'With his mammy and his nan having the same surname, I don't suppose there's ever been a father in Rory's life.'

'That would explain all – why they moved here when the lad was a wee bairn, and why his ma never spoke of the boy's father except to say he was dead.'

* * *

'This is where we keep the liquor when it comes out of the bonded warehouse.' Fergus pointed to the shelves filled with casks, stacked behind locked grilles.

Although he wasn't saying much, Hector appeared to be taking everything in with genuine interest.

'On the top-floor shelves we store items awaiting carriage clearance. As we don't know how long we're holding them for, we like to keep them out of the way.'

'What's your average storage time?'

'Two to three weeks.' Fergus pointed to several rolls propped up in a corner. 'We've had that sailcloth for going on three months. There's a dispute over the recipient's payment.'

'A bad deal for you, then?'

'Oh, no, the seller is paying us storage fees while he sorts it all out. Being custom-made it needs an experienced rigger, or it would have been long gone. It's cheaper to store it with us than ship it back to Lancaster while they engage one.'

'I could have done more of this sort of thing with Shackletons, but I've always thought it too risky.'

'And Shackleton & Company doesn't have the warehouse space. I keep the two businesses separate.' Fergus kept his thoughts on eventually working towards a merger to himself. Now was not the time.

'It's decent money for doing little,' he said. 'We employ men to load and unload as and when we need them. There's a surplus of labour in Whitehaven these days. I've found unemployed crew happy to do a few days' lifting and carting for a fair wage.'

'It must cost a fortune insuring all this.'

'The building is insured by us, but the depositors make their own insurance arrangements. We only have to provide the prescribed high level of security.'

'That can't come cheap.'

'No, but if we can keep the warehouse reasonably full, it makes us a tidy profit, which on top of the eventual carriage fees is promising.'

'What's on the other two floors?'

'The next one is more varied. Textiles, some household goods.'

'And the top?'

'At the moment we have agricultural tools and a small area of excess space, but we're thinking we may begin trading on our own account.'

'What are you thinking of? I've always thought there was a good profit in linen tablecloths from Ireland.'

'Yes,' said Fergus, 'that sort of thing.' He was tempted to reply with 'ivory chess sets and exotic jewellery', but that would divert his father down a road he did not want to travel just yet, and which, in any case, he might never need to.

'Trading can be lucrative, but it's additional work,' Hector said. 'I'd stick to carriage, son. It's the business you've been brought up in, and there'll always be a need for carriers picking up and delivering. I can take up some of the slack for you now I'm back.'

Fergus was going to bat away the idea of his father helping, but it was true he was busy, and his father was twiddling his thumbs at home. Perhaps a couple of mornings a week might not be such a bad thing. He would need to see how much his father had changed before suggesting it. Reformed Hector keeping his hand in could be advantageous; old prickly Hector had no place in the company, no matter how stretched they were.

'What about the trains I spoke of yesterday?' Fergus asked. 'They're beginning to transport goods all over the country. I see trading as a diversification of our business to help combat loss of carrier trade.'

'Bah! Trains aren't going to affect our business. You can't take a train across water.'

It was then that Fergus remembered how out of touch his father was with the changing shipping scene, and how he was seemingly unable to adjust his thoughts. Perhaps having him in the office was not such a good idea, after all – especially since Fergus had decided, whatever Bill thought, he was going to make serious enquiries about a steamship.

'While you're still here, we could visit the Seamen's Haven,' Fergus said. 'They'll give us a cup of tea and it's good to arrive unannounced sometimes.'

'A splendid idea, and as we're both trustees they can hardly turn us away at the door. It was a good thing Louisa did in setting up the Haven; it benefits the mariners of the town and keeps them out of trouble. Although I still think she was overgenerous in her will.'

Fergus looked at his father's ankle.

'Don't worry, I can walk that far,' he said.

Outside, the flagstones were still damp from earlier rain. Fergus put his arm out for Hector to take. Despite his ankle not being much trouble, his father had retained his walking stick. Fergus suspected it was because he'd got into the habit of lifting it in greeting, in the manner of someone raising their hat, and that he delighted in doing so.

'The mariners from the Seamen's Haven house, in the cottage next to ours, are no trouble because they're only offered refuge if they're sober. I understand from word on the ships the Haven's nickname is "the Grogless Heaven" – a reference to the lack of liquor and its Christian foundations.'

'Your mother thinks your cottage is too small and that you should move into Queen Street with us. I appreciate you don't want to at present, but when you have children, you may be glad of the opportunity.'

Fergus thanked his father for the offer, guessing he would also prefer it if they moved into Queen Street, but his parents wouldn't be touring the Continent for ever. With an eye to the future, Fergus knew Becky and his mother wouldn't last long under the same roof.

At the Seamen's Haven, the warden, on being advised they'd arrived, came out of his office and greeted them warmly by name.

'How fortuitous. We have another benefactor visiting today. Dr Fincham is delivering some books for the men and you are in time for tea. Please join us. I'll be a minute informing the kitchen.' He left them in the hall without waiting for an answer.

Fergus felt his father's body stiffen against him. 'Did you know he was going to be here?' he asked, in his irritated voice.

'I didn't know for sure. I sent a note to Nicholas yesterday saying we would be here, leaving the decision to him.'

'So, he was forewarned and I was not?'

'Yes, but he didn't have to come, and he is here. I see that as accepting the olive branch I was holding out – and surely better to meet again for the first time here than at the wedding?'

Hector shook his head. 'It is a damnably uncomfortable situation you have placed us both in. Me, especially.'

'If it's so uncomfortable for you, we can leave, but what better place to bring you together?'

'I am not happy about this,' said Hector, through gritted teeth. 'Not happy at all. It is a trick you have played against me.'

Fergus ignored his comment.

The warden returned. 'The doctor is in the day room talking to some of the mariners who came in from New Orleans last night.' He pointed to the open doorway leading into the day room. 'Please go through.'

As the warden disappeared down the corridor, Hector lingered and said in a hissing voice, 'I repeat, what the devil did you go and do this for?'

Fergus took a deep breath. 'I did it because I'm tired of two grown men anguishing over a series of events that took place years before I was born. We need to bring this to an end, or at least call a truce.' He held his father's gaze, feeling deep in his bones that if he failed to hold it, he would never be able to bring the two men together. He also realised this was something he wanted. He needed his father to meet with Nicholas and lay bad feelings to rest.

He felt a welcome surge of relief when his father broke their gaze, turned to his left, and started walking towards the open doorway.

I've got them this far – now what?'

Dr Fincham gave Hector a nod of recognition as they entered. He was sitting at a table with three heavily tattooed mariners, several books open in front of them. Fergus greeted Nicholas and the men, then picked up one of the books. 'Ah, *The Life of Horatio Nelson.*'

'We're discussing a man we all agree was one of our greatest admirals,' said Nicholas. 'And I've been reliving some of my sailing days with these fine men of the sea.'

Whether the men sensed the tension between Nicholas and his father, or whether they were just taking the opportunity to escape, Fergus couldn't be sure, but all three rose, made excuses and left.

Dr Fincham stood and, for a short time he, Hector and Fergus scrutinised each other in an awkward silence.

The warden returned with an assistant, who was holding a tea tray. 'Come, gentlemen, sit.' He pointed to a table in the bay window. While the men took their places, the assistant poured their tea, then left them to their discussion.

Fergus realised that if a reconciliation was to take place, it was *his* role to engineer it, but he was unsure how to proceed, and wondered if he'd bitten off more than he could chew. He was saved by the warden, who said, 'I take it introductions are unnecessary?'

Fergus recognised his opportunity and seized it. 'Indeed, but whilst your visitors are acquainted with one another, you are probably unaware that the three men sitting at this table all cared greatly for the Haven's late benefactress.'

'Louisa Shackleton? I know she was your aunt.'

'Yes,' said Fergus. 'You are taking tea with my father, who was her brother, with myself, her nephew, and with Dr Fincham, who was a special friend to her many years ago.'

'Goodness me,' said the warden.

'I am certain it will give her the utmost pleasure to know – and my faith tells me she *will* know – that we're gathered here today united in love for her, in a place she cared so much about. What better occasion could she hope for?' Despite thinking he sounded like a preacher, Fergus was confident he was doing and saying the right thing. He was certainly trying his best. The warden, unknowingly, was acting as a brake on the two men's reactions, for neither would want to make a scene in his aunt's beloved Seamen's Haven. They'd both kept their heads down while he spoke.

Nicholas was the first to respond. 'You are correct, Fergus. We all loved her in different ways, and had she not been taken so soon, she could have been sitting here with us today.'

Hector nodded. 'I cannot deny it would have brought her great pleasure to sit with us.' He fixed his eyes on Nicholas before adding, 'All three of us.'

'Actions from long ago could have been explained,' Fergus said. 'Reasons and apologies given.'

'Wounds stitched.' Nicholas shook his head. 'I came back too late. Perhaps I should not have come back at all.'

'I'm sure Dr Lennagon at least is glad to have you back as his partner,' said Hector. 'Even if others are not,' he added.

At these last words, Fergus gave his father what he later described to Becky as 'a look'.

Hector and Nicholas turned in their chairs to face each other, as opponents might.

The warden rubbed his hands. 'Regret in grief. It is the same for all who have lost loved ones. Things left unsaid, unresolved grievances taken to the grave.' He spoke as if he were aware of the circumstances they were alluding to, but Fergus knew it was impossible for him to know.

As though his homily about grief had brought their discussion to a close, the warden changed the subject. 'While you are all here, let me tell you about what's been happening at the Haven this month.'

The visitors were then treated to a detailed report on the Haven's recent charitable works. When that came to an end, they took their leave, Fergus promising to find time to call another day with some books he thought might be suitable for the library.

Outside, Nicholas said, 'I have never accepted losing Louisa and the life we could have shared together. I loved her more than life itself. But I did not return to harbour old grievances, seek out remorse, or proffer forgiveness for actions taken long ago, when times and attitudes were different. Let us work towards a mutual acceptance. The past may have shaped *our* lives, but it is no longer with us and it need not shape others' lives.'

He means Becky and me, thought Fergus.

'We did what we thought was right at the time,' Hector said.

Oh, Father, can you not give a little?

Nicholas extended his hand for Hector to shake. For a moment Fergus thought his father wasn't going to give an inch, but as it became obvious Nicholas wasn't going to withdraw, Hector accepted the offer. Nicholas acknowledged Fergus with a slight nod, then left.

Fergus escorted his father home. A walk completed, for the most part, in silence.

CHAPTER TWELVE

Mindful of his father's comments about chandlers, and uncomfortable with having to rely on Gudgeon's should the trip to Mauritius come to fruition, Fergus decided to visit Frisby's in Maryport. When he arrived, it was busier than he'd expected. He noticed immediately it was a tighter, more organised business than Gudgeon's could ever be. The assistants wore round black hats with peaks, like railway porters' caps, and clean white aprons that went from waist to mid-calf and were tied at the front. The shelves were plumply stocked, the premises spotless and, most importantly, there was an air of business. Fergus's plan had been to scout around, purchase a small item, then retire to the Queen's Head at the harbour-side to make a few general enquiries about the business amongst its customers.

He was examining a small trowel when he felt a tap on his shoulder. He turned to find Jeremiah Todhunter. The last time he'd seen Jeremiah was at the auction for the *Eleanor Bell*. He was the man in the tweed jacket who had bid against him, whom he'd nicknamed 'Mr Tweedy'.

'Fergus Shackleton, what are you doing here?' Jeremiah asked in a cheery voice.

An assistant stacking shelves a little way down from them stopped what he was doing and turned his head.

'Jeremiah, I do venture from home sometimes.'

Out of the corner of his eye, Fergus saw the assistant leave what he was doing and walk to the back of the shop.

'You'll take a drink with me at the Queen's Head, won't you?'

Whilst the Queen's Head fitted with Fergus's plans, he hadn't factored in Jeremiah. However, he could see no great disadvantage to accepting the invitation, and it could prove profitable, since Jeremiah had the reputation of knowing other people's business. So much so, Fergus knew word would go round Whitehaven before the day was through that he had been seen in Maryport.

'Yes, I have a thirst,' he said. 'That will be agreeable.'

'You've forgiven me for bidding you up for the *Eleanor Bell*?'

Fergus was about to answer in the affirmative when a middle-aged man with thick bushy eyebrows and untidy whiskers that both needed trimming, approached. He was wearing one of the white aprons, but not sporting a hat.

'Mr Shackleton, I believe? The Whitehaven shipper?'

'The same,' answered Jeremiah. 'I'll wager it's not often you see him in here?'

The man shook his head. 'No, and it is a most pleasant surprise. May I introduce myself as the proprietor of this fine establishment? Edward Frisby. I trust we can be of assistance?'

Fergus hadn't wanted to draw attention to himself, but it was too late. 'I'm here on business and just calling to pass the time.'

Mr Frisby gave a small sigh, as if disappointed, but he was not to be deterred. 'While you're here, please allow me to present you with our current product list and terms of business.' He passed Fergus several sheets of printed paper. 'I expect you deal with Gudgeon's?' He waited for Fergus to answer, but when nothing was forthcoming except a slight nod, he continued, 'We have several customers who call in from Whitehaven, and we can always deliver. We run our own carrier. Perhaps in the future we may call on *you*, Mr Shackleton?'

Fergus thanked Mr Frisby and would have asked a few questions, but with Jeremiah standing there listening, he didn't want to show too much interest. If the Glasgow contract came through, he would summon the man and they could discuss business in Whitehaven. He had gained something from his visit in that Mr Frisby would remember him now which, on reflection, was probably advantageous.

In the Queen's Head, Jeremiah paid for the refreshments.

'That proprietor is keen to do business with you,' he said, placing a pewter tankard in front of Fergus.

'I have to give him credit for coming forward touting his business.'

Jeremiah drank deeply. 'I wouldn't be surprised if they buy Gudgeon's out. How's business?'

Fergus spent the next half hour talking about Whitehaven and catching up on general shipping news. He was surprised to find Jeremiah a more agreeable gentleman than he had supposed and realised he had let their auction-bidding battles colour his thoughts and relations with the man. However, whilst they talked, Fergus did his utmost not to let slip anything about the Louisa Line's possible future plans.

They'd just reached an appropriate point to take their leave when Fergus realised Jeremiah could help him, especially now he'd changed his opinion of the man.

'Jeremiah, do you know of any steamships coming up for sale?'

Jeremiah gave a loud laugh verging on a guffaw that came from deep within his chest. 'You wait until we are about to part and ask me this?'

Fergus couldn't tell him why he hadn't broached the subject earlier; it wouldn't do their prospective business relationship any good to admit he'd previously regarded him as a competitor, even out of the sale room.

Fergus shrugged. 'My mind was on other things.'

'I may know of one or two steamships coming up soon. You're hoping for a private purchase?'

'Yes. Am I correct in thinking they don't often come up for auction?'

'Aye, and am I correct in thinking you're going into the steamship business?' Jeremiah searched Fergus's face.

'Perhaps,' said Fergus, scratching his nose.

'A man who scratches his nose is usually reckoned to be lying, but I'll wager on this occasion you're telling the truth. Don't worry, I may be known for liking a bit of gossip, but where it's business and likely to bring commission, I can keep my mouth tightly shut.'

They discussed the details and Jeremiah made some notes on a scrap of paper.

Outside, as he was shaking Fergus's hand, Jeremiah said, 'You know, I've always thought there's a bit of your granddad in you. He did well to start up the post-boats, and I know free advice is worth what it costs, but steam is the way to go now. We all know that.'

'We are of one mind. See what you can find me and I will engage you to negotiate for me.'

On the way back to Whitehaven, Fergus thought of the chance meetings that had occurred in his life and turned out to be important: Rory, Becky, Padraig Conran, and perhaps now this meeting with Jeremiah Todhunter.

* * *

Becky was nervous – so much so she sought refuge in her bedroom to gather herself. With three days to go to the wedding, people were fussing and it was suffocating her. She was waiting for a summons from the dressmaker they'd hired to add flourishes to the bodice. They were managing the flounces in sections, but putting the different parts together required space, and that was something the Indian Queen was short of.

How naïve I've been, she thought. No wedding can ever be a quiet one. Each person has their role to play and wants to be a part of it.

All was going according to plan: the banns had been read; no one had objected; the Waverley was in charge of the catering. Elizabeth and Hector seemed to have accepted the arrangements, despite perhaps not liking them much, and Fergus had told her he loved her more than ever. What could go wrong?

Fergus called for Becky at two o'clock. They were to visit Whittles to select dining-room furniture and general household items. The bed they'd ordered three weeks previously was arriving in two days. Everything was late in the day because of the overrunning of the decorating, and because of the bringing forward of the wedding date to support Rory's wardship. However, at last they could think seriously about moving into their new home. Hopefully the various deliveries would be made by the time they returned from their honeymoon. They were leaving Dolly to oversee such matters.

Elizabeth had offered them a green velvet button-back chair for their parlour, which Becky loved, and an old carved Welsh bed that they'd accepted for Rory's room. Elizabeth had offered much more, but most of it was far too big for the small rooms at Coates Lane, or not to their taste.

On arrival at Whittles they were greeted by the doorman. The very day they'd chosen to visit, Mr Whittle himself was in Carlisle; the doorman quickly introduced them to the under-manager, Mr Squires.

Mr Squires made the same mistakes Elizabeth had made – most of the items he suggested were too wide, too long or too old-fashioned. It was only when Becky mentioned Coates Lane that the man said, 'Ah, perhaps we should be thinking on a lesser scale.'

They spent an hour choosing household goods and smaller items, while Mr Squires made a list.

'Shall you require a dining table?' he asked.

'Do you have a circular one?' asked Becky.

'We have a circular one that can be enlarged with a central leaf.' He led the way to an upstairs showroom. 'And we have chairs to match.'

As soon as her eyes fell on the table, Becky wanted it. 'Fergus, it's perfect.'

'And the price?' asked Fergus. 'I know a good piece of furniture when I see it. This is a quality piece.'

Mr Squires ran his hand along the underside of the table until he came to a label. He bent down to check it. 'As you say, this is a quality piece. The cost is £8.'

Becky drew her breath in. This was two months' wages for a sea captain.

'And the chairs?' asked Fergus

'The chairs are £4, making the complete set £12.'

'Do you like it?' Fergus asked Becky.

Becky could only nod, because she was too excited to speak. She was already imagining the table *in situ.*

'Shall we take it, Becky?'

Becky didn't know how to respond. She was mesmerised by the ease with which Fergus was spending money. She came from a home where the need for anything new had to be thought through and discussed at length, before being carefully considered at least once more.

When she didn't answer, Fergus prompted her again.

'Aye,' was all she could manage, leaving Fergus to make the delivery arrangements.

CHAPTER THIRTEEN

On April 20th, their wedding day, Becky woke early. Pulling back the curtains, she saw bulbous raindrops on the windowpane. Judging by the dark colour of Church Street's flagstones, it had probably been raining for some time. One of her da's favourite sayings came to mind: 'Rain before seven, fine by eleven.'

She glanced at herself in the mirror; she was pale and her hair was all over the place. Her mother had insisted she wash it the previous evening, so it would settle down and "not be fluffy on the day". Becky wondered if she'd made a mistake, but it was too late. If she washed it again it would most definitely be fluffy.

There was a knock on her door and Dolly came in with a tray. 'I heard you moving about, so I've made a dish of porridge and put a dollop of treacle on it. I know how you love it, and you're going to need a lining to your stomach.'

Becky frowned at the bowl of porridge. 'Oh, Ma, thank you, but I can't eat a thing. I'm too nervous.'

'Don't spoil your day with nerves. There's nothing to be afraid of.'

'What if something goes wrong?'

'Such as?'

'I trip up, or Fergus changes his mind, or Mr Shackleton and Dr Fincham make a scene, or –'

Dolly put her arms out. 'Come here, silly lass, and let me give you a hug.'

Mother and daughter embraced for a while in silence, until Becky stepped back.

'I'm sorry, Ma. It's such a big day.'

'Nothing will happen. You're going to arrive at St James's as Miss Becky Moss and you're going to leave as Mrs Fergus Shackleton. There's an end to it. Now eat your breakfast and I'll wake Rory and make sure he has a good wash. I'll leave the porridge. Do try to get some down.'

Dolly disappeared and Becky looked again at her breakfast. She knew she ought to eat something, but she couldn't. Partly it was the thought of Elizabeth Shackleton, her soon-to-be mother-in-law. She'd been pleasant enough recently, but Becky was never sure what she was thinking, and it scared her. She held her hands out in front of her and was surprised to find they weren't shaking.

Her mother's voice rose from downstairs. 'Don't forget to bring your pearl necklace when you come down. We've to leave at half past ten.'

Dolly had negotiated a changing room at the dressmaker's shop for the big day. 'The last thing you want is for Charlie to leap up and scratch the lace with his paws, or shake hairs on you, and besides, there's no room big enough here.'

Becky agreed and so, on her wedding day, she found herself in her wedding gown and veil in the dressmaker's back room, watching her mother pace up and down as they waited for the carriage to take them to St James. Dolly was resplendent in royal blue, as befitted the widowed mother of the bride. Mary, Bill's wife, had collected the bridal bouquet from the florist, and with Rory in tow – dressed up to the nines in a new linen shirt, blue knee-breeches and his 'too-tight' waistcoat – she dropped the flowers off at the dressmaker's.

Mary paused at the door as they were leaving. 'You are beautiful,' she told Becky. 'A perfect picture.'

After she'd gone, Becky said, 'Am I really beautiful, Ma?'

'Oh, aye, lass, indeed you are. And your pearl is set off a treat.'

Becky touched the single pearl. She remembered how embarrassed she'd been when Fergus had first tried to give it to her, in the days before they were courting seriously. It had been such an expensive gift, she'd felt it incumbent upon her to refuse, until she knew him better.

'Would Da be proud of me?'

At the mention of her late husband, Dolly's eyes filled with tears and Becky watched her mother blink them away. 'He'll be with us in spirit, sending his love. I've no doubt on that.'

'And Fergus? Will he be proud of me?' Becky still couldn't quite believe that her Fergus loved her so much that he had once, for a time, forsaken his family for her.

'He's going to be proud of you today and the rest of

your lives. I warned you about coming from different backgrounds, lass, and I had misgivings, but I have to say, your marriage seems as true a love match as I've ever known.'

'I'm cold.' Becky put her fingers out for her mother to touch. She felt a bit light-headed, too. Perhaps she should have eaten something, after all.

'That's because you're nervous, and a good job, too. I'd be worried if you'd no sense of occasion. This is a day you'll remember all your life.'

* * *

Becky and Dolly heard a cabby call to his horses to pull over. It was time to leave. The dressmaker helped Becky gather up the flounced skirt and veil and she and Dolly eased her into the carriage. They were about to pull away when Dolly shouted to the driver to stop.

'We've forgotten the bouquet.' As she was struggling with the door-handle, the dressmaker appeared at the open window.

'You'll need this,' she said, handing the bouquet to Dolly then striking the side of the carriage with the flat of her hand, to signal to the driver to move off.

People going about their business stopped and waved at them. Becky had done the same to passing bridal parties on many occasions and now it was her turn to be the bride.

As they approached the church entrance, Becky was surprised to see a stranger standing beside Rector Longrigg. He was wearing clerical dress and his arms were folded over the large bible resting against his chest.

'Who's that?' she asked her mother.

'I've no idea, but he's got importance stamped all over his cassock.'

'Are we late?'

'Five minutes. Tradition demands it.'

The cabby jumped down as they came to a halt and opened the door. Dolly stepped out first and together they eased Becky out of the carriage and onto the path. Dolly adjusted the veil, making sure the two sides were even at the front, and then Rector Longrigg who had moved forward to greet them, led the way to the entrance, where the unfamiliar cleric was waiting and smiling.

The rector cleared his throat. 'This is Canon Frederick Allsopp. He is going to help officiate today.'

The canon spoke. 'I was in Maryport preparing candidates for confirmation, and when I learned my dear friend Elizabeth Shackleton's son was getting married, I knew without a doubt she would want me to assist. News of a big society wedding travels. I guessed she did not ask me for fear of my regarding it as a favour too far, but here I am, fortuitously nearby.' He was all smiles, yet Becky felt it was as if he were sacrificing his time to be there and that they should be grateful.

Rector Longrigg spoke in a low voice, as if imparting a secret. 'This is a great honour for us, Becky. The canon is from Carlisle Cathedral.'

Both men had fixed their attention on Becky, as if they were expecting her to do something – like curtsey.

Ah, they want me to thank him.

'I'm sure Mrs Shackleton is delighted you have found the time to be here. Thank you.'

'And we are delighted, too,' added Dolly.

Becky knew her mother's thoughts would be conflicting. How wonderful that Becky was to be married by a canon from the cathedral, and how typical of Elizabeth Shackleton to take control on the day, with no warning. Although to be fair, from what the canon had said, it appeared his arrival must be a surprise to her too.

Inside the porch, where they could hear the organ playing a lively prelude, the canon came to a halt. 'And who is to give the bride away?'

'I am,' said Dolly, smiling back at him.

The canon's friendly, if superior, demeanour disappeared. 'You?' he said, staring at her.

Becky felt her stomach lurch. *This is not promising.*

'Aye,' said Dolly. 'My husband passed away four years past.'

Canon Allsopp shook his head. 'This won't do. It absolutely will not do.' He turned to the rector. 'Why didn't you tell me about this? Were you aware?'

Rector Longrigg, who had paled, shook his head.

The canon sighed. 'You can't give her away – she's not yours to give.'

'What do you mean?' snapped Dolly.' Of course she's mine. I gave birth to her. She has my mother's distinctive grey eyes.' She grasped Becky's hand, as if signalling ownership.

'That is as may be, and I do not doubt it. The point is you are a woman, and women – even mothers – do not proffer a woman's hand in marriage.'

A big fat bee began buzzing inside Becky's head. Her

mouth was suddenly dry, and she felt dizzy. She put an arm out against the door frame to steady herself.

'That's rubbish,' said Dolly. 'I've never read that in the Bible.' Her cheeks were as scarlet as the rector's were pale.

The canon clucked his tongue. 'Can you provide evidence of a marriage you have attended where a woman gave the bride away?'

Becky could hear the voices around her, but they were becoming more distant with every second. Then the bee became one of many and she could hear nothing over the noise they were making. *Is the organ still playing?* She wasn't sure. Her vision was blurring, her eyelids were heavy. She shook her head to regain her senses.

'There must have been such an occasion,' said Dolly, her voice raspy. She placed the heel of her hand on her chest as if short of breath.

The congregation, who'd been standing waiting in their pews, had all turned round; people were staring towards the back of the church with curious faces. Becky knew Fergus would be at the front of them, but she couldn't see that far down the aisle.

The canon persisted. 'In all my years I have never –'

Becky didn't register his words; she felt she was no longer a part of the proceedings. It was as if she was watching herself get married. Black shapes swam before her eyes, and her bodice seemed far too tight. She felt her bouquet fall from her hands, and then the cold and damp of the black stone-flagged floor as her cheek came to rest upon it.

She came round to hear Dolly calling, 'A doctor, we

need a doctor.' Her voice rang out, bouncing off the walls. There were other voices, talking amongst themselves, and then she heard the familiar voice of Dr Lennagon, asking what happened. She tried to open her eyes, but the light was too bright, causing her to blink several times. As the people in front of her glided into focus, she saw an anxious Fergus, with Bill by his side. Elizabeth was holding a small bottle which she passed to Dr Fincham, who was kneeling on the ground. The stopper was stuck, but he managed to twist it off and waft the contents under Becky's nose. The smell assaulted and offended the soft tissues of her nostrils and she drew her head back, as if she'd received a heavy-handed slap.

'What happened?' asked the doctor.

Dolly's voice rang out again. 'It's his fault,' she said, pointing a finger at the canon. 'He upset Becky by refusing to let me give her away, because I'm a woman.'

The canon stuttered, 'It's n–n–not appropriate.'

Dr Fincham, ignoring him, took hold of Becky's wrist and felt her pulse. 'Did she eat anything this morning?'

Dolly shook her head. 'I tried to make her, but she said she was too nervous.'

Dr Lennagon, peering over Dr Fincham's shoulder, said, 'Probably the upset and nerves. Her colour's coming back.'

Becky still felt she wasn't a part of the proceedings; people were talking about her as if she wasn't there. She propped herself up on one elbow, and Fergus and Bill stepped forward to help her stand. When she was upright, she glanced down at her dress. It was crumpled, and probably dusty on the back from the floor, but she told herself she wasn't going to be looking at the back, so she wouldn't worry about it.

The rector, ill at ease, said, 'Sit yourself down in the vestry and I'll get you a glass of water.' He scurried off, while Fergus and Bill guided Becky into the vestry, where she sat down on an old pew. It was a small room, and with the two doctors, Fergus, Bill, Dolly, Elizabeth and the canon inside it, there was hardly any room to move.

Dolly stood turning the bouquet over in her hands, while Fergus moved a pile of dusty hymn books to one side so he could sit beside Becky. The rector returned with the glass of water.

'How do you feel now?' asked Dr Lennagon.

'I feel much better. I'm so sorry to cause such a fuss. I should have eaten something.'

'Is that the cause?' asked Fergus.

Dolly pointed a finger at the canon and said again, 'It's all his fault. He won't let me give her away.'

They all turned to the canon, who was leaning back against the wall. He seemed subdued, although from the firm set of his mouth it was clear he wasn't backing down.

Elizabeth spoke up. 'Canon Allsopp arrived unannounced, and uninvited as far as I am aware. In the short time he has been here, it seems he has upset the bride's mother and caused the bride to faint – all of which has disrupted your marriage ceremony.'

Fergus stood up. 'Rector, tell me, is it against canon law for a mother to give her daughter away?'

Rector Longrigg, transferring his gaze from Fergus to the canon, then back to Fergus, said, 'I have to say that whilst it is unusual, as far as I am aware it is not against the laws of the church. It is a social tradition based on economics – the father, as head of the household, with control of his daughter's financial affairs, passes on that control in the form of her dowry, in addition to her bodily self.'

'Ah,' said Fergus, 'then that is why women do not usually take on the role. Have you heard of a woman giving a daughter away locally, rector?'

'There was a case of it at St Michael's in Arlecdon some years back.' Then, glancing at the canon, he added, 'It was definitely somewhat of a curiosity, though, and some people did frown upon it.'

Dr Lennagon spoke, 'It appears *you,* Rector Longrigg, were happy for Mrs Moss to accompany her daughter down the aisle, until the canon raised his objection.'

'I have always seen my role in the church as one of a bringing together of Christian and social traditions. I understand I am thought of as a liberal cleric in the diocese. Is that correct, canon?'

Canon Allsopp nodded but made no attempt to speak. His arms were still enfolding his Bible and his jaw was tilted upwards, as if there were a bad smell in the room.

Fergus turned to him. 'Sir, it appears to me that you've disrupted our wedding for a personal prejudice. I find this incomprehensible, when you came here under the auspices of being a friend of the family – although I suspect your motive was less about the Christian aspects of the occasion and more about the feasting afterwards.'

Canon Allsopp raised himself to his full height, which was not insignificant. 'I have travelled here out of the goodness of my Christian heart. All I have to say is I am the senior cleric here and I will not stand and watch a woman give a bride away. That is final, even if it is a Shackleton wedding.'

Dr Fincham took the few steps necessary to stand in front of Becky, who was still sitting with Fergus on the pew.

'It seems we are at something of an impasse. Becky, were I to offer my services to give you away, would you be minded to accept? It would be a great honour for me, if your mother agrees.'

Dolly pulled Becky towards her and hugged her. 'You came here to get married, lass. I think we ought to get on with it, and I'll not stand in your way by insisting I give you away.'

Becky put her hand out for her bouquet. 'Aye, we've a job to do.' Turning to the canon, she said, 'Canon, I think your services are needed elsewhere. If you leave this minute, you can be back in Carlisle for cathedral Matins tomorrow.'

No one spoke – it was as if they were all holding their breath. Taking his cloak down from its peg and folding it over his arm, the canon said, 'I shall be reporting this to the bishop.'

'And so shall I, Frederick,' said Elizabeth. 'So shall I, and my account will not be kindly.'

With the canon departed, Becky felt an immediate change in the atmosphere. 'Dr Fincham, I would be more than delighted for you to give me away, but since the opposition has left and, if the rector agrees, I think that privilege still rests with my mother.'

'That will be in order,' said the rector.

While Becky and Dolly were waiting for everyone to resume their places and the organist to strike up again, Dolly said, 'This will be a wedding folk remember.'

Becky gave a nervous laugh. She didn't need her mother to tell her that. She wondered how Hector would have felt if Dr Fincham had given her away. 'We'll be the talk of the town, although probably not in the way my soon-to-be mother-in-law would approve of.'

'She stuck up for you, lass, in public, against a cathedral canon. You're family to her now, the mother of her grandchildren. Remember that, because it means she's on your side.'

Becky hadn't thought about Elizabeth's intervention in that way. She was still in awe of her as Mrs Shackleton, Fergus's mother, a *grande dame* of Whitehaven society. It was all going to take some getting used to, but first she had to become the new Mrs Shackleton.

She took her mother's arm. 'Lead on, Ma.'

CHAPTER FOURTEEN

In Becky's imaginings, their honeymoon began with a grand send-off witnessed by friends and relatives, so it was with some surprise and a little disappointment that she found herself alone at the station with Fergus, a porter and a small group of fellow travellers she did not know. It was Sunday and people were at church, some possibly still in bed nursing their heads after the partying the day before. Even as they boarded the train, Becky still didn't know where they were going, except that they were changing trains at Carlisle, and that they would be gone for a little over a week.

They'd spent their wedding night at Coates Lane and Becky smiled, remembering how, when the time came to consummate their union, Fergus had been tender, loving and thoughtful of her inexperience. Dolly had placed lavender bags amongst their linen and a small vase of flowers by the washstand.

Arriving in Carlisle, Fergus spoke to the porter out of earshot, so it wasn't until Becky heard one of the railwaymen shout out for passengers for the Edinburgh train, and Fergus stood up, that she discovered where they were going.

'Edinburgh! Oh, Fergus, that's wonderful. I've always wanted to see the castle. Can we go there?'

'It will be one of our first visits. Where did you think we were going?'

'I thought maybe south to Lancaster, until I realised we were getting the Carlisle train, and then I thought the Borders. I never imagined we'd go somewhere as exciting as Edinburgh. I am so happy.' She felt like a schoolgirl, euphoric at the thought that her whole life had changed, that she was to lie by Fergus each night listening to his breathing, knowing she need only reach out to touch him, and that they would journey through life together. And children? *Perhaps even now Fergus and I have made a child of our own.*

* * *

They were greeted in Edinburgh by stormy rain, which they woke up to again the next morning. The force of the cloudbursts meant there was no visiting the castle that day. It wasn't the organised kind of rain that fell evenly in straight lines – it came down in torrents, as if gigantic buckets in the sky were being emptied directly over them. The wind kept changing direction, and would make it impossible to keep dry under the widest and sturdiest of umbrellas.

During breakfast, while people outside passed by with hoods up and hunched shoulders, Becky said, 'Perhaps tomorrow morning, if it's dry, we can visit the castle or the cathedral.'

'Ah, about tomorrow – I've arranged to visit Mr Cameron, our shipping agent. There are a few points we need to discuss. Particularly regarding our competitors.'

Becky couldn't help feeling disappointed and hurt. *It's our honeymoon and he's thinking of work.*

He reached over the table and took her hand. 'You don't mind, my love, do you? They open the office early, so I should be back by eleven if things go as planned.'

'You made plans before you left Whitehaven?'

'Yes. It seemed foolish to come all this way and not meet with him. Don't worry, we have plenty of time to spend together.'

And if things don't go as planned, will I be sitting in the hotel room twiddling my thumbs until teatime? Is this how it's going to be?

'You can go out on your own.'

'Aye, I suppose I can.' *But it won't be the same.*

* * *

The next morning, Fergus set off to see Mr Cameron. His offices, on St Mary's Street off the High Street, were austere. The chairs in the reception area were straight-backed and uncomfortable, the reception clerk was dressed completely in black, and there was an odour of mustiness in the place. Fergus was relieved when Cameron, in a dark jacket with matching trousers, spectacles perched precariously on the end of his nose, suggested they adjourn to a nearby coffee house.

'First, my congratulations on your marriage, Fergus. I think you will find Edinburgh a most suitable place in which to spend the first days of your married life.'

'So far it has done little else but rain.'

'Aye, we are rather prone to particularly heavy April showers. However, you are not here to discuss our inclement weather.'

'No. You have been our Shackletons' Edinburgh agent for many years – and a most reliable one, I would add. My partner, Bill McRae, and I have established a new business, the Louisa Line. We run two ships at present and are seeking to expand. Would it be a conflict of interests to ask you to act for us as well?'

Cameron curled the right side of his moustache between thumb and index finger. 'The situation presents the possibility of competition between the two companies, and my first loyalty must lie with Shackleton & Company, since they have first call.'

'I understand that. It was my father who suggested I speak with you and enquire about such an arrangement, and since the Louisa Line is my own company and I am a major shareholder in Shackletons, then I would regard competition as unhelpful to both.'

'You're carrying the same cargoes, so there has to be competition.'

'We need an ear to the ground. I'm not asking you to pass on confidential information – I'm talking about coffee-shop and club gossip that is in the public domain, but which we are too far away to hear. For instance, we're planning a visit to Glasgow next month, to Macintosh & Warrilow, and we know little about them.'

'I don't know much about them myself.'

'But I'll wager you're in touch with people who do?'

Cameron scratched his head. 'Certainly. But don't you have your own agent in Glasgow?'

'We do, but we'd like to keep a veil over our visit.'

'A new contract?'

'Exactly. You've put two and two together and come up with four, which is exactly what our competitors will do if they get wind of it. We remain undecided but would like to keep the opportunity open.'

'Possibly an enquiry from an Edinburgh agent would not suggest any link with Whitehaven although I cannot be sure. I can make enquiries for you and report by the end of the week. My links with Shackletons go back a long way and they have always been cordial. In the coming months, if any interesting gossip comes to my notice that I think may be of interest, and which will not harm my other clients, I'll see what I can do in forwarding the information to you.'

'Thank you.'

Fergus asked a passing waiter to bring the coffee-house account. When it arrived, Cameron leaned forward and picked it up. 'Away to your bride. I'll see to this. Think of it as a wee wedding present.'

They shook hands and Fergus made his way back to the hotel. He was conscious of Becky's concerns that he'd put business before *her*; he had made a mistake not mentioning his visit to Cameron in advance. He would make a point of telling her all about his meeting and spend the rest of the day doing exactly what she wanted to do.

CHAPTER FIFTEEN

Fergus was relieved to find Becky in good humour when he returned to the hotel. They enjoyed a light luncheon before setting out. Determined to include her, Fergus began relating the meeting's details, until he understood from her expression that it wasn't necessary He then outlined briefly how Mr Cameron would be looking into Macintosh & Warrilow and left it at that.

The walk up to the castle was steep. Becky held Fergus's arm, and both of them took particular care on the uneven cobbles. Arriving within the main area they stood side by side, close up against the ramparts, peering down on the city below.

'It may be we'll return one day and remember standing here,' said Fergus. 'Perhaps with children by our side.'

'Maybe even our children's children.'

'That's a thought. It would mean we've grown old together.'

'Isn't that what we both want? To grow old together?'

'Yes, that's what I mean – and between then and now so much will happen that we cannot possibly imagine.'

'What do *you* want to happen? What are *your* wishes?' Becky leaned in to Fergus's shoulder, as much for a display of affection as for warmth.

'I could wish for us to be happy, but I have no doubts over that, so it would be a wasted wish.'

'What else?'

'That we and our family enjoy good health – and I include Rory in that.'

'Of course.'

'And that we enjoy a comfortable life, with no tragedy.'

'You mean death?'

Fergus thought for a moment. 'We're bound to experience death. Mother, Father and Dolly, in due course, but I hope that their passings will be part of the grand scheme of things – that they will not die prematurely and, when they do, that it will be peacefully. What are *your* wishes for our future?'

'That we have healthy children and they live to stand here with their children's children.' She laughed. 'It's good we share a sense of family history. Some people seem to live just for the day or the year; they have no sense of what has shaped them, and I think that's their loss. I realised you had this sense of family when you named the Louisa Line.'

Becky seemed to have forgotten that the name was Bill's idea. He was going to remind her, but to do so might spoil the moment.

After they'd finished admiring the view, and had taken a walk round the castle, Becky paused by the guard house and said, 'You know I'm not particularly religious. I mean, I believe in God, but I don't shout about it like some folk do.'

'Yes?'

'I think it would be nice to walk back down to St Giles's and say a prayer. To thank God for bringing us together, and to pray that He'll watch over us and our family.'

'If you would like.'

'Aye, I would. It's something I would very much like to do.'

* * *

That evening they attended a concert at the Assembly Rooms and Becky wore what she called her 'Dublin dress' – the one she'd made from the purple linen silk mix Fergus had brought her. They arrived by carriage and a doorman in red and gold livery came forward to help her down onto the pavement.

Inside, everything was touched by the glow from the gas lights and candles. Becky had never seen so many candles alight in one place.

'Fergus, it's like midsummer daylight in here, and yet it's pitch-black outside.'

Men in blue livery were escorting the audience to their seats and the musicians were tuning their instruments.

'It's magical.'

'I thought you would enjoy it. We can come every evening, if you would like. There's a variety evening, a choral concert and after that a play.'

'I'd love to.' Then she thought, *but I only have the one dress*. 'Perhaps not.'

'Why not?' asked Fergus. It took him a while, but he was able to coax out her thoughts. 'We can soon change that. This is the great city of Edinburgh. I'll enquire at the hotel. There will be dressmakers here who will be only too happy to come to our rooms and fit you. Shall we say two dresses?'

Becky could hardly believe it. To have one new dress would be wonderful – to have two at the same time was something she had never experienced. All the way through the concert she kept thinking about how her life had changed, and that the cost of things – something she had grown up to be aware of – no longer seemed to matter.

* * *

On the sixth day of their Edinburgh honeymoon, on their return from a choral concert, Fergus was handed an envelope by the doorman.

'Who can that be from?' asked Becky.

'It's likely the report on Macintosh & Warrilow I'm expecting from Mr Cameron.'

In their rooms, Fergus gave the letter to Becky. 'You read it.'

Becky, in one of her new dresses, collapsed into a deep chair with broad arms and opened the letter.

'You're right, it's from Mr Cameron.'

'What does it say?'

Becky didn't answer at first. It was a short note. She read it again.

'And?' asked Fergus, moving towards her.

'It's a note. It says there's been a message from Jeremiah Todhunter for you. He has found a steamship. It will be in Whitehaven until the 29th. Are you able to inspect it?'

Fergus, instantly bright and alert, took the letter from Becky's outstretched hand.

'What day is it today?'

'The 27th.'

'If we leave tomorrow early, we can be back late on the 28th. The concierge can make the arrangements for us.'

Becky was aghast. She didn't think she had heard him correctly. 'Leave? Tomorrow?'

'Yes. If we don't, I may miss this ship.' Then, as if it had only freshly occurred to ask her, he said, 'Would you mind? It's only one day.'

Do I mind? That our honeymoon is being cut short? That we have tickets for a gala evening tomorrow? And that I've been saving my second new dress for it?

Fergus was watching her, waiting, she supposed, for her approval.

'How did Jeremiah Todhunter know how to contact you?' She knew her voice was spiky.

'I told Dicken in an emergency to contact Mr Cameron and he, or Bill, must have passed Jeremiah's message on to him.'

'And this is an emergency?'

'Don't you see? It could be exactly what we need for the Mauritius trip.'

'A trip which so far has not been confirmed and which consists solely of the exchange of appointment letters.' Now that the full enormity of his suggestion was dawning on her, and she could see he was serious, Becky was beginning to feel angry. Besides, apart from the loss of the day and the gala, she would lose face. Who returns from their honeymoon a day early? What would people think? What would Dolly and Elizabeth think?

'What do you say?' asked Fergus.

'What *can* I say? That you would suggest such a thing has taken my breath away.' Then a thought came into her head and she played it as a gambler plays a trump ace. 'That is the sort of thing your father would have done, before he mended his ways.'

Fergus stepped back as if she had dealt him a physical blow. 'I'm sorry, you're right. I should never have suggested it. We'll stay. There will be other ships.'

'No, we'll go back. Everything is spoiled now. I could never enjoy the gala evening knowing you resented me for wanting to stay.'

'I don't and won't resent you.'

'You say that, but you'd resent me if you lost the ship. You have to be back for the 29th, and so leave we must. You're right, there is time for you to inform the night porter we shall be leaving tomorrow.'

Becky was in bed when Fergus returned, her back towards him. He undressed and got in beside her. She waited for him to reach out and touch her, so she could rebuff his advance, but there was no approach.

Sleep eluded her. She thought back to her mother's words, that she would come down the aisle as 'Mrs Fergus Shackleton'. Her mother had made no reference to 'Mrs Becky Shackleton' and now Becky understood the difference between the two. She was Fergus's wife, and his needs and wishes came before hers.

CHAPTER SIXTEEN

In Whitehaven, late in the afternoon on April 28th after what had been rather a strained and sombre return trip, Fergus was infuriated to learn the steamship had left early and was now in Douglas, on the Isle of Man. He paced up and down in Jeremiah Todhunter's office, his hands behind his back.

Jeremiah was full of apologies. 'The owner received word there was genuine interest in Douglas and she wasn't prepared to wait for what she called a "maybe" buyer who was on his honeymoon and unlikely to rush back.'

'I'm not one for waiting around,' Fergus rapped out. 'Are you sure the owner wants to sell? And did you say "she"?'

'It's the *SS Ketton*. Jacob Grainger's widow is selling her.'

'I know his name. He travelled east, didn't he?'

'Yes, he traded in India. His widow wants to secure her family's future and is liquidating her husband's estate. With six children, every penny counts for her, and while she was tied up here there was also the matter of Whitehaven's harbour fees, which are far more expensive than those in the Isle of Man.'

'You say there's competition?'

'So it would seem.'

'And the crew? Would they come with the ship? The engineer, stoker, and greaser?'

'They'll be needing new positions, so I expect you could employ them. Built in 1853 from Napier & Sons in Glasgow for Cunard. She's 268 by 37 feet. A useful size for an oceangoing vessel.'

Fergus cursed out loud, something he rarely did. *A ship tried and tested in the waters he and Bill were hoping to travel, and an experienced crew. And just what they wanted, with a seller who needed the money. But now there was a competitor.*

'You're sure she's in the Isle of Man?'

'Certain. She said if you were interested enough, you'd come to her.'

'She's canny, then?'

'Don't make the mistake of thinking she doesn't know what she's doing. She told me before he died, Jacob gave her instructions for selling. She wants – and, more importantly, *needs* – to sell.'

'What did her husband die of?'

'Consumption.'

'And the price?'

Jeremiah told him, and Fergus whistled.

'Still interested?'

Fergus nodded, running over the figures in his head. He

wouldn't make the mistake he'd made last time of using all his own money; he'd take out a loan or maybe two.

'I wouldn't recommend you rush over to Douglas,' Jeremiah said, 'but I think the *Ketton* is precisely what you need. I'm anticipating you've got your eye on Boston, or perhaps New York.'

Fergus didn't correct him. All the better if Jeremiah thought they were planning to go west. 'I could go today,' he said.

'You could catch the ferry to Douglas if you hurry. I'm so sure this is the right ship for you, I'll cover your expenses there and back. It's only two and a half hours.'

'Would you consider coming with me for the introduction?'

'Most certainly. There's always business I can see to in Douglas and, to be frank, we have my mother-in-law here from Frizington, and an excuse to get out of the house on business is a welcome diversion.'

* * *

Fergus found Becky at the Indian King, and from the expression on Dolly's face, he had no doubt she was fully aware of the reason they'd returned early.

Becky was in the kitchen. She'd changed out of her travelling clothes and was wearing a plain tartan day dress. She was drying cutlery and putting it away. When she saw him she put the drying cloth down. 'You've finished already?' she asked. 'Was the ship no good?'

He explained what had happened, finishing with, 'Do you want to come to Douglas? I know you've never been.'

'When?'

'Today. There and back.'

Becky laughed. 'Oh, aye? At least two and a half hours there and the same back, when I've spent the last day travelling? No, thank you. Ask me another time.'

'Are you sure?'

'Sure as eggs is eggs. Now get off and do what we came back for. Check over that ship.'

'I'll hurry back, but I may have to stay over.'

'I'll not wait up, then.'

He kissed her. 'I'm doing this for us and the family we talked about. Our children's children.'

'We're not going to have any if you're always gadding about.'

Fergus was shocked and sucked in his cheeks.

Becky picked up the drying cloth and flicked it at him. 'Go on, you've no time to dilly-dally talking with your new bride.'

* * *

When the ferry arrived in Douglas, Jeremiah pointed to a line of three steamers. 'There she is,' he said. 'The one in the middle. She's the reputation of being a good runner. Iron-hulled, a combination ship, propelled by steam and sail.'

'Meaning sail can take over if the coal runs out.'

'Correct. And a screw propeller, which makes her efficiency consistent, regardless of the depth at which she's operating.'

'Much better than the old paddle wheels and, being

submerged, her propeller will be less prone to damage. I've done my homework.'

'I expected no less from you, Fergus. Meet me back here in an hour. By then I will have checked the lay of the land regarding the other potential buyer and paved the way for your inspection.'

Fergus pulled out his pocket watch and checked the time. 'It's one o'clock now, so that will be two o'clock. I'll be back in plenty of time if I go into town.'

Fergus stood on the quay for a few minutes and watched Jeremiah board the steamship. His first impression was the ship's size – three masts and two funnels. What surprised him was how graceful she was, despite this.

From where he was standing, she appeared to be in good shape. The sails were furled and there were men working on the deck.

Am I seeing the future of the Louisa Line?

Fergus turned his back on the quay. The town was busy with shoppers and mariners. Fergus sauntered towards a large painted sign attached to the side of a warehouse that said 'SHIP'S CHANDLERS'. He slipped inside, but it being a smallish business there was little of interest. However, he asked for a product and price list, which he folded and put in his pocket.

Back on the quay, three bare-footed dark-haired boys were mud-larking, digging for treasure beside some rowing boats hauled up on the sandy slipway. They were scooping up globules of wet sand and squeezing it in their fists, then letting the sludge drop through the gaps between their fingers. Their faces were mud-streaked, their jackets short and too tight, and their trousers stopped halfway down their legs. All three were wearing the poor boys' uniform. Thinking of Rory, Fergus took three pennies from his pocket and called to them. When he had the attention of all three, he threw the pennies down onto the sand, saying, 'A penny for each of you.'

For a moment they were startled; then they were laughing and scrabbling for the treasure. The first to get one raised his arm and held it high.

'Thanks, mister, you're a good 'un.'

Fergus gave the boy one of his best smiles. It was worth more than the three pennies it had cost him to see the surprise and delight of the boys. He walked along a little way, absorbed by the different vessels and their hard-working crew, then stopped to buy some fancily packaged aniseed balls and liquorice for Dolly and Becky respectively. With time to spare, he bought an *Isle of Man Times* newspaper, before settling down to read it in a busy coffee shop.

At five minutes to two, Jeremiah was waiting for him by the *SS Ketton.*

'I saw you talking to those boys,' he said. 'How's that young lad that works at your warehouse?'

'Rory? He's a good worker. I'm training him up for all sides of the business. He's a reliable cook's assistant and quick with figures. I can see managing potential in the boy, but to do that he must be acquainted with all branches of the business.'

'If you've a mind to it, as a favour I'll be pleased to take Rory in the office for an afternoon or two. Give him a grounding in being a shipping agent, show him the ropes.'

'Thank you. I'm sure he'll leap at the chance, but I warn you his heart's set on travelling the world. He's a mariner through and through, so I'll not force him into the business side. He must make his own decisions when he's old enough.'

They were at the gangway when Jeremiah said, 'What do you think of her close up?'

'She's got smooth lines.'

Fergus was introduced to the master, then to the engineer and the stoker. The greaser was described as "being in a poor way, having had four teeth pulled that morning".

After he'd shown them the upper decks, the engineer took them below to view the two compound engines.

'I'm a duck out of water here,' said Fergus, as soon as he saw the pipes and cylinders.

'That's why you have an engineer on board,' said Jeremiah.

As he was being shown around, Fergus kept wondering what Bill was going to think, and how important it would be that he got on well with the engineer. After finance, that relationship would be one of the deciding factors.

After an hour, they adjourned to the captain's quarters.

Jeremiah handed Fergus an envelope. 'I've listed the specifications for you, but the most important statistic for you will be the internal space.'

Fergus nodded, then turned to the engineer. 'You said there were how many watertight compartments?'

'Six. The goods tanks, in the centre of the ship, are 45 feet in length and 18 feet in height, and the coal bunkers are sited either side of the tanks.'

'What is her history?'

'Her maiden voyage, in 1853, was to New York. In 1854 she was requisitioned for Crimean War Transport. After the war, Cunard sold her to Captain Grainger, and she's spent the last years travelling to India – particularly Bombay. Now, as you are aware, his widow has put her up for sale.'

'Why is she not going to auction?'

'Captain Grainger knew he didn't have long to live, and a few days before he died, he gave his wife instructions. These were that she was to sell the ship to raise capital, but not through an auction house, because paying them commission was "a waste of brass". I understand his words were "Companies'll be clamouring to own our ship".'

'I see.' Fergus was struggling to conceal his excitement. A steamship with a crew who had so much experience in sailing to India was a dream come true. 'And the other buyers?'

'Mrs Grainger is waiting to hear from them. They called yesterday and left, stating they were consulting with their accountant. We understand from their agent they're genuinely interested.'

'And the crew? Do they come with the ship?'

'I've spoken with the men,' the engineer told him. 'Negotiation is possible.'

* * *

Fergus returned to Coates Lane intending to wake Becky to tell her the news, but he found her sitting up for him by the range, winding wool into a ball from a skein slotted over the back of a chair.

'The ship's perfect and we have to buy her,' he told her.

'Slow down, Fergus, you're rushing ahead. Bill hasn't seen her yet.'

'They're bringing her over for an inspection, so Bill will have plenty of time to consider her. I promise you I won't proceed unless Bill is behind me on this.' That wasn't exactly true; what he meant was, *I shall make it my business to see that Bill is behind me for this purchase.*

'Can the company afford her?'

Fergus remembered the moment he had learned the asking price. He'd then seen it confirmed at the end of the specification sheet Jeremiah had given him. It was an awful lot of money, and he didn't have that much. Even so, he had told Jeremiah if the ship passed inspection, he was prepared to offer Mrs Grainger fifty pounds over the other potential buyer's offer.

'With investors, some capital input and a small loan, I don't see a problem,' he told Becky. 'And I trust Todhunter. He's a good eye for a ship.'

'What if you don't secure this Mauritian contract?'

Becky was voicing Fergus's worst fear. He was assuming all would go as he wished. But the proposition they had for Macintosh & Warrilow made so much sense to him, he felt the manufacturers couldn't possibly turn it down.

'We need a steamship, regardless of Macintosh & Warrilow. We'll just be getting one sooner than we planned. There are government contracts we could apply for, like moving troops, that sort of thing.'

They talked things over until gone midnight. Fergus finished undressing and Becky was in bed when she said, 'Did Hector discuss Shackleton & Company's business with your mother?'

'Not as far as I know. I don't think she was that interested.'

'I'm interested. Ma and I always discussed the business.'

'That's no surprise. You were living amidst it.'

'You don't have to share the day-to-day running – I'm saying you can always discuss your business plans with me. I know it's not a thing most husbands do, but I've a business head on my shoulders, and I've learned a lot about finance listening to men talk on the other side of the bar.'

'Of that I've no doubt,' said Fergus. 'I've told you about Mauritius and how we need a steamship. I'm not hiding anything. I don't want to burden you with unnecessary detail, that's all. You've always said you worry about me turning into my father, that I'll think only of the business and talk of nothing else.'

'There's a difference between living the day-to-day business at home and sharing your thoughts for the future. It's my future, too.'

'I see our future as bringing up a family in a happy home. Don't you?'

Becky felt a tightness in her throat. *He's talking about children. My role as a mother.* 'But it's all about sharing. I enjoy you telling me about the big things that happen. Dicken's purchase of another marbled stock-book is amusing, as are your other tales about him and his pernickety ways, but I'm interested in hearing about the next ship purchase and the big contracts.'

Fergus grinned at her. 'I'll bear that in mind, but while we're waiting for the family to come along, we could put in some practice.'

'Now?'

'Why not?'

* * *

The next morning at the office, Dicken greeted Fergus's return with a request for their cleaner to come in twice a week, rather than once.

'You are the bookkeeper,' Fergus reminded him. Dicken's tidy ways were beginning to grate on him, and sometimes the sound of his pen scratching on the paper made Fergus want to shout out. 'I think you will agree your suggestion is an unnecessary expense.'

Dicken ran his finger along the counter separating the company side of the office from the public area, making a dust trail in the wood. 'Each time the loading door is opened and they bring in more barrels and sacks, the counter becomes covered in dust. It comes in at the loading doors and floats down from the upper floors, and in through the entrance too.'

Fergus sighed. 'Are you telling me you've no idea what a dusting cloth is for?'

Dicken sucked his top lip. 'I do, but I'm the bookkeeper.'

'I've promoted you to chief duster, in charge of the office counter,' said Fergus, smiling. 'This is a small company and we all have to pull together.' Had Dicken not been such an efficient bookkeeper, Fergus would have dismissed him before now, but he'd held back.

Sitting on top of the pile of post waiting for him in his office was the report from Mr Cameron on Macintosh & Warrilow, in a larger than usual envelope. Fergus sent Dicken out to arrange a meeting with Bill before the *Sophie Alice* sailed for Dublin.

The report confirmed Dr Fincham's general overview of the firm, which was reassuring; Macintosh & Warrilow was a sound company, had been in business for over thirty years, and its current chairman and board of directors were all well respected in Glasgow. However, the more congenial founding chairman, whom Dr Fincham had met, had died the previous year and his son, Guthrie Macintosh, was a tighter businessman, who did not suffer fools gladly.

After Fergus had read the report again, he turned his attention to making an appointment for the next day to sign the legal documents concerning Rory, and to enquire about a loan for the *SS Ketton*.

Bill arrived carrying a jar of pickled herrings, which he presented to Fergus. 'These are for you. I know you like them.'

Fergus laughed, thanked him, and took the jar.

Bill continued. 'I've arranged for the *Sophie Alice* to enter dry dock to undergo repair after her next Dublin crossing. I'm unhappy about some of the planking. Not worried enough she isn't safe to sail – it's just that twenty nails driven home now will secure the job, rather than having to use sixty in two months' time.'

'I'll take the opportunity to set Rory on working at the warehouse. Here's the Macintosh & Warrilow report.'

After he'd read it, Bill said, 'We still need a steamship before we can even consider such a voyage.'

'I've found one. The *SS Ketton*. Here's the specification sheet.'

'Things *have* moved on,' Bill said, scanning the sheet.

'It'll be here soon, so you'll be able to inspect her. In my mind, she's perfect, but we cannot make any commitments until we have your decision to be master. There's no one else I would trust with the company's future. What do you say? Do we invest and move forward?'

'My reservation is that I've never captained a steamship, but the way I see it, it's how things are going. I've learned there are masters' courses with practical training in Maryport for precisely my situation.'

'And you'd be prepared to take such preparation, at the Louisa Line's expense?'

'I think it's a necessity, whether we sail for Mauritius or not.'

'So, what are you saying?'

'I'm saying if the ship passes the inspection, if I like the feel of her, and we're both happy with the arrangements with Macintosh & Warrilow, then, yes – I'll happily take our ship to Mauritius and back. Providing, of course, we can afford her.'

Fergus stood up and slapped Bill on the back. 'Good man. We can make this work.'

'If the *Ketton* hadn't already proved herself with trips to India, I would advise that we hold off on the purchase until we have a firm contract, but I agree – she is perfect for our needs.'

'If she's sound on the gridiron and passes A1 with Lloyds, then I'll buy her. Either way, I'm coming with you on the next Glasgow voyage.'

'That's planned for the 19th,' Bill said. 'Two weeks on Sunday. I'm sad to say you were right. We've received written word from Campbells that the next load of Hebridean textiles will be ready for collection. It may be our last.'

'As well as Macintosh & Warrilow, you could speak with our agent about trains taking over our carriage business. I want you to hear what he has to say with your own ears. We may be able to salvage something.'

'He may have ideas, especially since he's losing commission. The details of the sugar machinery and Mauritius we can discuss later, and during the voyage up there.'

'Agreed,' said Fergus. 'There's one final thing.'

'What's that?'

'I'm signing wardship papers for Rory tomorrow. It doesn't outwardly change anything, but it means I'll be officially recognised as a significant adult in his life, should there be an accident, or anything like that.'

'He's a lucky lad,' said Bill.

'People will think so, but Becky and I are the lucky ones. Strange how he literally fell into my life, and then into Becky's.'

* * *

Later, Fergus, having related his conversation with Bill over supper with Becky, he entertained her with Dicken and the dusty counter.

She laughed. 'He's like an old woman, yet he can't be more than his early twenties. Next thing he'll be demanding a clean doorstep. It's a good job he's not living here, with all the dust the workmen have left. I keep cleaning and it keeps appearing.'

'It'll settle down now the workmen have finished. I'm looking forward to bringing my books from Queen Street. I miss having them to hand.'

Becky clasped her arms around Fergus's neck and he drew her in. 'I can't believe we have our own home at last,' she said.

'You haven't travelled far, with the Indian King being only two minutes' walk. If we listen carefully, we'll probably hear Dolly telling a tipsy collier to pipe down.'

'That's true enough, but it's *our* home and that makes it extra special.'

'From tomorrow it will be Rory's home, if he wants it. I'm going to sign the papers.'

'Are you taking him with you?'

'No, he's not needed, but you can come with me. In fact, I'd like you to. It's an important day for us both, and it will show Mr Needham we're truly united in wanting to care for the lad.'

'You called him a lad. I haven't heard you say that before. He's always been a boy.'

'The more he grows, the less he seems a boy, but he's not yet a man. The crew call him "the lad", and I think it suits him. I can't call him son, because I'm not his father.'

'In that case, what is he going to call you? It will sound queer him calling you Mr Shackleton when this is his home.'

'I've thought about that. What about Mr Fergus? He calls you Miss Becky and Dolly, Mrs Dolly.'

'And when he's on-board ship? What then?'

'Whatever the master of the ship instructs him to call me.'

CHAPTER SEVENTEEN

After Rory's ward documentation had been signed and witnessed by Mr Needham and was pronounced ready to forward to the Justice of the Peace's clerk, Becky left to go home. Fergus himself stayed on; he didn't want Becky involved in the financial discussions with Mr Needham surrounding his plans.

'There is the matter of a steamship. I've seen one I can purchase.'

'This comes as no surprise. Tell me more.'

Fergus outlined their plans, including the Mauritius voyage, and stated how much money he needed.

The solicitor pursed his lips. 'Let's work in percentages.'

Fergus pulled a paper from his pocket. 'Here's some calculations. You can see I've a shortfall of twenty percent.'

'Are you sure this is the correct time for such a venture?' asked Mr Needham in a doubtful voice. 'Wouldn't you prefer to build up more capital first?'

'It's something Bill and I have been planning for a while. The future is in steam, not least because of timetabling and a release from the vagaries of the wind. The Mauritian voyage is behind our swift decision, and now we have the perfect ship on our doorstep.'

'Don't you think you should at least wait until you've heard from Macintosh & Warrilow?'

'I have great hopes there.'

'If I may say so, many such hopes have hit submerged rocks, resulting in the loss of all hands. Fergus, as your solicitor I must point out that you have a propensity for rushing in. My considered advice is to wait.'

'But I don't want to. I could lose this ship.' Even to his own ears, Fergus knew he sounded like a petulant child. 'I see her as the future of the Louisa Line. If I get the Glasgow contract, they will pay me a deposit, which I can use to offset a loan. The *Eleanor Bell* and the *Sophie Alice*, both making good profits on their regular runs, will also create capital which I can use to offset debt.'

'Your reasoning makes some sense. However, the important word here is "if". You'll also need to engage a new captain for the *Sophie Alice*. If you don't receive the Mauritian contract, then your two current ships will not raise enough to draw down your debt. You will then need to seek out alternative contracts, which will take considerable time and effort.'

'I have investors I can turn to. Here's a list.'

Mr Needham ran down the names. 'You are determined, I see.'

'If I can secure this voyage, it will ensure the Louisa Line's future.' *And if I don't, I will lose all Aunt Louisa's inheritance.*

'In that case I suggest you follow up on these investors individually, rather than bring them together as a group, even though it's more work. That way one will not influence another, and they won't know who their fellow investors are until later. In the meantime, I'll enquire about raising finance from the banks on your behalf for the purchase of this steamship. You realise you may have to take out a mortgage on the warehouse?'

Fergus nodded. *And if it all goes totally wrong, on Coates Lane, too.*

* * *

Two days later there was a delivery from Mr Needham to the warehouse containing the official wardship papers. They'd been signed and returned by the Justice of the Peace and were now covered in various stamps and seals. Taking the documents, Fergus went in search of Rory. He found him on the second floor, sitting on a barrel, adding up columns of figures.

Rory stood up when he saw Fergus. 'I heard your steps,' he said. 'I knew it was you because Dicken creeps about, and *your* steps are heavy. Anyways, if it'd been Dicken, Charlie would have started barking. They don't get on, those two. I'm checking the latest Cockerm'uth delivery for Cardiff.'

'Come here,' said Fergus, beckoning the boy forward. 'You've a cobweb in your fringe.' He pulled it off and showed it to him.

'Good job I'm not a lass,' said the boy, peering at the black and dusty, sticky threads hanging from Fergus's fingers. He put out one of his own to touch them.

'Why's that?' asked Fergus.

'Lasses are scared of spiders. You'd not get any of them up here. They'd be running down the stairs, screaming their heads off so loudly, they'd hear it in St Bees.'

Fergus found a flat surface on the top of a new barrel, took out his handkerchief and stretched it out, then laid the document on it. He kept hold of one edge to prevent it from rolling up.

'Here you are, Rory. These are your wardship papers.'

'Does that mean I'm yours and Miss Becky's now?'

'It means you're what's called my ward, and the law of the land says I'm allowed to care for you. For the three of us, it means we can all live together. Are you happy about that?'

Rory's shoulders shot up and he called Charlie over to him. 'I've exciting news! You and I are wards, Charlie,' he said, scratching behind the dog's ears. Charlie cocked his head at his master, then checked with Fergus. Rory deliberated a moment, before adding, 'Although I do like it at Mrs Dolly's. Those pies she makes when the races are on are reet tasty.'

'I'm sure Miss Becky knows how to make them. You enjoy being at sea, don't you, Rory?'

'Aye, I love it, and I'm a canny cook's assistant, but I like it here, too, in the warehouse – putting things straight, counting the barrels. Charlie loves it, especially when there's a rat under one of the shelves.'

'I know it's a long way off, but when you're fifteen you can be apprenticed. What about that?'

'I know all about it. I've heard the others talking and they get £20 a year.'

'It'll probably be even more in four years' time. I want you to know that it's something you can do if you want to, when the time comes.'

'Will it mean I can go to America and Canada?'

'All over the world. India – and China, even.'

'Is that the truth?' Rory sounded impressed.

'If you're an apprentice and work your way up, like our two captains, to become second mate and then first mate, there's nothing to say you can't be a master in time.'

Rory glanced down. 'What about my leg?'

'I've spoken to Dr Fincham about that. He thinks as you grow taller and stronger you'll be able to manage better and get about faster, with greater ease. He mentioned something I'd never thought of. When he was a ship's surgeon, he worked alongside mariners with only one good leg, and some with a wooden peg from the knee for the other. You see them working in our harbour sometimes.'

'Were their legs bitten off by crocodiles hiding in swamps?'

'I'm not sure of that, you'll have to ask Dr Fincham. More likely hit by a piece of falling wood or caught up in an anchor chain. What he means is, one-legged mariners are working on ships, and he thinks, in time, you may be able to do so too, out in the open on deck in most weathers.'

'Maybe I could go to that place Mauritius he talks about. I'd love to see the French fort at Port Louis, with all the cannon and those plantation houses. Do you think I might be able to go there? I think it's near the top of Africa.'

'No, that's Madeira. Mauritius is much farther away. You have to go down the west coast then round the bottom of Africa, and then across a bit of the Indian Ocean. I think it's safe to say you may go there some day.'

* * *

Becky was both excited and nervous at the same time. They were having lunch at Queen Street and had brought Rory, too. It was the first time they'd been invited as a family. She wondered what Rory would make of all the finery.

'You'll remember not to talk with your mouth full, won't you, Rory?' she reminded him as Fergus knocked on the door.

Rory sighed. 'Yes. And to sit still, be quiet, not make a fuss and not run around.'

The door opened and Samuel ushered them in. 'The master and mistress are in the drawing room.'

Although they were now in May, a fire was burning in the grate. The room, as always, smelt of polish, and the silver gleamed. Becky saw a new, green-upholstered chair had been added to the room.

Elizabeth greeted them warmly.

Rory, looking from Elizabeth to Hector then back again, took hold of the front of his waistcoat and pulled it down.

'What do you say to Mr and Mrs Shackleton?' prompted Becky. They had practised this.

'I say "good morning", but I can't remember which one you said I was to say it to first.' Out of the corner of her eye Becky saw Elizabeth's lips turn up as she stifled a smile.

Hector came forward and put out his hand. 'Good morning, young man.'

Rory put his hand in his. 'Good morning, sir, how do you do?'

'Very well, thank you.'

He turned to Elizabeth. 'Good morning, ma'am, how do you do?'

Elizabeth gave a gracious nod. 'Good morning, young sir. I am in good health, thank you.'

'I think this is for you, Rory.' Becky put her hand in the small of his back to guide him towards the new chair.

When they were all seated, Elizabeth asked about Edinburgh. 'You came home a day early?'

'Yes, I went to inspect a steamship.'

Hector's eyebrows shot up. 'Where?'

'The Isle of Man. Jeremiah Todhunter found it for me.'

'And?'

'I'm thinking of buying it.'

'Goodness,' said Elizabeth. 'Although I can't say I'm surprised.'

Hector frowned. 'With the loss of the Campbell contract you feel able to expand in this way? It won't be cheap.'

'Father, let's discuss this another time. We are here socially.'

Hector regarded Elizabeth, then Becky. 'You're right. No need to discuss business in front of the ladies.'

Becky bit her lip. *What's wrong with discussing business with the ladies?* She was about to say something, when Samuel came in to announce luncheon was served.

With Hector at one end of the long table and Fergus at the other, Becky and Elizabeth were placed opposite each other, halfway down, with a chair placed next to Becky for Rory. Becky thought it a north, south, east, west way of sitting, with big spaces between them.

As the soup was being served, Elizabeth cleared her throat, then glanced at Hector as if she was expecting him to say something. He either didn't see her look, or he ignored it. There was a short pause, before Elizabeth said, 'How are you finding Coates Lane, Becky?'

'Very well, thank you. It suits us.'

'You don't find it too small?'

Becky shook her head. 'No, not at all.'

Elizabeth turned to Rory. 'You're still living at the Indian King, I understand.'

'Aye,' said Rory, twirling his spoon and making waves in his soup. 'Mrs Dolly says I have to give Mr Fergus and Mrs Becky time to settle in.'

'Yes, of course. That is a good idea.' Elizabeth's next words were directed at Fergus. 'You don't think it is going to be a little crowded when Rory moves in, do you?'

I know where this is going, thought Becky.

'And there's no room for a maid?' Elizabeth went on, asking a question to which they all knew the answer.

'I don't need one,' said Becky. 'I'm trained in keeping a house. If I didn't have the house to care for all day, what would I do?' She wanted to add she was no giddy, empty-headed wife who'd been waited on all her life, but that would be devastatingly rude to Elizabeth.

'She does all the cleaning,' said Rory.' I've seen her.'

'I'm used to it,' Becky said, 'and I've plenty of time now I'm married and not working at the Indian King.'

'I realise that may be the case right now, but when the children come along, that will be quite different.'

Becky blushed. She was uncomfortable talking with her mother-in-law about her role as a potential parent at the best of times, and she thought it a little insensitive in front of Rory. She had no idea how he would take to another child in their family and had been hoping, when the time came, she would be able to bring the subject up in a gentle way.

'I may help Fergus. He enjoys discussing the business with me.'

Elizabeth's eyes widened and she cast a glance at Fergus, who was seemingly absorbed in his soup.

'I help Mr Fergus in the warehouse,' piped up Rory. 'I like it – all those boxes and casks and sacks going off to faraway places. It's exciting. Although that Dicken is a bit sour. I don't think he likes dogs o'er much, either.'

'I'm sure you do enjoy it,' said Elizabeth, 'but, Becky, whilst I saw a lot more women on the Continent working in hotels, and in some cases whole families working together in street-side coffee shops, I do think the creation of a home is paramount.'

'I agree, it's important,' said Fergus, 'but I recognise Becky is interested in the business and I'm happy to talk to her about it.'

Becky would have preferred it if he'd said 'share it with her'.

Elizabeth was not to be discouraged. 'An ordered house is a sign of virtue and respectability, you know, and

I like to think our household here in Queen Street was, and remains, a refuge from external business trials and tribulations.'

'What are tribulations?' asked Rory, speaking with his mouth full.

'They're troubles,' Fergus explained.

'Like winds and storms and high tides?'

'They can be,' said Becky.

Elizabeth continued, 'I'm sure you will find Coates Lane far too small when you are blessed with little ones, and you won't have time for anything to do with business. When Rory is living with you, where will you put the nurse?'

'The nurse?'

'Yes. When Fergus was born, I had a nurse live in for two months until I felt able to cope.'

Fergus came to Becky's aid. 'Mother, we can talk about this when the need arises. We are not moving into Queen Street with you; we have discussed this several times.'

'I know,' Elizabeth spluttered, 'but that was before you were married. I'm asking in case you now find it too small.'

'I would love to live here,' said Rory. 'There's nice things.'

'I'm sure you would enjoy it,' said Elizabeth, seeming to warm to the idea, perhaps as an encouragement to Fergus and Becky. 'You could have your own room.'

Fergus raised his eyebrows. 'Mother,' he said firmly.

'All the same,' said Hector, 'it will be nice to have young people in the house sometimes.' He smiled at Rory over his water glass, before adding, 'Especially if they're as polite as you are – not running around with high-pitched voices, making a mess everywhere.'

'Rory's on his best behaviour,' said Fergus. 'Aren't you? He can make himself heard with the best of them when he wants to.'

'Aye, and I've remembered not to tuck this piece of cloth in my neck.' He held up his napkin and started waving it around.

Becky was beginning to think she needn't have worried about Rory and the Shackletons. They both seemed to find him amusing – Elizabeth particularly so. It seemed she was going to accept Rory as part of the family, which was something Becky hadn't expected. Perhaps it was because she was so desperate for a grandchild, and because she had nothing of substance with which to fill her days.

After lunch, Elizabeth said she'd like to take Rory and show him something. They returned with Rory holding a large wooden train and Elizabeth behind him, holding two carriages.

'My train,' said Fergus. 'I'd forgotten all about it. You've kept it all these years?'

'That's another advantage of having a large house,' Elizabeth said. 'We have an attic to store things.'

Rory set the train down on the expensive carpet and directed his attention to attaching the carriages, while Hector invited Fergus to join him in his study to deal with some papers.

'Can I take this train home with me?' Rory asked Elizabeth.

'You could, but why don't you leave it here? Then you have an excuse to visit me.'

Rory put his head on one side. 'That's a reet grand idea. I can come sometimes after work, when I'm not at sea.'

'He's not always this neat and tidy,' Becky said. 'You won't want him down on his knees in here if he's come straight from the warehouse covered in dust.'

'Then we'll visit the horses outside,' said Elizabeth.

Seeing Elizabeth reach out for the companionship of an eleven-year-old lad, Becky realised how lonely her mother-in-law must be. She was even more determined to make sure she had a purpose in her own life other than as the mother of Fergus's children.

While Rory was occupied with the train, Elizabeth went to a desk and took out two notebooks.

'Becky, come sit by me.' She sat down on the chaise longue and patted the seat beside her, then passed one of the books to Becky. 'This is my household account book.' As Becky took the book from her and began to leaf through it, she went on, 'This is my first book. I'm on my fifth now. I've been keeping household accounts and notes since the first week we were married, nearly twenty-five years ago.'

Inside Elizabeth's book was the date of her marriage – October 15th 1836. Then, in Elizabeth's copperplate writing, came an inventory of their wedding presents. Glued to the next page was a newspaper clipping, with the heading *Notes on Keeping Servants and Their Duties*. The clipping contained menu lists and tips on household cleaning, and how to rid clothing of stains. Becky turned over more pages and saw Elizabeth had recorded what must have been the whole history of their Queen Street house: the weekly menus, the cost of the laundry, the purchase of new curtains, the cleaning of the chimneys, the purchase of new kitchenware.

'This is an encyclopaedia of this house and your life in it,' said Becky, in surprise and awe.

'It has been my Sunday evening task all these years.'

'Every Sunday?' asked Becky.

'Mostly. When we've been away, I have written an account of our visit upon our return.'

'Then this is a daily record of life in this house? A diary?'

'Not a normal diary. It's a household account, not a personal one. It is a factual record.' Elizabeth handed her the other book she was holding. 'Here's a new account book I bought at Croxall's for you.'

Becky was unsure how to respond. She was stunned into silence. She could see the value of keeping a record of some things, such as how to remove stains, but daily life in such detail? She could never record all that, and nor did she want to. Finally, she said, 'Thank you for my book, it will be most useful. I will do my best to keep it up.'

Elizabeth laid her hand over hers. 'Don't worry. I don't expect you to follow my example in such detail, but it is useful to keep accounts. That way you have a tally of the important things, like tradesmen's charges year on year, that sort of thing.'

Becky was beginning to see Elizabeth in a completely different light. To have had the discipline to create such a record, and to have done it for twenty-five years, was an enormous achievement. She had learned two things that afternoon – that Elizabeth was lonely, and that she had assumed the role of domestic scribe to keep herself occupied for quarter of a century.

* * *

A week passed during which Fergus approached each of the potential investors on his list. It being Wednesday, Dicken was working at the Seamen's Haven, and he was able to report to Bill at the warehouse.

'We've secured Nicholas Fincham, our own Captain Jessop, and three businessmen – Messrs Nubley, Heslop and Dickinson.'

'I've heard of Nubley,' Bill said. 'He's connected with the foundry. But I haven't heard of Heslop, or Dickinson.'

'Heslop's a flax-spinner from Cleator way, and Dickinson's the sail-maker on George Street. We may be able to sign up a few more. Mr Needham is making enquiries; he knows everyone in the business world in Whitehaven. I'm pleased to say our plans have been enthusiastically received.'

'Has the ship's report come back yet?'

Fergus shook his head. 'I'm expecting it the day after tomorrow. I have a further meeting with Mr Needham. Are we decided to go ahead if she passes? It seems we have the financing in place.'

'If you're sure we can finance it. As soon as we get her, I'll sign up in Liverpool for the masters' steamship instruction. I've had a thought – if we retain her current captain in our employ, he can support me, and then when I depart for Mauritius, he can take over the *Sophie Alice*'s runs.'

'I was wondering about that. He might also be available to take a second run to Mauritius, if the first is successful.'

After Bill left, Fergus gathered up the account books and spent the next hour projecting the company's income, including factoring in the loss of the Campbell textile account. The *Ketton* could be purchased; his credit was good, but it was going to be a close run, and so much was out of his personal control. Even if the contract came through, they hadn't given enough thought to what they were buying in Mauritius, or how they were going to sell what they brought back.

If I'm going to pull out, it needs to be now. I can walk away today, instantly sleep easier at night and probably have fewer headaches.

He closed the account books and put them back, then found the file they'd marked "THE FUTURE". The envelope he'd placed in it was still there, as was the piece of paper inside, on which he'd written "MAURITIUS?"

* * *

'Are you sure you wish to proceed without a firm contract from Glasgow?' Mr Needham was regarding Fergus in a kindly manner, as an uncle might. 'I've mentioned previously it may take you some time to build up business for a steamship without it.'

'It's not solely about Glasgow; it's about the future of the Louisa Line.'

'I understand that. I'm not sure whether I admire your courage and forward thinking, or whether I fear for your recklessness.'

Fergus gave a nervous laugh. He'd spent the previous night tossing and turning, keeping Becky awake. As dawn broke, and the sun rose to promise a bright day, he'd experienced a strong feeling of optimism. He would go ahead, because he knew if he didn't, he would always wonder if he should have done. It wasn't a sound argument, but it was one he was prepared to defend.

CHAPTER EIGHTEEN

Becky was rearranging the mantelpiece ornaments above the range when Fergus came home from the office a few days later. She was holding one of a pair of flat-backed Staffordshire figures, which she laid down on the kitchen table.

'I heard you singing like a canary,' Fergus said. 'I can tell you're happy.'

'Indeed, I am.' *What's not to be happy about? A new bride in her own home.* 'All spick and span and ready to receive your books.'

Fergus sat down, putting his hat perilously close to the Staffordshire figures.

'Not on the table.' Becky picked it up and ran her fingers along one side to feel its smoothness. 'You haven't told me why you're home now. I thought there was a Shackleton & Company monthly board meeting.'

'There is, but that's this evening at the Waverley. I thought, since you're making such headway with the house, and most of the dust and confusion has gone, that we could visit Whittles and spend some more of Father and Mother's wedding present money. Would you like to?'

Becky touched her hair. 'Oh, Fergus, I can't go like this.' She pointed to her apron, which was splattered with marks, and laughed. 'Such visits need planning. You're thinking like the bachelor you used to be. Things are different now. You've a wife to consider.'

Fergus took in the worn dress Becky had changed into for the cleaning as though seeing it for the first time. 'True. I'm not used to having a lady in the house to share things with.'

'I'm sure you'll soon get used to it. And apart from my messy appearance, I'm expecting Rory. I promised him a batch of his favourite ginger and almond biscuits before he leaves for Dublin, and I'm about to make them.'

'Will it take you long?'

Becky saw the beginnings of a smile on his face. 'No. Why? Is there something else?'

'I'm thinking, if we're not going to Whittles, and you've some time to idle away then we could…' He undid his bottom waistcoat button.

Becky was shocked, but in a happy way. 'Fergus Shackleton, if you're thinking what I think you're thinking, then shame on you.'

He drew her towards him.

'In the middle of the day?' she asked.

'Why not?'

Becky couldn't think of any good reason why not. It would be another hour and a half before Rory was due to appear. Plenty of time to accept Fergus's invitation and then set to making the biscuits.

'All right, but lock the door. It would be just our luck for your ma to decide to call unannounced and catch us.'

Later, when Fergus was buttoning his waistcoat, getting ready to return to the warehouse, Becky asked him, 'When are you bringing your books?'

'Mother and Father are leaving for Carlisle tomorrow. Mother has a cousin she's going to visit, so I thought I'd pack them while they're away. Otherwise, she'll take it upon herself to help me, and whilst I appreciate the sentiment, I'd rather take care of things myself.'

'Have you missed your books? Or should I say, have you missed your library?'

'I've been rather busy recently, and I used to read a great deal at night in bed, but these days…'

'You've found something else to occupy yourself with.'

'Becky, that is an immodest remark.' Fergus laughed, raising his arms in mock shock.

She joined in his laughter. When they'd composed themselves, Fergus said, 'I've thought about why I love reading so much. Partly it's the appeal of the story or of learning something new, but it's also the books themselves. The bindings, the tooled leather, the smell and feel of a brand new book. Or with an old book, wondering who has held and read it before me. I like to lose myself in them, to transport myself somewhere else.'

'It can be a solitary occupation, reading.'

'I'm an only child – that explains a lot.'

'So am I.'

'Yes, but living at the Indian King there must always have been something happening. In our house, I used to read for company.'

'It was never peaceful at the pub,' Becky admitted. 'But unlike you, it was solitude *I* craved. The joy of finding a quiet corner. Sometimes I would go into one of the empty guest bedrooms and hide, just so I could read. Now we're married we can read together.'

'And to each other,' said Fergus.

When Fergus left, Becky went to the door and watched him walk away, his hands clasped behind his back. *Sometimes I am so happy, I think I will burst with the thrill of it all.*

* * *

The next day at Queen Street, after supervising the last case being loaded onto their carriage, Elizabeth gave her travelling valise to Samuel to hold, while she put out her arms to Fergus.

'We shall be gone just over a week,' she said. 'I'll send word immediately we are safely arrived.' Turning back to Samuel, she went on, 'I have no further instructions regarding the house other than those we discussed last evening.'

Samuel inclined his head, returned her valise, and helped Hector into the carriage.

Watching them depart, Fergus gave an audible sigh of relief. 'That homecoming passed without major incident,' he remarked to Samuel.

'Apart from the fracas with the cook over the seasoning of

the tomato soup, the rind on this year's batch of marmalade being cut too thinly, and the light in your father's study running out of oil, I think all went smoothly,' said Samuel.

'We got away lightly, when you think back to the old days when the slightest thing would set him off. I think running the business was what made him so tetchy.'

'If I may say, sir, it didn't appear to come as easily to him as it did to your grandfather – or to you.'

Fergus had never considered others might liken him to his grandfather, the founder of Shackleton & Company. 'Do you think I am like him? He died when I was nine so I only have a young boy's memories of him.'

'Not in character, but in business. From what I hear, you are up to date and planning for the future.'

Fergus lurched inside. 'What do you hear and from whom?' *Does he know about Mauritius? Have any of my potential investors spoken?* He would have hesitated to prompt anyone else about his reputation, but he knew Samuel would tell him the truth.

'I hear about you at the Seamen's Haven and at Friends' Meetings. In particular, your own Captain Jessop speaks highly of you.'

'He's been a great success with the Shamrock Run. He came from Shackleton & Company to take over the *Eleanor Bell*, allowing Bill to oversee the Dublin and Glasgow runs in the *Sophie Alice*. He's a sound fellow.'

'He's the one says you've an eye to the future, which these days must be a good thing.'

'Let's hope so. However, I can't stay chatting about the business with you, Samuel. I have work to do.'

'You're right. Standing here won't buy the baby a new bonnet.'

Fergus set off for the warehouse, mulling over Samuel's words. It was pleasing his reputation in business was satisfactory, but he wasn't sure it was correct. Outwardly, he aimed to project a capability he did not feel. There were times when goods arrived late, when things did not go as planned, when he had a queasy feeling in his stomach, or he felt angry. It was at moments like these that he had more understanding of the pressures his father had been under. Seeing his father now so much more relaxed, he felt it was clear it was the business that had been behind his difficult nature. Worst of all, Fergus knew Becky would never forgive him if he became like his father, after he'd assured her he would never do so.

'I must not lose hold of "bookish Fergus",' he told himself. 'My father had nothing to turn to when the business caused him to lie awake at night tossing and turning, but *I* have my books and my wife.'

* * *

Rory was still living at the Indian King while he worked at the warehouse, and Dolly suggested he remain with her a while longer, since Becky and Fergus were so recently wed.

'Plenty of time in the future to take him in,' she said. 'It's best you have the place to yourselves for a few months. It's hard enough getting used to being married, without a young lad taking up your time and watching over you.'

Becky had thought Fergus might want them all to begin

living together as a family right away, but he'd surprised her.

'It's good starting as you mean to go on, but I think your mother's right. Although what about having him here at Coates Lane when I go to Glasgow? You'll not be on your own and it will give him a chance to get used to the idea.'

'Don't you need him on the ship?'

'Not this trip. Besides, the warehouse could do with tidying up and he likes organising things. Dicken can keep an eye on him during the day. What do you think?'

'It's a good idea. I mean, we all need time to adjust to living together as a family.'

'Don't forget we'll be getting Charlie, too. That'll turn things upside down.'

'I wouldn't have it any other way,' she said.

Since they'd returned from their honeymoon, Dolly had asked Becky several times if she thought she was going to be lonely at Coates Lane. 'You can move back in when Fergus is at sea, if you don't like the silence,' she'd told her.

Becky had put on a brave front. 'I have to get used to it, and you're so close, it's as if I'm still living here at the Indian King. Besides, not having me sleep there means you can use my room for bed and breakfast.'

In the end, they'd decided Becky would call in first thing when Fergus was away, to see if Dolly needed any help. If they were going to be busy, she would take care of supper so Dolly had something warm to eat when she'd finished. Becky suspected this arrangement was more to keep her mother happy than to save herself from being lonely. Besides, it was strange to see the new girl her mother had taken on doing all the chores she used to do. The one job she had retained was the doling out of wages on a Friday. She was good at it, the men trusted her, and she would rather do it herself than have to go to the bother of teaching someone else to do it.

CHAPTER NINETEEN

The *Sophie Alice* departed for Glasgow with a full load of general cargo. It was a while since Fergus had been at sea, and the sounds of the ropes and chains, and the chatter and sea shanties, brought back memories of previous voyages. They left Whitehaven in heavy rain but the winds were favourable, and when darkness fell the weather cleared up and the air grew lighter. The ship kept her way close enough to the coast to see the lights on land, but not to make out landmarks in the dark. For a ship known as a bit of a pitcher, there wasn't a great deal of movement, and Fergus was thankful for that. He'd never considered himself a sailor – more someone who was interested in ships and the culture and traditions that surrounded them.

Bill instructed the first mate, Sven, to keep a close eye on some of their Shetlanders in port to make sure they didn't run off. It didn't happen often, but recently several had absconded from two of Brocklebank's ships to return to their islands. Crew were easy to replace, but it was an inconvenience Bill wanted to avoid. The journey being uneventful, Sven set several of the crew on painting, and Fergus spent most of his time sitting in Bill's cabin, reading.

On arrival in Glasgow, after seeing their discharging was proceeding as planned, Fergus and Bill called on their agent on West Clyde Street. The agent confirmed to Fergus all that Bill had relayed about the rising importance of the railways and the inevitable shifting of freight from ship to train.

Later, over supper on board accompanied by several glasses of Madeira, Bill and Fergus put together their strategy for discussions with Mackintosh & Warrilow. After he'd retired to his cot, Fergus couldn't settle. Too many thoughts were playing havoc with his brain, and he was irritated with himself for having the second glass of Madeira. After half an hour, he got up and went and stood by the ship's rail. Even though it was past midnight, there were lots of men about. Some were obviously working, transporting goods on their backs and on barrows, calling out for people to make way, while others were just milling around. A few women with dresses cut far too low to be seemly were plying their trade; those finding custom disappeared for a short while, before returning to the same spot to await further business. Fergus wondered idly whether they agreed pitches between themselves, or whether it was a question of who got there first for the best spots. He knew standing by the rail wasn't going to bring sleep, so he returned to his cot and was thankful when, after putting his head down, he yawned. His last thought was to picture Becky asleep, safe and sound in their bed in Whitehaven.

The next morning, waking much earlier than usual because of the unfamiliar sounds on board, Fergus was refreshed and excited despite the lack of sleep. He and Bill watched the post loaded before disembarking and heading for Bill's favourite dockside coffee house, where they ordered full breakfasts with extra griddle pikelets to see them through the day.

In Macintosh & Warrilow's office lobby there were several mahogany plinths upon which rested strange metallic tubes, metal containers and gear parts. On the walls were gold-framed certificates from various trade exhibitions at which they'd won silver medals.

After Fergus and Bill had introduced themselves and had been invited to 'wait a wee while', their attention was drawn to a portrait of an elderly gentleman dominating the wall to their left. A recently polished brass plaque attached to the base of the frame informed them he was the company's founder, Cameron Macintosh, and that he'd passed away in 1860. There was also a short biography, and Bill and Fergus were reading this when the receptionist informed them Mr Macintosh had arrived.

Even though he was dressed for the city, Mr Macintosh carried himself with the air of a Scot who had recently stepped off a Highland moor. He was tall and thickset, with dark red hair and a beard that would not have seemed out of place on a Viking warrior. For a split second, Fergus imagined him holding a fighting axe in one hand and a shield in the other. His Scottish accent, while melodious and appealing, was so strong it took Fergus a few minutes to attune himself to its pitch and rhythm. He guessed Mr Macintosh was going to prove to be a no-nonsense man, a trait he respected when negotiating in business.

Bill and Fergus were shown into a walnut-panelled boardroom, in the centre of which, to their surprise, was a dining table laid out for luncheon. A man holding some booklets stepped forward.

'This is our works foreman,' Mr Mackintosh said. 'He's been with the company many years and is an expert in our products. After coffee he'll guide you through a short tour of our works. We realise you're not here to purchase our products, but it would be remiss of us not to show you our wares and working practices. Besides, we are extremely proud of our workmanship. We won several prizes at the Great Exhibition at Crystal Palace.'

'We're looking forward to seeing it all,' said Bill.

'Excellent,' said Mr Macintosh. 'I will leave you now and join you later for luncheon. We're serving Scottish beef. That will set us all up splendidly for what I trust will prove a fruitful discussion.'

'I'm sure we will find the tour interesting,' said Fergus, wondering how he was going to eat a full luncheon after their generous breakfast. He glanced at Bill, confident he was sharing similar thoughts.

A steward poured the coffee and, while it was being served, the foreman ran through the company's history before presenting them with one of the illustrated booklets he was clutching.

'We have these catalogues especially printed for exhibitions,' he said. 'It lists our products with descriptions, sizes, weights, etcetera. I should warn you that although I will do my best, the works are necessarily noisy, and it may not be possible to explain things on site, so you may wish to keep questions until we have returned.'

The foreman hadn't exaggerated the noise. Fergus could see that, as the weavers in the Lancashire cotton mills were expert lip readers, the same skill was required by Macintosh & Warrilow's workmen. Hammers were flattening metal, lathes were humming, and strange, complicated machines with rotating parts were making high-pitched clanging sounds, while metal shards were cascading onto the floor. Fergus thought the only way he'd be able to describe it to Becky would be to tell her it was like being made to listen to a conductor-less brass orchestra, where each instrument was out of tune while engaged in a battle to drown out its neighbour.

On the way back to the boardroom, both men's ears were buzzing.

'It'll have to be typhoon strength before I complain about the sound of the wind at sea again,' said Bill to Fergus. 'We know we can ride through a storm, but these workers, they have to endure this daily.'

'If this afternoon's discussions go as we hope, you may find yourself in a real typhoon soon enough,' said Fergus.

'We're used to it,' said the foreman. 'You probably noticed some of the men have white material jutting out from under their caps. They take raw cotton, wrap it in soft twisted linen and stuff it in their ears. I thought with you being sailing men you wouldn't find it so difficult, because the chains and ropes on a ship must create noise. I must sincerely apologise. I expect wherever men work they become accustomed to sounds that are difficult for outsiders.'

'Don't worry,' said Fergus. 'It was a most interesting tour.'

Back in the boardroom, Mr Macintosh was holding a sherry and talking to a shortish, bald-headed man with a gold-rimmed *pince-nez* set high up on his nose.

'May I introduce my partner, Mr Warrilow.'

'Gentlemen.' Unlike Mr Macintosh, Mr Warrilow seemed perfectly at home in city office surroundings. Fergus wondered if he had ever even visited a Highland moor, never mind hiked over one. He was surprised to hear Mr Warrilow speak with an educated southern English voice. His pronunciation was exact, each consonant perfectly formed and articulated. Fergus hadn't given it any thought prior to their visit, but he would have expected a Scottish company to be run by two Scots. No matter, there was no doubting the company's partners were interesting in different ways. Still, he was unsure whether he could do business with them. Whilst they were not unfriendly, neither were they particularly welcoming in manner or speech. Their guards were up.

The lunch looked and smelt delicious, but Fergus, between being nervous and already full, only just managed to attempt it.

They talked about Mauritius, with Mr Macintosh beginning the conversation.

'My father,' he said, 'whose portrait you saw downstairs, was in Mauritius some years ago.'

'When he met Dr Fincham?' asked Fergus.

'Quite so. We had several orders for full set-up, which he accompanied, but more of the business side later. My father arrived in February and found it extremely uncomfortable and hot, with many mosquitos.'

'Dr Fincham mentioned the mosquitos.' Fergus wanted to find some common ground with the two men, but was aware he was getting nowhere. For a start, Mr Warrilow had hardly said a word and seemed content solely to observe.

'Without the meeting between Dr Fincham and your father, we wouldn't be sitting here,' added Bill.

'I was surprised to learn from your letter he had returned to England. It sounded as if he'd built up a decent practice in Port Louis. We received a report from our agent that he tended to one of our crew, who needed a toe amputated after it became caught in a moving chain link, and gangrene set in.'

'Certainly, he was sociable,' Bill told him, 'and we understand the ladies liked him. Although he's never married.'

'It doesn't suit some gentlemen,' said Mr Warrilow. 'Myself included. If a man can find a capable housekeeper who can cook and manage accounts, if he has a brother to carry on the family line and prefers the company of men to wittering women, then I would advise him against it. I am perfectly content.'

Bill gave an embarrassed laugh. 'Fergus has only been wed one month.'

'Then I say good luck to you, sir,' said Mr Warrilow, not appearing in the least embarrassed. 'You must like the company of women?'

'The company of one woman.' Fergus wasn't enjoying the conversation, but he knew he couldn't show irritation – the investment of others in this contract was helping them to purchase the steamship they needed.

'If you want to avoid trouble, keep it that way, eh, Macintosh?'

'Mrs Macintosh and I have been married this last twenty years and have three sons. My wife tells me we are blessed. The amount their education has cost me, I think she may be mistaken.'

Mr Warrilow, chasing a roasted onion around his plate with his fork, turned to Bill. 'What about you, Captain McCrae? You'll have Scottish blood in your veins with such a surname. I'll bet you've a cautious Scottish nature, too.'

'I've a wife of three years and we're awaiting a son or a daughter any day. As for my Scottishness I'm told my relatives accompanied Bonnie Prince Charlie to Derby, liked what they saw and settled in Cumberland.'

'A Jacobite,' said Mr Warrilow, leaning forward with a raised eyebrow.

Fergus laughed, despite not being sure it was a joke. He didn't know much about Scottish history, but he did know Bonnie Prince lived in the eighteenth century and was long dead. He had to keep reminding himself he must remain alert. They had yet to cover the business – the overriding reason for their visit.

After the steward serving the coffee had left the room, Mr Macintosh wiped his mouth with his napkin, screwed it into a ball and put it on the table.

'Gentlemen, I think it is time to discuss business.' He laid out some papers. 'Mr Shackleton and Captain McRae, we assume you're sitting here because you're of the opinion we can work together for mutual benefit.'

'That is correct,' said Fergus. He was experiencing a cold sweat and it was making him feel clammy.

Mr Warrilow addressed them. 'From our side of the table, I trust you will not take this amiss, but now we've met, we realise you are both extremely young in years.'

Allowing neither Bill nor Fergus the chance to answer, Mr Macintosh butted in with, 'Mr Shackleton, I should mention that raised as you were in a well-established shipping firm, we have confidence in *your* knowledge, ability and contacts.'

'We represent the Louisa Line, not Shackleton & Company. I should make that quite clear.'

'But the two companies are part of the same business, are they not? I'm confused.'

'No,' said Fergus. 'The two firms are run separately, but I hold an interest in both.'

There was a pause before Mr Macintosh spoke again. 'We were not aware of that.' Fergus saw something unspoken pass between the two men.

That's blown it. We've lost the contract and we've hardly opened our mouths.

He tried to rescue the situation. 'There was no intention to deceive. At no time have we mentioned Shackleton &

Company. I would suggest you have made assumptions from my name.'

'So it would seem,' said Mr Warrilow.

Fergus glanced at Bill, then at the door. It was a glance Mr Warrilow caught and interpreted correctly.

'Let us not be hasty. Captain McRae, what is your background and experience? For example, what do you know of ocean travelling?'

'Some years ago I travelled on a regular basis to the west coast of South America as a second officer. You will appreciate this entailed passing round the Horn, often in winter. Following that, I received my Master's Certificate from Leith, and since then I've commanded ships to New Orleans, Quebec and Montreal for Shackleton & Company. I am currently with the Louisa Line. I'm an experienced master, older than I appear. I was apprenticed at fifteen, and during those early years served under a hard master, which has benefited me tremendously.'

'I have a question for you both,' said Fergus. 'Do you honestly think I would risk sending one of our ships as far as Mauritius under Captain McRae's command, if I did not have complete confidence in his ability?'

'You raise a good point,' said Mr Macintosh, fiddling with his collar. 'You understand we have to ask such questions, for ourselves and our shareholders. We're not questioning your judgement, Mr Shackleton.'

Fergus knew that was exactly what they were doing. 'Captain McRae and I both run the risk of the ship going down,' he said. 'For you, that would be an expensive loss, but for us it would mean the end of the Louisa Line. We have far more to lose than you.'

'Certainly,' confirmed Mr Macintosh. 'I have another question. It is obvious why we need you, but on your part, you run a fledgling business, as we now realise. That being the case, why do you want to undertake such a risky venture?'

Mr Warrilow's gaze was fixed on Fergus as if everything depended on his response.

'That's simple. Confidentially, we have an enticing business opportunity in Mauritius which requires the positioning of an empty vessel out there. To facilitate this, we necessarily require cargo for the outward journey. Dr Fincham suggested we approach you.'

Mr Macintosh appeared to consider this reply, then spread his papers out. 'From our side we have a ready-made market for our specialist products – sugar-plantation production machinery and, most importantly, spare parts. These parts are of particular importance since, as you will appreciate, without them machinery lies idle, production falls, competitors move in, prices rise and/or become volatile. However, carriers do not seem to like calling at Mauritius.'

Fergus nodded. 'Yes, we assume their sights are set on crossing the Indian Ocean for bigger markets and more varied produce.'

'Exactly. As a result, to access the few that do call there we have to haul our goods to London, which not only adds to the shipping costs, but requires a great deal of administration. Also, bear in mind that some items are of considerable size and weight.'

'It's this section of the journey we feel able to help you with,' said Bill. 'As you put it earlier, for our mutual benefit.'

'Continue,' said Mr Warrilow, in the manner of a Latin teacher asking a young boy to resume translating.

'We shall be willing to collect the orders from Glasgow, thus eliminating your transit costs to London. I know the customs and excise work much faster here than they do in London, so you would also be saving time and effort. Not to mention agents' fees, which are always higher in the capital.'

'What about your competitors?' asked Bill. 'There must be others making machinery for the sugar plantations.'

'The French? Their components and ours are incompatible and I have no qualms in saying ours are of far superior quality. That is a comment we receive many times over at exhibitions. However, with any new plantation establishing itself, we run the risk of them choosing a French production model over ours, exclusively due to the erratic shipping of our parts.'

They talked for another five minutes before Mr Macintosh moved his chair back. 'I think we can all agree that this has been an interesting meeting and that we should now break to consider our options. We'll speak with our agent and we'll talk again tomorrow. Perhaps we may visit your ship?'

Fergus was taken aback. 'You're welcome to do so, but it's not the ship we will be taking to Mauritius. We have regular textile business between Whitehaven and Glasgow, and I've travelled here as part of our normal operations. I saw no need to bring the steamship.' *Besides, until all the payment details are signed off, there is no ship,*

Mr Warrilow raised a hand. 'One moment. May I

mention at this point that we will require A1 documentation from Lloyds as proof of seaworthiness?'

Mr Macintosh addressed Fergus. 'That will be in order?'

'Certainly. All our ships are inspected annually.'

'Thank you,' said Mr Macintosh. 'Shall we say eleven o'clock tomorrow?'

'It will be my pleasure to welcome you on board at that time,' said Bill.

Out on the street, Bill and Fergus strolled a short way before turning into the nearest pub to order what Fergus regarded as well-earned ales.

'What do you really think?' he asked.

Bill fiddled with the handle on his tankard. 'For a start they thought we were a big shipping company. They'd not have laid on such a grand meal if they hadn't.'

'After they'd learned we weren't actually part of Shackleton & Company, I detected a certain frostiness. Do you think they were only going through the motions?'

'What do you mean?'

'Finding out what we have to offer, without having any intention of following up on our visit?'

'They've called another meeting, and they're talking with their agent. There's one thing I don't understand.'

'What's that?'

'Why don't they have a warehouse in Mauritius they can keep stocked with the smaller parts they need?'

'I wondered that, too. Maybe it's a responsibility too distant. Managing it would cut into their profits. Still, there's possibly an additional opportunity there.'

'For us?'

'If we're going to make this a regular trip, we'll need a good agent. Hopefully the one Dr Fincham is introducing us to will work out profitably. We'll also need someone to manage a small warehouse?'

'Mary will put up with one voyage, but I think I'll have a problem being away six months or more year on year if we're contemplating annual trips.'

'You're right. It's asking too much and the warehouse is purely an idle thought for now.'

'It could still be a good one. Would you allow Captain Jessop to make the trip?'

'Certainly.'

'Then we could alternate.'

'In due course I think you could take Rory.'

'I thought that was a given.'

CHAPTER TWENTY

The next morning, while Fergus and Bill were enjoying another Glaswegian breakfast with extra pikelets, in Whitehaven the Indian King had just opened up. Sergeant Adams came in with his one-eyed dog Molly, and they took their reserved position by the door. The sergeant was much earlier than usual. He lit his clay pipe, and Becky, who'd been chatting to her mother, remarked that he seemed thoughtful.

'I know you're not meant to be working here anymore,' Dolly said, 'but can you take the sergeant's ale over?'

'Aye, and I'll get a bowl for Molly.'

When Becky drew near, the dog sat up and fixed her one good eye on her.

'I know what *you* want,' said Becky, pulling something from her pocket. Molly's head shot up. 'Here you are.' She held out a ginger biscuit, which Molly took and swallowed in one gulp. Her nose twitched as she moved her head seeking more, but none being forthcoming, she settled down again, resting her head on Sergeant Adams's thigh.

Becky was turning away when the sergeant pointed to the seat across the table from him. 'Sit yourself down a moment, lass. I've something t'say may be of interest. On second thoughts, get your mammy over here, too. It's for both your ears.'

Mystified, Becky called out to Dolly. When they were both seated, Sergeant Adams said, 'You knows I sometimes drink elsewhere.'

'Aye,' said Dolly. 'The Three Tuns.'

''Appen I can sometimes be found in there, but yesterday I was in the Dog and Duck in George Street, seeing an old regimental comrade. This burly fellow comes in. All muscles, and he's definitely been in the wars. Broken nose, ruddy cheeks. I thought to myself – he's one of them wrestlers or bare-knuckle fighters, and to top it he had shorter hair than is usual these days. You know, like professional fighters, so's it can't be grabbed or flop down. He was kitted out in fashionable attire, but the cloth was cheap and worn. Aiming to give folk the impression of being the gentleman he ain't.'

'Who was it?'

'He didn't give his name and didn't speak directly t'me. I may appear a bit daft and dozy, an old soldier seen better days, but there's nowt wrong with my hearing.'

'Is he local?' asked Becky.

'He's not from round here, because I knows most folk, and when he speaks, it's with a more northern accent. Probably up-country – Carlisle way, or maybe from the borders. Anyways, I'll get to the point of my tale so's you can get back to your chores.'

Becky had a feeling of foreboding. For Sergeant Adams to call them over, it had to be important.

'The man had no time for niceties,' the sergeant went on. 'He came in, went up to the bar and straight away asked if anyone knew Rory.'

'Rory? Our Rory?' asked Dolly, her back stiffening.

Becky's heart sank. From the sergeant's description of a fighting man, no good was going to come of such a man's interest in Rory – an out-of-town stranger, to boot.

'Aye, Rory Rooke,' he said. 'So, it's your Rory, all right. Got to be – there's no other Rory Rooke round here.'

'Go on,' said Dolly.

'He said an innkeeper had told him the boy's mammy was passed o'er, but he said nowt about why he wanted him.'

'Did anyone in the pub say anything?'

'No. They shrugged their shoulders. The barmaid asked him what he wanted to sup, and when he said he wasn't there to drink, she scowled and turned away. Then he left. I wasn't minded to say owt, and I would've come straight round, but 'twas too late for me by the time I left my comrade. So, I'm here first thing.'

'Thank you,' said Dolly. 'There's an ale on the house for you today.'

'And a large helping of beef and onion pie later,' Becky added. 'With an extra bit of meat on the side for Molly.'

'I'm thanking you. Like I says, I didn't say owt, but no doubt he'll find you soon enough.'

Back behind the bar, and out of earshot of their few early customers, Becky said, 'To my mind this reeks of trouble.'

'I'd like to correct you, but I'm feeling the same. We've not much to dwell on, but he knows Amy is dead. Why is he asking questions?'

'Perhaps he knew her.'

'Or someone who did.'

Dolly called over to Sergeant Adams. 'What's the difference between boxing, wrestling and bare-knuckle fighting?'

'For a start, boxers wear gloves and there's rules and it's legal. Now, you take wrestling – again, it's legal and has rules that once t'other man's on the ground, that's it, there's a winner. Bare-knuckle fighting is vicious, unregulated and illegal. A man can get beaten up something dreadful, but if he wins, the payment can change his life. Besides, there's always a clear winner, because they keep on fighting until one man can't go on or submits.'

Dolly thanked the sergeant, then, lowering her voice, said to Becky, 'This couldn't have come at a worse time, with Fergus in Glasgow and Rory here.'

'And Hector and Elizabeth in Carlisle,' Becky agreed. 'There's no one we can call on to help.'

'We need a plan for if he turns up here.'

'*When* he turns up you mean,' said Becky.

'But perhaps we're getting ourselves het up over nothing. He's probably an old seadog from a previous voyage.'

'Could be. Fergus says all the men enjoy Rory's company. Perhaps he's got a treat for him, or a story to tell.'

'If that's the case, he only has to call at the office and ask. Going round pubs not giving your name reeks of subterfuge.'

* * *

Fergus spent the night worrying he had foolishly overstretched himself financially. He'd been certain Macintosh & Warrilow would greet them with open arms, but they hadn't. He knew Scots had a reputation for being canny and cautious; were they too wary to attempt anything new? Even if it was going to save time and money? Such thoughts whirled around his head as he waited to receive the two men.

When they arrived, he invited them to adjourn to Bill's cabin.

'Gentlemen, we thought we would change the agenda this morning and discuss business before the tour of the ship. If our first mate, Sven, is correct, then the slight drizzle we're experiencing should have cleared in half an hour, and we'll have no need for tarpaulins or umbrellas.'

'Sven isn't always right, but most times,' added Bill.

Mr Macintosh took some papers from a folder and put them down on a table already groaning under charts and papers. He looked around the cabin. 'I don't know how you do it, travelling for such a long time in so small a space.'

'That's because you're from the Highlands,' said Mr Warrilow. 'Used to wide open spaces and vast expanses of sky. We city folk prefer stone walls and pavements.'

'We enjoy plenty of open space and fresh air at sea, I can assure you of that,' said Bill.

'You'll take refreshment?' asked Fergus.

Both men shook their heads. Mr Warrilow explained, 'We've a Corporation luncheon to attend.'

Fergus interpreted this as an indication they would not be staying long. *Is this also an indication all is lost?*

He decided to carry on, regardless of his thoughts. 'You've spoken with your agent?' he asked.

Mr Macintosh removed two pages from his papers and handed one each to Fergus and Bill, saying, 'This is an example of a *pro forma* contract for a past engagement with our current shipper. Perhaps you would like to peruse it and comment. You will see it lists terms of engagement, dates, collection place, timings, taxes and packing requirements. You have the individual product details in the catalogue we gave you yesterday, which provide all the information you need for loading up.'

'No prices?' asked Fergus.

Mr Warrilow raised his eyebrows. 'You will appreciate we don't want to influence you in that respect. This *pro forma* is from our agent, to be clear as to what we would expect of any quotation you might offer us in the future, should we ask for one.'

Bill and Fergus studied the invoice, while the other two men continued their examination of the cabin.

After putting his head on one side and raising an eyebrow at Bill, Fergus said, 'At first glance there are no surprises here. Would you agree, Captain McRae?'

'The contents appear to be in order. I see no irregularities.'

Mr Macintosh retrieved the papers. 'This provides you with an indication of how we conduct business.' Then, after a slight pause, he added, 'Should we decide to proceed.'

Fergus wanted desperately to ask how long it would be before they came to a decision, but he couldn't run the risk of seeming badly in need of their business, so he just nodded.

Mr Macintosh stood up. 'It would seem all that remains

is for us to commence our tour of the ship and to confirm that we will contact you in due course.'

In due course? A week? A month? Three months? Damn them, why can't they say yea or nay?

The first mate was proven correct. The drizzle had cleared away, although the sky remained somewhat overcast and grey for May.

Bill apologised for the frenetic activity on board. 'I'm afraid you can't inspect the hold, as it's almost full. The crew have been loading up with textiles and whisky all day.'

'Don't apologise for having a full load, Captain McRae. It's something you can be proud of, and business is obviously thriving.'

After a brief tour of the deck, during which he took an active interest in the rigging, Mr Warrilow said, 'We can see you keep a tidy and a sound ship, Captain.'

'Only a fool doesn't keep his ships and his men in fine fettle,' said Fergus, knowing he was telling them something they were well aware of.

After the two men had left, Fergus, leaning against the ship's rail, watched them walk along the quay to flag down a cab, then excused himself and went to lie on his cot. He had one of his headaches. He couldn't remember packing Dr Fincham's linctus, but found thankfully that he had. He took a double dose, and within ten minutes the sleep that had evaded him for the last two nights came quickly. When he woke, several hours later, he noticed someone had covered him with a blanket. The rocking of the ship and the sounds around him told him they were out at sea and on their way home. He was in two minds as to whether the trip had been worth the effort.

CHAPTER TWENTY-ONE

At two o'clock, as Fergus was sleeping off his headache and the *Sophie Alice* was heading home, back at the Indian King Becky asked Rory to tidy away his books and go upstairs, saying she had some jobs for him in the guest rooms. Then, not quite simultaneously, but close enough to warrant being regarded as a close shave, as the kitchen door closed behind Rory, the pub doors opened and a stranger entered. Becky knew immediately, from Sergeant Adams's description, that this was the man who'd been asking for Rory. She glanced at Sergeant Adams who gave a slight nod. *I've got Rory out of the way just in time.*

Dolly, behind the bar, turned her attention to the stranger. 'Good afternoon, sir.'

The man swaggered over to the bar. 'You've got my lad, and I want him,' he said.

Becky's stomach turned over. Dolly, after an initial pause, tilted her chin and looked down her nose. 'Your lad? Who might that be?'

Becky braced herself for what she knew was coming, but even so it was a terrible shock.

'Rory. Rory Rooke.'

'Your lad?'

'Aye, my son. I know you've got him. Where is he?'

Rory's da? Becky cursed herself for not having run back, taken Rory home with her and locked the door, even though she knew it wouldn't have taken much for the man to find her. But on the other hand, she would then have been alone and vulnerable. If there was going to be a confrontation, better it be here with people to act as witnesses.

'And your name is?' Dolly said.

'What's it to you?'

Dolly gave a hollow laugh. 'You expect, because you stroll in here saying you're the boy's father, that I'm going to give him over to a stranger without knowing his name or authority? If that's your game, you're wasting your time and breath here.'

Becky was repelled by the man, yet she couldn't remove her eyes from him.

The stranger frowned at Dolly. Becky was hoping against hope her mother might have frightened him off and given them time, when the kitchen door opened and Rory came in. With a cheeky grin on his face, he said, 'I've come back down for my paints.'

All eyes fixed on the man.

'You must be Rory?' he asked.

Rory examined him and nodded. 'Aye, I'm Rory Rooke.'

'No, you're not,' he said. 'You're Rory Loadman and I'm your father, Walter Loadman'.

Rory stared at Loadman in astonishment, then at Dolly and Becky.

Becky went over and put her arms around him. 'Don't worry, it's nowt to worry about.'

'When's your birthday?' asked Loadman.

Rory appeared to be struck dumb.

'Can you tell the man your birthday, Rory?' prompted Dolly.

'Yes,' said Becky. 'Tell the man. It's all right. It will be a mistake.' Although in her heart, she knew it wasn't.

'My birthday's November 11th.'

'What year were you born?' Loadman stared down at Rory as a headmaster might, in order to intimidate an errant pupil accused of cheating.

'1849. I'm coming up twelve.'

'Here.' The man pulled a piece of paper from his pocket and held it under Dolly's nose. Becky moved to her side so they could read it together.

'What's that?' asked Rory.

'It's your birth certificate, lad.' He turned to Becky. 'Can the boy read?'

Becky could only nod; she couldn't speak. All she could think was how they might be going to lose Rory to this dreadful man, and how upset Fergus would be when he got back.

Loadman beckoned Rory nearer. The boy took three steps forward but remained behind the bar, leaning against it to examine the paper.

Pointing with his finger, Loadman said, 'See, you were born in Lancaster on November 11th 1849. There's my name, Walter Loadman, and there's your mother's, Amy Rooke. Your birth was registered on December 18th.'

Rory began sniffing and Becky tightened her grasp on him. There was fear in his eyes and his gammy leg was twitching, which was always a sign he was upset. The atmosphere in the pub had become one of nervous tension.

'Have you nowt to say to your da?' asked Loadman.

Rory shook his head.

'I've come to bring you home.'

Becky gasped.

'No, I've not got a da, he's been dead a long time. Mammy told me that, and I know she'd never lie to me. Lying's a sin and she was God-fearing. I'm going to be a master mariner and travel the world. I'm not coming with you.' His face puckered up and Becky could see he was fighting hard not to cry.

Loadman turned to Dolly. 'He's got some wild ideas. I'm taking him – he's my son and I'm entitled to him.'

'You're not taking him with you unless the constable comes and tells me so,' said Dolly, standing with her arms crossed. There were murmurings from their few customers, who up to that point had been looking on silently. Becky hoped Loadman could sense the room was against him. Perhaps seeing the logic of Dolly's insistence, he said, 'I'll be back on the morrow with the law. Have his belongings packed.'

He stared at the bottles on the shelves behind the bar. 'It would be good to have some light refreshment for my lodgings tonight. It's blowy up on the hill and the geese next door are noisy. Some grog will help me sleep.'

Dolly hesitated then reached up and took down a small bottle of port.

He checked the bottle label and said, 'It'll be a long night. I'll be awake until the early hours, as I've business to see to.'

Dolly exchanged the bottle for one twice the size.

'I know the lad can read,' Loadman said, 'but what's he like with figures?'

'I can do my sums,' said Rory, with pride in his voice.

'All the better,' said Loadman. 'I'll bid you all farewell. I'll return first thing.'

After he'd gone Becky's first thought was to comfort Rory and she put her arms around him.

Then, turning to her mother she said, 'I'm surprised you gave him that port.'

'It's the cheapest and roughest there is, and if he drinks enough, he'll wake with a head from hell. I wanted to get rid of him and that seemed the quickest way – to agree with his underhanded request.'

One of the drinkers came up to the bar. 'Can I give you a bit of advice?'

'Aye,' said Dolly.

'Have you got a solicitor?'

'My husband has,' said Becky.

'Then I suggest you get yourself down there and tell him what's up. He'll know what to do.'

Dolly spoke to Becky in a crackly voice: 'I'll tend to Rory; you get down to Mr Needham.'

* * *

Less than twenty minutes after Loadman had left the Indian King, Becky was sitting opposite Fergus's solicitor.

She had burst into his offices demanding to be seen immediately.

'You can't see Mr Needham without an –' began the reception clerk.

'Believe me, sir, Mr Needham will want to see me when he learns what has happened.'

At this juncture, Mr Needham stepped out into the corridor. 'Mrs Shackleton, whatever's the matter?' Speaking to the clerk, he said, 'Let Mrs Shackleton pass. I can see she is distressed. What has happened? Has there been an accident? Is your husband well?'

For once Mr Needham's desk was covered with documents; he was obviously in the middle of something.

While Becky related what had happened, Mr Needham listened, making no comment. When she'd finished, he leaned forward and steepled his fingers.

'If the birth certificate is a valid one, and Mr Loadman can produce documentation that he is the person named on the certificate, I'm afraid there is nothing we can do.'

'Nothing at all?'

'No. The boy is a minor, and the man is his father. He is correct – he has a right to collect his son and remove him from another's care.'

'What about what Rory wants? He's distraught.'

'I've no doubt about that, but as the law stands, this Mr Loadman, as his father, is his legal guardian.'

'And Fergus's wardship?'

Mr Needham hesitated before saying, 'Null and void. He is now a "stranger in blood" to Rory.'

'That's it, then?'

'I am sincerely vexed to state that is, indeed, the truth of the matter.'

Becky, who had been leaning forward in her chair, slumped back and put her head down.

'There is one thing you could consider,' Mr Needham went on.

'What's that?'

'You could consider solving this financially.'

'Pay him off, you mean?'

'Yes, but I have not suggested this.'

'No, no. I understand.'

'Although you run the risk of him coming back for more. Whilst I can't think of anything else right now, leave it with me.'

'We could hide Rory. Send him to Dublin.' She was thinking of Padraig Conran. 'If he's disappeared when Loadman comes for him tomorrow, there's not a lot he can do.'

'I'm afraid there is. The head constable would think most dimly of such action. You, and probably your mother, would be detained in the lock-up in Scotch Street before you could sneeze. You would be charged with kidnap of a minor, depriving a parent of his child, and a host of other offences. If you are tempted to follow this path, remind yourself there is nothing you can do for Rory from within the walls of Carlisle Gaol. You must accept things have to run their course.'

'The mystery to me is why he would want the boy after all this time. He must want money.'

'My thoughts, for what they are worth, are that the boy will be a novelty for a while, then Loadman will return with him in tow and suggest a financial deal. Does he know the boy is lame?'

'I don't know,' said Becky. 'I don't think so. How is he going to treat Rory before he brings him back? He has some plan for him, of that I am certain. He asked if the boy could read and do arithmetic.'

'That's interesting. We'll have to sit this out for a while. Be there tomorrow when he takes the boy, so you are a witness, and so Rory can see you are there for him. Let Rory know he will always have a home with you. Is there anyone who can be there tomorrow? We need another reliable witness. I'd come myself, but that would mean I could not act, were the case to go to court. I know Mr Shackleton is away in Glasgow.'

'My mother will be there.'

'Is there anyone else? A gentleman would be more intimidating to Mr Loadman and, although it may not be fair, a court of law will take more notice of a male witness than a female.'

'I don't think there's anyone. Mr Shackleton senior is in Carlisle.' Becky cast her eyes around the room. The answer came straight to her when she saw the deed box with LOUISA MAY SHACKLETON stamped on the side.

'I could ask Dr Fincham.'

'An admirable choice.'

'I will call on him right away.'

'Direct him to me if he has any questions.'

Leaving the solicitor's offices, Becky broke into a run, all the while telling herself that there must be something they could do. It was a warm afternoon and there were a lot of people strolling in the sunshine, forcing her to dodge between them. With thoughts elsewhere, she stepped into the path of a carriage, had to jump back, and was cursed loudly by the driver. She was out of breath when she reached the surgery.

A woman with a sour expression opened the door. From what she'd heard about her, Becky assumed this must be Constance, the doctors' housekeeper.

'I must see Dr Fincham immediately.'

'Who are you?' asked Constance.

'Mrs Shackleton.' *And I'm not going to let you stand in my way.*

'Mrs Fergus Shackleton?'

'Yes, also known as Mrs Becky Shackleton. I simply must speak with Dr Fincham.'

'Is it a medical matter?'

'For goodness' sake, what does it matter? It's an emergency.' Becky was conscious she had raised her voice and that it sounded tight.

'The doctor's writing up reports in his room. I am not to disturb him.'

'Good, then he'll be able to hear me.' Becky drew in a deep breath and shouted as loudly as she could, 'Dr Fincham.' Then again, 'Dr Fincham, it's Becky.'

Constance made an 'Oh!' sound that forged surprise with horror. A door opened and footsteps could be heard coming down the stairs. Becky sent up a prayer. *Please, dear God, let it be Nicholas.*

Her prayer was answered. Dr Fincham appeared.

'Becky, my dear, whatever is the matter?'

'Rory's got a da and he's coming to take him away tomorrow.'

CHAPTER TWENTY-TWO

The next day, when Walter Loadman arrived at the Indian King with the head constable, Mr Mastin, Becky realised Mr Needham had been right – there was nothing they could do to keep Rory, who was sitting ashen-faced, with Charlie on his knee and a packed bag by his side.

Mr Mastin refused Dolly's offer of a seat, saying, 'This business won't take long, ma'am. All seems in order.'

'Aye,' said Loadman. 'I've appointments to keep, and I've been here a day too long already. The less time I spend in this spit-and-sawdust of a pub, the better.'

'Be civil,' said Dr Fincham, taking a step towards the man.

Loadman's head shot round. 'Who the devil are you?' he asked with a sneer.

'I'm the boy's doctor.'

'Is he sick?' Loadman glanced at Rory.

'No, I am here to see to the boy's welfare. He may have been to sea, but he's still no more than a child.'

Dolly put a hand on Loadman's arm, but he bristled, so she removed it. 'Can't you see the lad doesn't want to go with you? He's shaking with fear. He's happy here and cared for. You can visit him.'

Loadman snatched his arm back. 'A boy's place is with his da.'

'If that is the case, then where have you been all these years?' asked Dr Fincham.

'It's none of your business, but since you ask, I've been searching for him – don't doubt that, any of you. His ma upped and ran off. A man's got a life to lead. Can't spend all hours on a lost bairn. Like I say, what business is it of yours?'

Mr Mastin cleared his throat. 'Let's attend to the legal business to hand. Mr Loadman is here to collect his son. He has produced a birth certificate to prove paternity, and a porter's licence made out to him for identification purposes. The law is satisfied he has blood ties with the lad and that he is his father. As well as that, I think you will agree, now that I have seen the boy, it's obvious there is a distinct familial resemblance.'

Becky had to admit it was true – Rory and his da shared the same colouring, shape of head, hair colour and jaw.

Mr Mastin turned to Loadman. 'You are free to take your son.'

Rory, who up to now had been sitting quietly stroking Charlie, stood and said, with pleading eyes, 'I don't want a da, I want to stay here.' He made a dash, as best he could, for the door leading to the kitchen. In his haste and unsteadiness, his foot caught a chair leg, and he and the chair went crashing down. He hadn't gone far, but it was enough to display his disability.

Becky saw Loadman hone in on Rory's leg.

'Strike me down, he's a cripple.'

Becky helped Rory get up. 'He had an accident and we've been caring for him.' She hugged him, her wide skirt wrapping itself around him. 'Mr Shackleton has employed him as crew on his ship.'

'An accident, eh?'

Becky could see Loadman, by the puckering of his brow, was thinking, and she imagined him reassessing the boy's usefulness.

'Compensation paid?'

'To his mother. There's nothing there for you.'

Dr Fincham asked, 'Have you changed your mind?'

'He's *my* boy, and he's coming with *me*. He can't be that crippled if he can serve on a pitching ship.' He went over to Rory. 'Come on, lad, time to leave.'

Rory stepped back and, seeing the man move to take hold of the boy, Charlie's head shot up. He let out a low-pitched, menacing growl then leapt forward and nipped Loadman on the ankle. Loadman yelled and cursed. He took aim and gave Charlie's rear end the full force of his boot.

'Vicious creature!'

With Loadman cursing, Rory calling out to him to stop, the dog whimpering, and Becky's sobs, the noise in the bar was deafening.

Dolly stepped forward. 'This is *my* public house and it's my job to keep order here. All of you, hold thy noise.'

When the room had quietened down Mr Mastin spoke. 'Young lad, this is your father. He's a stranger to you now, but you'll get to know him as kith and kin and, in my experience, the best place for a young'un like yourself is with his blood family.'

Dolly opened her mouth to contradict him, but Becky nudged her in the ribs and whispered, 'Let him go. We're only making things worse for Rory.'

Mr Mastin led Rory to the door ahead of Loadman and took him outside. Charlie made as if to follow.

'We're not taking that mongrel snapper,' said Loadman, 'specially after the bastard's gone and bit me.'

'He's Rory's best friend,' Becky said. 'You can't leave him here. The dog is his shadow, they are inseparable. He was only trying to protect the boy. He'll settle down when he knows you mean Rory no harm.' She was so angry, it was all she could do not to step forward and slap the man.

'Watch me give the mangy cur what he deserves,' said Loadman, putting his boot out again. This time Charlie was ready and sprang out of the way, but Loadman wasn't going to give up. He cornered the dog beside the fireplace, put his boot out again and caught Charlie's right side.

Becky felt fury invade her throat, like rising bile.

'Enough!' Dr Fincham shouted.

Loadman took two steps forward towards the doctor and raised his fists, then seemed to think better of it. Becky wondered if he was remembering the presence of Mr Mastin outside.

With a nasty snarl, he said, 'You're in luck. I get paid for using my fists. I don't doubt I can knock you out, old man, with a single blow.' Then he turned, picked up Rory's bag and stormed out.

The coloured glass in the pub's doors shook and rattled as they closed behind him.

'We didn't say a proper goodbye,' sobbed Becky.

'He's a smart lad,' said Dolly, in an uncharacteristically shaky voice. 'You told him this morning he'll always have a home with us. He knows we love him as our own.'

'That's as may be, but even though he's Rory's flesh and blood, I can't see that beast taking care of him. I mean, why does he want him, anyway? And after all this time? It's not clear.'

'The situation is murky, I agree,' Dr Fincham said.

Struggling with controlling her anger, while coping with the sudden loss, Becky said, 'My guess is he was in the area and was curious. What man isn't interested in his offspring, especially if it's a boy? He's found Rory, seen he's living in comfortable circumstances –'

'Aye, and he's seen there's a bit o' brass behind him,' added Dolly.

'Correct,' said Dr Fincham. 'And he's probably thought he'd reclaim the boy, make sure we feel the pain of the loss, then come back to demand money in exchange for him.'

'You mean he'll bring Rory back?' asked Becky.

'Within the month, I'd say.'

'It's going to cost him to keep him,' said Becky. 'Apart from anything else, he eats for all Cumberland and beyond.'

'I'm surprised he didn't have the cheek to ask us for

money straight up,' said Dolly. 'Especially after he more or less stole that port from me last evening. He was quick enough to think of accident compensation, too.'

'I expect he knew it would look bad in front of the head constable,' said Dr Fincham.

Sergeant Adams, who had been watching from his usual place by the door, with Molly's head still resting on his thigh, spoke up. 'I think I can answer some of your questions. He'll use him as a bottle boy.'

'A bottle boy?' asked Becky. 'What's that?'

'You'll pardon me, Becky, but I've lived in his world. He'll train the boy up to collect bets, fetch, carry, mend his clothes and so forth. When he's fighting, he needs someone to hold his water bottle and fill it. That's why these young lads are called bottle boys.'

'But how will Rory cope with his leg?'

'It must certainly have been an unwelcome surprise for Loadman,' said Dr Fincham. 'But he could hardly back down after calling out the head constable, could he?'

Sergeant Adams shook his head. 'Nay, and apart from anything else, fights are held in fields, where it's often muddy and uneven underfoot. I don't want to upset you further, but there's no doubt in my mind the lad'll find it hard.'

'Then let's hope Loadman will realise Rory is no good for his purposes,' said Dr Fincham, 'and will bring him back sooner than he intended.'

Dolly took a bottle of brandy from the shelf. 'I know it's early, but I think we could all do with one of these. The trouble is, Rory's such a good lad. Instead of using his leg to make a bad job of things, he'll try his best and make a half-decent job of it, so Loadman may decide he's useful and keep him.'

'There's one good thing about his leg,' said Sergeant Adams. 'If you want to keep tabs or track them down, all you have to do is ask for the fighter with the crippled lad. Rory'll stand out like a pickle on a parson's pudding.'

'A what?' asked Dolly.

'I think he means Rory'll stand out as something that's been put down in the wrong place,' said Dr Fincham.

CHAPTER TWENTY-THREE

As soon as Fergus came in the door Becky lost control and burst out crying. She'd considered meeting him on the quay, but it would be dark when they returned from Glasgow. Better to leave a note asking him to return to Coates Lane immediately the *Sophie Alice* docked.

After she'd calmed down and was able to tell him what had happened, Fergus began pacing the room.

'Tell me again. The head constable told you to stand by while Loadman walked off with Rory?'

'Aye. There was nowt we could do.'

'I'd never have allowed it had I been here.'

'Fergus, will you please listen to me? I spoke with Mr Needham about hiding Rory, or perhaps even sending him away, but as he will no doubt explain to you too, we would have been charged with kidnapping and depriving a parent of their rightful child. How clearer can I put it than to say we ran the risk of being gaoled?'

'How can we be sure he was Rory's father?'

'Had you been there you would have seen it was

obvious. Apart from having the papers, he looks much like him.'

'Where did they go when they left?' Fergus was gesticulating while he spoke – something he did only when agitated.

'I don't know.'

'Didn't anyone think to follow them?'

As soon as he said the words, Becky realised that was what they should have done, but it hadn't occurred to any of them at the time. They'd been in shock and Fergus didn't seem able to grasp that – probably because he was now in shock himself.

'You had to be there to know what it was like. He was a horrible man, a fighter, a big man obviously not afraid to use his fists. He was no gentleman and he had a horrible tattoo on the back of his neck.' Becky began to cry again.

Fergus went over and put his arms around her. 'I'm sorry. It's such a shock, and you're right, I can't imagine what it must have been like for you and Dolly to have to go through it. Thank goodness Mr Needham suggested you have a witness. I'll go and thank Nicholas tomorrow. If only we'd taken Rory to Glasgow with us and I hadn't asked him to stay behind to work in the warehouse.'

Although he hadn't said it, Becky guessed Fergus must also be thinking *...and if I hadn't thought Becky might be lonely.*

The next morning, Fergus left Becky and went out to make enquiries in the town. When he returned, she was dismayed to find he'd learned that Loadman and Rory had left Whitehaven in a carrier's cart, bound for Maryport.

'They could have boarded a ship and gone anywhere by now.' She hadn't been able to think about anything all day except the sadness on Rory's face and his drooping shoulders as the head constable led him away. The memory haunted her.

'Sergeant Adams was right,' Fergus said. 'A fighter with a lame boy will stand out. I expect we'll have news soon enough. Although under the law, this man has done nothing wrong.'

'We may never hear from Rory ever again.' Saying the words out loud seemed to make them more likely, and Becky wished she'd kept her thoughts to herself.

They were both sitting at the table staring at the country pie Becky had made, that neither could eat.

'Can we fetch Charlie to stop with us?' Becky asked. 'I know the Indian King's where he's used to being, but he'll be searching for Rory all the time, and Ma hasn't got time to walk him and play like Rory did. I can do that.'

'You're right. The least we can do for Rory is take good care of Charlie. Maybe, in time, the dog will forget about Rory – undoubtedly faster with us than if he's left with Dolly. But if we take him in, *we* will be the ones with the constant reminder of Rory.'

Becky couldn't believe what she was hearing. Her head shot up. 'The way you say that it sounds as if it's a bad thing. I can tell you right now there won't be a day, as long as I live, I don't think of Rory. If we never see him again and I live to be over eighty, he will be in my thoughts. I shall pray for him each and every day. Having Charlie will be more than a small comfort to me.' All the anger she'd felt during the past days seemed to have polarised, and she wanted to shout out and bang her fists on the table. She clenched them in readiness.

'Becky, I don't mean it to be a bad thing. We won't forget Rory. I plan to do all I can to get him back here with us, where he belongs. Surely you don't doubt that? Until we have him back, we must hold him in our hearts.'

'Stop it,' she snapped. 'You sound like you're talking about someone who's died and you're going to see them again at the Resurrection. That's what they say to comfort people about the dead. "Hold them in your heart".'

'Becky, *you* stop it. You're not thinking properly. You know I don't mean any such thing about Rory. The situation is bad enough without you allowing that dreadful man to be the root of our first serious quarrel.'

Becky knew he was right, but she was so upset and angry, she couldn't help herself.

Fergus stood up. 'I'm going to check the warehouse. I left Dicken to lock up.' At the door he paused. 'Shall you be all right on your own?'

She nodded.

After he'd gone Becky lay down on their bed and wept.

When Fergus returned an hour later, he had Charlie with him and was carrying his wicker basket and favourite blanket. Charlie wagged his tail when he saw Becky. He leapt onto the bed, licked her cheek, which was still wet with tears, and then, while she got up, he proceeded to inspect each room. Seemingly satisfying himself there was nothing, or no one, of interest, he lay down on the floor next to Fergus. After seeing him put his paw on Fergus's calf and gaze at him soulfully, and then at her, Becky said, 'He's hungry. I'll give him some of our country pie, unless you've found your appetite.'

Fergus shook his head. 'I'll eat some, but today I'm sure Charlie will enjoy it more than either of us will.'

After Becky had filled a bowl for Charlie and he was concentrating on wolfing it down, she put her arms out to Fergus. 'I'm sorry I was so sharp with you.'

'We're all hurting. It would be odd if we weren't. We mustn't let it rule our lives. What's happened has happened. Loadman may act and sound like a brute, but we have to remember he's Rory's father, and that must count for something in his treatment of him.'

'Perhaps Rory will find a new family with loving aunts, uncles and cousins,' said Becky – although she knew if he did, it would be a long time before she could see such a development as positive. She would always think Rory's home was with her and Fergus.

CHAPTER TWENTY-FOUR

Three more days passed with no word of Loadman and Rory. It was as if there had been a death. Becky was constantly on the verge of tears, Dolly becoming short-tempered and abrupt with her staff, and Fergus was unable to concentrate properly. He was worried about Rory, about Becky, his finances, and whether they would get the Macintosh & Warrilow contract.

Fergus was waiting for Bill at the warehouse. They were to have a planning meeting. He was on the point of sending Dicken to find him, when Bill burst into the office.

'It's a boy!' he cried. 'We're calling him William, and he's going to go to sea.'

'That's pretty definite,' said Fergus, patting Bill on the back.

'He's destined to be a mariner.'

'I know you're excited he's made his appearance, but he may have other plans when he's all grown and taller than you. Can you stay for our meeting or would you like to postpone it?'

'To be truthful, there's so much fuss and bother at home, I'd rather be in our meeting.'

Fergus laughed and picked up his hat. 'Dicken, we're going to retire to the Waverley,' he said, 'and when we've decided on the Louisa Line's future, we'll be celebrating the new arrival. I'm leaving you in charge.'

'Right. Will you be back later?'

'Unless the celebrating gets too rowdy, most certainly.'

At the Waverley they found a quiet spot out of earshot and ordered coffee.

Fergus took a small notebook out of his coat pocket. 'Right. The way forward. We've heard nothing yet from Macintosh & Warrilow. What do you think?'

'For an arrangement that suits both sides it doesn't bode well. Even so, I've written out a chandlery list in readiness.'

'I've been preparing, too. While you were in Dublin, I contacted Cameron in Edinburgh, asking him to make enquiries "confidentially on behalf of a client" about carrying machinery to Mauritius from the East India Docks in London. He's come back to me with some quotations. Here.'

Bill read the letter. 'This smacks of carriers over-quoting so they don't have to take on the job. Exactly what Dr Fincham told us about. We can match these quotations, can't we?'

'Match them *and* some, but I think we've made a miscalculation. We've always thought it was about price and not having to transport machine parts to London. It's not about price for Macintosh & Warrilow, it's about something else.'

'Inertia?' asked Bill.

'Possibly. We're young and have the future in our sights. We've sound business with the Shamrock and Glasgow runs, yet we're working to better the company by moving into steam and going to Mauritius. Strange as it may seem to us, it may be that Macintosh & Warrilow are content with their status quo.'

'I'll not hold back, Fergus – you've been impulsive going after this steamship without a contract, but I do agree we can't afford to stay still. Take Shackleton & Company. Your father's refusal to contemplate even reading about steamships has put it on the back foot with its competitors. We don't want that happening to us. Do you think the two companies will ever merge?'

'I think, if we manage the Louisa Line competently and invest soundly in its future, in due course we may take over Shackleton & Company.'

'Or if your father dies?'

'Perhaps. They're back from Carlisle this evening. He's quite sprightly still. Who knows? In the meantime, we'll have to sit and wait and hope we hear from Macintosh & Warrilow.'

'How long do you think that will be?'

'I don't know, but I think they're gentlemanly enough to write to us with their decision, whichever way it goes. Now, about that celebration brandy…'

Fergus hoped he'd been putting on a good show. The whole time they'd been talking about the new arrival and the Louisa Line, his thoughts were focused on how much he was going to be in debt and what was happening to Rory.

* * *

Becky was finishing the ironing when Fergus came home unexpectedly, mid-afternoon.

'We should get a young girl in to help you.'

'I don't need help, and besides, I haven't got enough to do as it is. And now there's no Rory, I've even less.' She bit down on her bottom lip and rubbed her upper arms, as if to soothe herself.

Fergus put an arm round her. 'I only mention it because you know if you change your mind, we can get someone.'

'I'm busy today because I want a day clear of chores, ready for the Seamen's Haven's whist drive tomorrow.' *Fergus is uncomfortable, I know that shoulder shrug.* 'Have I got the wrong day?'

'Ah. About that.'

'What?' *He's going to cancel.*

'I've an important business meeting tomorrow. I've come home to tell you so you can send apologies.'

'Tomorrow?' she said, although she knew that was when he meant. 'What for?'

'I have to see an investor.' He didn't feel the need to tell her he was going to sign a mortgage document for their Chapel Street warehouse towards the purchase of the *SS Ketton*.

'And you have to go tomorrow? They're expecting us at the Haven.'

'It's important. I'm sorry. They won't miss us, I'm sure there'll be quite a crowd. You could always go on your own.'

'It's a paired invitation, and anyway, I don't want to go on my own. The joy for me is being there with you.'

There was lots Becky wanted to say about putting the business first and cancelling at the last minute, but she bit her tongue and turned away. It wasn't just that she was looking forward to the afternoon – she'd planned to wear the new blouse she'd finished.

A new pattern was emerging. What had begun as arriving home half an hour later than when they were first married had now become sometimes an hour later. Then, when Fergus did come home, he seemed distracted, as if something were bothering him. Fearful she was going to cry again in front of him, Becky gathered up the freshly ironed laundry and went into the bedroom to busy herself putting it away.

She waited until he'd left for the warehouse, then picked up her shawl, more from habit than for warmth, and left for the Indian King.

Dolly's surprise at seeing her was too much and, seeing her ma's arms as the safe pair she needed, Becky burst into tears.

Dolly ushered her into the kitchen. 'Whatever's wrong, lass? Is it Rory? Are you expecting? I was tearful when I was expecting you.'

'No, I'm not. We're not going to the whist afternoon at the Haven now.'

'Did he promise you?'

'No, but we accepted. They're expecting us.'

'He's not broken a promise, then. What's made him change his mind?'

'An important meeting for business.'

'Shackletons, or the Louisa Line?'

'It's to see a potential investor. That's all I know. I didn't tell you, but we had an argument the day Rory was taken.'

'Don't fret, lass. It was a dreadful day and we were so upset. All married couples argue.'

'This was a serious quarrel.'

'Mark my words, it'll not be your last. As for changing plans at the last minute, he's a busy man building up a business and you've time to spare. A bairn will keep you busy, you'll see.'

'Mam.' *Not the bairn business again.*

'I know, it's early days, but what I say is true.'

Becky wondered how her ma could be so glib. The message she'd received, albeit in a not unkindly way was: 'You've made your bed, now lie in it.'

This message was reinforced by Dolly changing the subject. 'If you've time, you could see to those curtains in the back room,' she said. 'The hem's down and I've folk coming by later this evening.'

* * *

After signing the mortgage document, Fergus called in to see Todhunter, to check on progress regarding the *SS Ketton* purchase. As he was about to leave, Jeremiah asked after Rory.

'It's been a terrible business,' Fergus told him. 'We are all troubled, especially Becky and Dolly.'

Jeremiah sighed. 'I know. I was bidding at the Indian King auction on Friday and Dolly told me all about it.'

'Unlike Becky, Dolly seems to find comfort in talking

to people about Rory. She says the more people know about the event, the more likely they are to pass on news of him.'

'What have you heard?'

'It's been close on a week now, and not a single word.'

'Have you made enquiries?'

'My solicitor suggested a man who traces missing people, but when we approached him, he said he couldn't see a problem – Rory was with his long-lost father, and what was wrong with that?'

'Some folk in Whitehaven say the same.'

'What do *you* think?'

'You want an honest answer?'

Fergus nodded.

'I hesitate to speak my mind on this and plant seeds of doubt that can only make things harder for you, but I reckon it's a reet "rum do", that man turning up out of the blue. There's something not quite right in my mind. In fact, it's downright peculiar.'

Jeremiah's words cut deep, but he hadn't planted any seeds of doubt in Fergus's mind – Fergus already knew there was something wrong about the whole episode. What Jeremiah had done was stimulate the growth of seeds already sprouting. The appearance of this man had all been too sudden.

CHAPTER TWENTY-FIVE

As soon as she opened the pub doors, Becky could hear Dolly's voice, even though she was in the kitchen with the door closed. It was the high-pitched frustrated tone she saved for events over which she had no control.

As Becky passed, Sergeant Adams put an arm out to stop her. 'Your mammy's in a state. They've moved your pie stand at the races. She's been ranting about it for o'er half an hour.'

Becky grimaced. *This is bad news on top of everything else.* She scratched Molly's head and braced herself. When she entered the kitchen, Dolly was examining a stall plan she'd spread out over a table.

'I can't believe it. We've had that stand siting for four years, maybe more.' Dolly jabbed her finger at the end of a row of boxes.

Becky took the plan from her. It was true – instead of being at the centre of the food section, they'd been put right at the end, farthest away from the finishing post. 'Oh, dear,' Becky said.

'Dear? It'll cost us dear, that's what it'll do. Rory gone, and now all this.'

'Why have they moved us?'

'Turn it over. It says they've decided that instead of having all the food stands together, they're splitting us up and mixing us with general traders. What good is it going to do us if we get stuck beside someone selling caps, or fancy pots, I ask you?'

'Is that so bad? It'll mean more space surrounding the stall.'

'But that's exactly it. It's a disaster. Think of the number of times people have been queuing either side of us for our competitors' pies. Take Mrs Jenkins from the Pack Horse. Folks standing in her line glance across, see and smell our pies, then leave her and move over to us. Her pastry's dry and thick and ours is thinner, so there's more meat.'

It was true. Becky had seen people glance across, check back with Mrs Jenkins mutton pies, return their gaze to Dolly's beef pies, then move across.

'I'm going to complain to the organisers,' Dolly said.

'You can't complain, Ma. They'll say if they move us then they have to reorganise all the stall-holders. With two days to go, they're not going to do anything. Anyway, we've enough on with Rory gone.'

Dolly disappeared into the larder and came back with a small sack of flour. 'I suppose the best we can do is get on and make the pies.'

They were rolling out the first batch of pastry when Dolly said, 'We're always slow here when the races are on. What if I get one of the bar lads to walk the course pathways, ringing a bell advertising our pies?'

Becky frowned. 'With all the noise and the crowds, that'll never work. I've a better idea.'

Dolly put down her rolling pin. 'What?'

'Why don't we abandon the stall completely and apply to sell the pies in the ale tent?'

'Where the gentlemen go? Where the ale's more expensive?'

'Aye.'

'If we could, we'd make a fortune, but they don't have food in there.'

'It's all about making brass, Ma. We could offer to pay a bit more for a stand if it was in such a premium position, couldn't we?'

Dolly thought for a moment, then said grudgingly, 'I suppose so.'

'I'll go up there now to the estate office and suggest it, and see what happens.'

'They'll never go for it,' said Dolly, turning her attention back to the stand plan.

'They won't if Becky Moss asks, but I bet they might if Mrs Fergus Shackleton asks, and offers to give a donation to the Seamen's Haven from the proceeds.'

'You mean make money from the Seamen's Haven?'

'I wouldn't put it like that – that sounds grabby – but people hold fêtes and bazaars doing the same thing for churches. I'll need to check with Fergus, but I can't see as how he'll mind.'

* * *

Fergus didn't mind at all, as long as it wasn't Becky selling the pies, to which she was happy to agree. She didn't ask him to explain why, because she knew: he didn't want people to think he'd married a purveyor of pies.

'There's nothing to prevent there being a presentation at the end, with Mrs Shackleton accepting the donation, and a report about it in the paper. It'll be good publicity for the Seamen's Haven. Shall I come with you to the estate office?'

Becky thought about it. 'No. I can do this. Charity is women's work. I think they're less likely to turn *me* down than a man.'

Becky thought perhaps she was on a fool's errand, but it was worth a try. On arrival at the estate office, she was passed through several people until she came face to face with Lord Lowther's steward.

'It is indeed a novel idea, Mrs Shackleton,' he told her, after listening to her suggestion. 'And I am sure it would be warmly received by the gentlemen in the bar. However, if I allow the Indian King to sell its pies in the ale tent, this will result in other pie-sellers understandably protesting, and in point of fact other charities will want...How can I put it?'

'A bite of the cherry themselves?'

He laughed. 'A choice turn of phrase. You understand my dilemma?'

'If anyone questions the arrangement, my suggestion is you tell them this is a worthy experiment. Something different. After all, you've already changed the arrangement for the stalls.'

The steward scratched his head. 'There is another problem. It's Lord Lowther who usually makes such decisions, but he's abroad and won't be present.'

'Then you are his representative.' She stated his position as fact, not as a question.

'Yes, but –'

Becky bathed him in one of her sweetest smiles. 'Since I can see you obviously agree with my suggestion, and in Lord Lowther's absence you are, in fact, in charge, I'm sure you'll want my husband to be able to tell His Lordship the next time he meets him in the Gentleman's Club how wonderful it was that the Seamen's Haven was able to benefit from the races.'

The steward rubbed his palms together and Becky thought he was going to turn her down.

'I grant you it's a worthy idea, and I know Lord Lowther does make an annual donation to the Seamen's Haven. It's the Indian King's involvement that is the problem.'

The solution came to Becky in an instant. 'What if the Indian King supplies the pies, and your staff sell them? Will that solve the problem?'

'We would have to add a premium to the cost. The charitable donation, the loss of stall rent, and –'

'Your commission,' Becky finished.

'Oh no, I can't do that.'

'We could let you have a few extra pies for the staff kitchen.'

'Mrs Shackleton, I hope you don't mind me saying this, but you are a shrewd businesswoman.'

When Becky arrived home and told Fergus, he roared with laughter.

'Who would have thought you had such a business head on your shoulders you could run rings round the lord of the manor's steward? You sold all the pies in one transaction, made money for the Seamen's Haven, and your mother gets a day out at the races in front of the stalls, rather than behind them.'

When Becky explained the arrangement she'd brokered, Dolly was delighted. 'I don't care how much extra they slap on for the toffs in the gentlemen's bar. Selling two days of pies in one go at a good profit, with the Seamen's Haven getting a slice, and me not having to stand there all day, is an excellent arrangement. Even if it's a one-off.'

* * *

At the race course, Dr Fincham having won a modest amount on the fourth race and declaring himself done for the day, and with Fergus curious as to how the sale of Dolly's pies was going, the two men agreed that a welcome ale would not go amiss. They were placing their order in the gentlemen's bar when Mr Needham beckoned them over to his table.

'Welcome, gentlemen,' he said. 'Do join us. May I introduce my cousin, Oliver Trenchard? He's visiting from Carlisle.'

Fergus saw a man of slighter build than Mr Needham, of similar age, with a cheerful demeanour.

'I travelled down by train two days ago,' Mr Trenchard said, after the introductions were made. 'A most scenic route along the coast.'

'You've picked the perfect time to coincide with the

races,' Fergus told him. 'Although sometimes it can be so blowy up here on Harras Moor, it ruins the whole meeting.'

'And you're here at the right time for the pies.' Mr Trenchard nodded in the direction of the pie table, where a small queue had formed. 'You should try one. Such an interesting idea to include that seamen's charity.'

Fergus hoped Mr Trenchard wouldn't wander out of the tent and notice the pies outside were on sale for two thirds the price.

Dr Fincham, aware of the story, caught Fergus's eye and winked.

Mr Trenchard continued, 'I aim to come down once a year and Edgar comes up to me similarly. You know how it is for us legal people. There's always some case or other keeping us tied to our desks.'

Fergus had never thought of Mr Needham as 'Edgar', although he knew it was his Christian name.

'Oliver is also a solicitor, as were both our fathers,' Mr Needham explained. 'The law has to be in our blood, as the sea must be in yours, Fergus.' He turned to Dr Fincham. 'And are you from a medical background, sir?'

'My father was a doctor, but having spent so many years as a ship's surgeon, I cannot say for sure whether it is medicine in my blood or the sea.'

'Perhaps both,' said Mr Needham. 'I'm sure you have tales to tell.'

Encouraged by Fergus, who was confident the others would be entertained, Dr Fincham went on to regale them with some of his more hair-raising tales of being at sea, and the joys of living in Mauritius.

Fergus was about to take his leave and join Becky for the donation presentation when Mr Needham said, 'How is your wife bearing up under the strain of the Loadman business? Have you heard anything of the boy?'

Fergus shook his head. 'No, nothing as yet. Sadly, perhaps we never will.'

'Loadman?' asked Mr Trenchard, leaning forward.

'Yes,' said Fergus. 'I have – I mean I had – a ward whose father we believed to be dead.'

'I arranged the court papers,' said Mr Needham. 'A most interesting legal case, if Mr Shackleton doesn't mind my mentioning his private affairs.'

Fergus shook his head. 'Not at all, in this case. Allow me. It seems the father wasn't dead at all. Two weeks ago, this Loadman fellow arrived, claimed the boy and took him, with the full consent of the local constabulary. The head constable himself, no less.'

Mr Trenchard was now leaning so far forward in his chair, with such an air of excitement, Fergus thought he might be tipped out onto the grass. 'Loadman is an unusual name,' Mr Trenchard said. 'What's the boy's Christian name?'

'Rory,' said Fergus, wondering at his interest.

'Rory? Was his mother called Amy?'

Fergus put a clenched fist to his chest. 'Yes! Have you word of him?'

Mr Trenchard pinched the bridge of his nose. 'I don't know the boy, but I think I know the man. Please describe him to me.'

'I haven't seen him,' said Fergus.

'But *I* have,' said Dr Fincham. 'He was a strong man – stocky, you might say – with a broken nose, a handlebar moustache, his hair closely cropped and a tattoo on his neck. We thought he might have been in a recent fight, as his knuckles were cracked and sore. An old soldier who saw him thought he could be a professional bare-knuckle fighter.'

'You have news?' Fergus asked again.

'Yes, I do. The boy, how old is he?'

'Coming up twelve. He's like his father.'

Mr Trenchard hesitated. 'I sincerely hope not. From your description, I agree the man is a bare-knuckle fighter, but the man you are describing is not Rory's father, because that man is dead.'

'Are you sure?' asked Fergus.

'Definitely. Walter Loadman died in Carlisle Gaol last February, and I was one of the last to see him alive. The man you describe is a Loadman all right, but he's Rory's uncle, not his father. He's Adam Loadman, Walter's brother.'

'You mean he's passing himself off as Rory's father?'

'From what you have told me, it would appear so.'

CHAPTER TWENTY-SIX

'Where's Fergus?' asked Becky. She was standing by the finishing post, next to the prize-winners' podium.

'I don't know, lass,' said Dolly, 'but you'll have to begin. They're ready and the crowd's gathered.'

'Fergus was going to say some words.'

'You'll have to do it. Thank them, say it's an honour... Oh, I don't know. You'll think of something.'

The steward asked for quiet, then invited Becky to join him on the podium. 'Ladies and gentlemen, what a successful afternoon we have had.'

A voice from the centre of the crowd shouted out, 'Speak for thisen. Ah've lost a packet.'

There was a ripple of laughter and the steward raised his hands, as if about to conduct a choir.

'I stand corrected,' he said. 'Perhaps not so successful for all of us. We've made some changes this year, and one of them has been to introduce a charitable event in the Gentlemen Members' Bar. It behoves me now to present Mrs Fergus Shackleton with a note of our donation to the Seamen's Haven – the sum of £8.'

The crowd clapped enthusiastically, and when the noise had died down, the steward indicated Becky and said, 'Mrs Shackleton.'

'It is an honour to be here today to accept this donation,' Becky began. *What shall I say now?* 'Thank you.' *What now?* Her brain was empty. *Oh, I know.* 'I don't have to tell you that the name Shackleton is known for its shipping business. What many of you may not know is that Louisa Shackleton, who passed away last year, was a founder of the Seamen's Haven and a great supporter of the charity. I take it as a great honour to be here today to accept this donation in her memory.' *Have I said enough?* 'Thank you.'

She stepped down and noted there was still no Fergus.

A middle-aged lady in an expensive dress came forward. 'I am Lord Lowther's steward's wife. You will join myself and some of the other officials' wives for tea in the Lady Members' Area, won't you? We so want to get to know you better.'

'Thank you, but I ought to find my husband. He was to join me for the presentation.'

A man stepped forward. 'I've just come from the members' area and Mr Shackleton is enjoying an ale with that new doctor and two other men. Their conversation was animated, to say the least. I'd accept the tea invitation.'

Becky managed to thank the man, despite being furious. How could Fergus have forgotten and left her stranded? *Where's Ma?* Dolly seemed to have melted away into the crowd. *Am I to be totally deserted?*

* * *

While Becky was accepting the donation, Fergus, in conversation with the two solicitors and Dr Fincham, had paled so quickly, the doctor called over a waiter to order large brandies for them all.

'Go on,' said Mr Needham. 'Who is this Adam Loadman, pretending to be Rory's father?'

'Strike me down,' said Dr Fincham. 'What happened?'

'I was summoned to see Walter Loadman in Carlisle Gaol in February,' Mr Trenchard said. 'Definitely then, because I remember it being so cold walking there, and I was anxious to arrive for some warmth, but his cell was as cold as outside.'

'What was he in for?' asked Mr Needham.

'Horse-stealing. A second offence. He can't have been bright, because usually men who steal horses sell them on quickly, or make some effort to disguise them, but he was caught bold as brass with his accomplice riding a stolen horse in Penrith. And on market day, too.'

'How did he die?' asked Mr Needham. 'Horse stealing isn't a hanging offence anymore.'

'He and his accomplice were sentenced to six months imprisonment for stealing a horse and I was called out because I represented him at the trial. You can't truthfully say I defended him because there was no doubt over his guilt. Anyway, he asked for me because he knew he wasn't going to last the night. He told the governor he had business to see to.'

'What was wrong with him?' asked Dr Fincham.

'He had a poisoning of the blood. It started in his left thumb, which became hugely swollen, and spread through his whole body. When I saw him, it was obvious he was dying; he had that yellowing of the skin signifying impending death.'

Dr Fincham nodded.

'Despite being in pain, he was *compos mentis,* calm and resigned to his fate. When I arrived, the governor met me and presented me with a hessian bag, which he said contained all the prisoner's effects, and that if Loadman had summoned me to make a will, as far as he knew, that was all the man had to bequeath.'

'Was there anything of interest?' asked Fergus.

'I'm coming to that. There were some clothes, which I told Loadman I would donate to the workhouse. Then Loadman asked me if there were any papers in the bag. I felt around the edges and came across a goods carrier's licence, and a birth certificate for a boy called Rory. The mother's name was Amy and, if I remember correctly, her surname was some sort of bird.'

'Rook,' said Fergus, 'Rook with an "e". That's Rory's name. Rory Rooke, so it has to be our Rory.'

Mr Trenchard nodded. 'The prisoner confirmed he was the boy's father, that he was nineteen when the boy was born and Amy eighteen, and they'd lived in Lancaster. They never married. He asked me what I thought St Peter was going to say about his not having acknowledged or provided for his child? I think he thought a deathbed acceptance of the boy as his son to a solicitor was going to secure him a place in heaven.'

'What did you say?'

'He was a dying man. I told him what he wanted to

hear, although I didn't believe it. Then I suggested he ask for a reverend. I don't know if one visited.'

'Dolly told me the man pretending to be Rory's father asked him his birthday,' Dr Fincham said, 'and when Rory told him, the date matched the certificate he was holding.'

'The impostor, Adam Loadman – let's refer to him from now on as the fighter, to be clear – called at my office two days later, asking for his brother's chattels. The governor had directed him to my office. I told him the clothes had already been despatched to the workhouse. To be truthful, my clerk couldn't get them out of the office quick enough, mumbling about gaol fever and lice. I suspect they never made it as far as the workhouse and ended up in a ditch somewhere. Anyway, my impression was the brother was hoping there was going to be some money.'

'He must have been disappointed,' said Mr Needham.

'Did he say anything?' asked Fergus.

'Yes, I remember his words exactly, as they were so callous. He said, "Left me nowt, the cheap bastard".'

'What did you say to that?' asked Dr Fincham.

'I said, "He may have left you more than you anticipated. You have a nephew," and I gave him the certificate and the licence which, as next of kin, he was entitled to.'

'Did he say anything about the birth certificate?' asked Mr Needham.

'I remember him picking it up, peering at it, holding it close, and squinting at it. It was then I decided he had to be a bare-knuckle fighter, for his fingers were twisted and covered in scars. When I examined him more closely, I noticed further old scars on his face, and how his nose was bent, as if it had been broken. He said "Oh yes, the lad," and I didn't say anything further. It was my impression it was something he knew about, but that he'd forgotten. Had I any idea of what he was going to do with the certificate, I would have retained it in our files.'

'What am I going to tell Becky?' Fergus said. 'That an imposter strolled in and took the boy we were going to bring up as our own son?'

'No,' said Mr Needham. 'Adam Loadman will be arrested for impersonation and abduction of a minor under false pretences. As your solicitor, I advise you to tell Becky when we catch up with this fighter. You will then say Rory will soon be home again.'

'And will he be my ward?'

Mr Needham turned to his cousin. 'It's a most unusual case, but I think you'll agree, Oliver, that under the circumstances a judge will be happy to confirm a reinstatement of Mr Shackleton's wardship. Besides, our bare-knuckle fighter will be in no position to protest, since he's going to be locked away for a long time.'

'But why didn't he just say he was his uncle?' asked Fergus.

'I've been sitting here thinking about that,' Mr Trenchard said. 'Because saying he was his father gave him an unrivalled claim on the boy. The man's feckless, always after the main chance. I think he obtained the papers, thought about it, then realised there could be money in it. He's shrewd. He arrives here, learns Amy is dead, picks up information in town, learns the boy's been taken in by people with money, anticipates there's a family resemblance and that he can benefit from it.'

'But why did he take the boy?' Dr Fincham asked. 'Why not make a demand?'

'I think I can answer that,' Fergus said. 'To get the boy he had to prove paternity, and that had to involve the constable, so after that he had no choice but to take him. I'm surprised he hasn't brought him back yet.'

'How did he know to come to Whitehaven?' asked Dr Fincham.

'That's a question to ask when you find him,' said Mr Needham.

Mr Trenchard took his snuff-box from his waistcoat pocket. 'On my return I will speak with the gaol governor. Loadman had a partner in crime; perhaps he will be able to tell us more. We must inform the police. I'll see to that in Carlisle.'

'I'd like to meet this accomplice,' Fergus said.

'Why don't you come back with me when I return to Carlisle, the day after tomorrow? We can visit together. I'll send ahead and make an appointment with the prison governor and I'll engage an investigator I know to make enquiries on our behalf.'

'Thank you. Please do. We must do all we can, as soon as we can.'

* * *

Becky was still sitting with the ladies at tea when a steward informed her that her husband was waiting outside. She made her excuses and left. She was still angry and was about to launch into the reprimand she'd been practising, when she recognised something was wrong. Fergus didn't greet her with his usual 'I missed you' smile. Instead, his face was grave, as solemn as an expression might be when about to tell someone a loved one has died. Her first thoughts flew to Rory.

'What's wrong?'

'I'm sorry I missed your acceptance speech,' he said, 'but important business kept me away. Business about Rory.'

'What have you heard? Is he all right?'

'I don't know. It's a long story, but we have reason now to go after them. Reasons that mean a search will be supported by the law.'

They were promenading along the course rails and people were nodding at them.

'I take it you accepted the donation on the Haven's behalf?'

'Yes. I've been having tea with the steward's wife and others.'

'Good. That means we can leave.'

'Can't you tell me now?'

'Not like this, here. We'll take a carriage, collect Charlie and go for a long walk.'

CHAPTER TWENTY-SEVEN

Later, when she thought back, Becky could never understand how she'd managed to contain herself in the carriage home. Fergus had sat beside her, deep in thought. She'd tried to extract information, but he wouldn't be drawn.

'You're not being fair. You deserted me for the presentation, now you're holding back news of Rory.'

'I didn't desert you, I was held up. Trust me. I need to settle my thoughts. Walking with Charlie will help us both.'

Charlie welcomed them with great delight, leaping up, then running around like a berserker and wagging his tail. He wasn't usually left on his own for more than an hour or so, but with dogs not being allowed near the race track, and Fergus and Becky expecting to be busy, they had left him at home. After showing his appreciation for their return, he went and sat by the door.

'It's all right, Charlie, we're taking you out straight away,' Becky said.

Fergus waited while she changed her bonnet for a smaller one and took off the sturdy boots she'd needed for negotiating the racecourse grass, and then they set off. She wasn't surprised when they turned in the direction of the harbour. The town was quiet, with the usual crowds up at the races. Later, the main streets would come alive with folk celebrating their winnings or drowning their sorrows.

As they walked along, Fergus told Becky what he'd learned.

'I can't believe it,' she cried. 'We stood by and watched that man steal our Rory! You must go to Carlisle. I agree with Mr Trenchard. The story originated there – you never know what you may learn to help us find him.'

'We have the authorities on our side now,' Fergus said. 'The police will be going after an impostor, not a man reunited with a long-lost son.'

'And a boy with a crippled leg. That's a good thing, it makes Rory stand out. You'll be going to the police first thing in the morning?'

'Yes. I'd go this minute if they weren't all busy at the races, but don't think I'm going to leave it up to them.'

'What are you going to do?'

'After the police I'm going to do what Loadman did. I'm going to go round the pubs and ale houses here, asking people for information, but I'll be asking about *him*. Any slip he's made about where he was from, or where he was going, may provide a clue we can follow up. Then I'm going to track down the carrier who took them to Maryport and take it from there. I'll put Dicken in charge of the day-to-day running of the business, to give me time.

I'm going to find Rory and put that man in gaol, if it's the last thing I do.'

Despite the shock of the impostor and the false pretences, Becky had to admit she was experiencing a certain joy at seeing Fergus putting their family life before his business interests.

* * *

The next day at ten o'clock, having made his report to the police and signed a statement, Fergus set himself to calling on the town's ale houses and inns. Although it had gone round the town that Rory's father had called for him, it was twelve days since anyone had actually seen him. A few recollected him. 'Thought he were a fighter,' they said, or 'I think he were about six foot, or 'He were well over six foot.' There was nothing, though, that Fergus hadn't already heard. It wasn't long before he felt he was wasting his time, since it seemed those who'd been at the Indian King when Loadman took Rory were the ones who knew most about him.

He went home to Becky and hadn't been a minute in the door when she said, 'I've been thinking. Where did Loadman spend the night? If we can find that out, perhaps the innkeeper or landlady can tell us something. He made a comment to Dolly when he asked for the port. What was it?' She drummed her fingers on the mantelpiece clock. 'Oh, what was it?'

'Think back. He asked your mother for port. Did he?'

'I've got it!' She grasped Fergus's arm. 'He said it was blowy where he was and that the geese next door made a noise.'

'Blowy?'

'Yes, blowy, he had to be up on the hill.'

'Which hill?'

'That was all he said, but my wager is he was up by St James's. The wind always blows sharp up there. We need to find a guesthouse that has geese next door.' She reached for her coat.

'Where are you going?'

'I'm going up there now.'

Fergus shook his head. 'Let *me* go.'

'No, this is my task. You're going to Carlisle later, you've things to see to. I want to play my part.' She didn't say it, but she was thinking a toff appearing at folk's door asking questions would put people off. They might respond more easily to her, a local lass on her own.

'I can't let you. What if something happens? I'll come with you.'

'I'll be perfectly safe. I've lived here all my life and come to no harm. It's broad daylight, there's plenty of folk about.'

'You don't know who's going to open the door.'

'I promise I won't go inside any house. Let me do this. It's important and makes me feel I'm helping. You go to the warehouse and finish off what you need to do before you leave tomorrow.'

'All right, but take care.'

Becky marched up Queen Street until she reached St James's Church, then turned right along High Street before turning into Charles Street. All the while she listened out for geese. She wandered down to the junction with Peter

Street, still hearing nothing, then retraced her steps. At the top end of Scotch Street, still with no clues, she began to think she was on the wrong side of the town.

She was on Charles Street again when a group of children ran past her, shouting and laughing, and suddenly there was a cacophony of honking. It was as if the geese had heard the children, thought about it, then decided to warn of their presence. It was easy to pinpoint the noise – but which side was the guesthouse where the fighter had stayed?

Becky looked in the windows for a notice indicating to a visitor that this was a guesthouse. There was nothing in either. She knocked on one of the doors. After a while she heard a shuffling, and the door opened. An elderly lady, who must have been in her early eighties, was standing there in apron and slippers.

Becky smiled. 'Forgive me, but do you run a guesthouse?'

The lady shook her head. 'I used to, like, a long time ago, when my Frederick was at sea, but no longer. Why?'

'I'm asking after someone, and all I know is he stayed near here about two weeks ago.'

The old lady shook her head. 'Left you in the lurch, has he, lassie?' She gave Becky a sympathetic smile that revealed a single front tooth.

'Oh, no, nothing like that. It's a long story. He has a young lad with him I'm trying to trace.'

The woman brushed back the string of grey hair that had dropped onto her shoulder. 'I see. This is number 8. You could go and knock up her that lives at number 4.' She pointed back up the hill. 'I hear she sometimes takes in people. Men only, from what I hear.' She winked. 'I guess the crimps send them up here and get a cut for themselves. Know what I mean?'

Becky knew exactly what she meant. Her own mother ran a respectable business, but in a town awash with men back on land after months at sea, she could understand why there was a market for casual liaisons of the paying kind.

'Thank you. I'm sorry to bother you.'

At number 8, the paint on the windowsills had peeled and the wood had become unprotected. There was a heavy black iron door-knocker in the shape of a fox's head. Becky lifted it and let it drop. The door was opened almost immediately by a young girl not much older than her.

'Yes?'

'I'm sorry to bother you. I'm asking about someone who may have stayed here recently.'

Fear spread across the girl's face. She made to shut the door, but Becky put her foot out to act as a wedge. 'No, please don't. It's about a missing lad. You may be our only hope of finding him.'

The girl stopped pushing. Whether it was the urgency in Becky's voice, or whether she was just curious, Becky couldn't be sure.

'Please,' she went on. 'He could be in real danger.'

'A lad? How do I know what you're saying is true?'

'Would I be standing here doing this, wasting my time, if it wasn't?' Becky was aware it might look as though she was attempting to trace an unfaithful husband or lover and had come with a made-up story. She took a chance. 'The lad's name is Rory. Rory Rooke. Folk have been talking about him in town.'

'Oh, the lad with the funny leg?'

'Aye,' said Becky, relief flooding through her. 'Do you know him?'

'Nay, but my ma knew his ma. She worshipped at church here.' The girl tilted her head in the direction of St James's. 'Then she died. I've heard about the lad. His da turned up, didn't he?'

Becky nodded.

'What's it to do with us?' the girl asked.

'The man lied when he said he was Rory's father. He's not.'

The girl took two steps forward in her curiosity, almost closing the gap between them. However, Becky needed more than a greater show of interest.

'We think this man stayed here the night before he took Rory away,' she went on. 'Is there anyone inside who might know anything about him?'

The girl thought. 'When did you say it was?'

'May 20th.'

'The missus keeps a guest book. I could ask her?'

'Perhaps the missus would come out and speak to me?'

The girl disappeared to be replaced a few minutes later by a pretty, middle-aged woman. 'What's all this about Rory?'

After Becky had explained the circumstances again, the woman sighed. 'We do take in lodgers, but so many I can't always recall them, especially strangers who turn up for one night.'

'We think he was a bare-knuckle fighter. Tall, dark hair, a tattoo round the back of his neck.'

'There was one like that – I remember the tattoo. I'd have sworn it was back end of April, though, but I can check. Would you like me to?'

'If it's not too much bother. Please.'

The woman came back, holding a large black book. 'You're right, it was more than two weeks ago. Time rushes by. What is it you're after?'

'Anything you can tell us about him so we can find Rory'

'To start with, he didn't say much, but he'd got a bottle of port, and the more he drank, the more talkative he became.'

'That's the port Ma gave him to get rid of him.' The woman looked puzzled, so Becky went on, 'It's my mammy runs the Indian King, where Rory was taken from.'

'You're Dolly Moss's lass?'

'Aye.'

'I thought I recognised you. You come to church with her, don't you?'

'Yes, and I was wed there recently.'

Becky tried not to frown. The woman was wasting time. 'But what do you know about the man who took Rory?'

'As I said, he drank quite a bit, and started talking about Carlisle, which is where I thought he came from. Then he seemed to want to impress me, because after a couple of glasses he started talking about his fights. Seems he does some local ones Carlisle way and in the Borders, and a couple of big ones each year.'

'Did he say where the big ones were?'

'I wasn't paying that much attention, you understand. I was nodding, saying "Oh, really," that sort of thing, but I do remember he talked about Carnforth. I remember that because I've an aunt lives close by. He said he made a lot of brass there last year taking wagers.'

'Did he say when?'

'There are a few throughout the year. He never said 'owt about Rory. I'd no idea it was him took the lad.'

'From what you've said, especially about the tattoo and the port, it was him all right.'

'We don't get many bare-knucklers in here, which is lucky, because if we did, I have to say he wouldn't have stood out.'

'Is there anything else you can say about him?' asked Becky.

'Nay, but if I do, I'll drop by the Indian King for a glass with Dolly. You can tell her you've seen Helen – Helen from Charles Street. She'll know who you mean. I hope you find the lad.'

CHAPTER TWENTY-EIGHT

Fergus and Mr Trenchard arrived at Carlisle Station at two o'clock. They were collecting their bags when a smartly dressed young man approached them.

Mr Trenchard performed the introductions. 'This is Mr Shackleton,' he told the young man, 'and he will be staying at the Crown and Mitre and will be with us for a day or two.' Addressing Fergus, he said, 'This is our office boy, Richard. He'll look after anything you require. I will leave you in his care and he will escort you to our offices in Devonshire Street, while I go ahead and see if there are any messages.'

The young man summoned a porter and they stepped out in silence until they reached the hotel, where Fergus took a room and deposited his luggage.

He was in Trenchard & Son's waiting room half an hour later, where the office boy offered him a copy of the *Carlisle Journal* and asked him to wait. Fergus ignored the 'For Sale and Wanted' advertisements on the paper's front page and turned straight to the news. He skimmed an article about the American Civil War and was halfway through an account of a North London Railway accident when Mr Trenchard entered. Fergus put the journal down and stood up.

'My dear sir, I am so sorry to have kept you waiting. We'll take tea in my rooms. I have received information from the investigator.'

Mr Trenchard's rooms housed the usual type of solicitor's office accoutrements, with a large desk, deed boxes and ostentatious inkstand, and leading off it a smaller room, with wide armchairs and a small table.

'I use this room for interviews and meetings of a more informal nature,' Mr Trenchard said. 'Witnesses find it less daunting than my being behind the big desk – especially children. I am a governor at the Grammar School and the Fawcett Schools.'

'You have news?'

'Yes. The prison governor has agreed to meet with us and has authorised an interview with Will Stead. He's Walter Loadman's partner in crime and they were sentenced together. We have an appointment for tomorrow morning.'

'Excellent,' said Fergus. This was all good news.

'Let me tell you what I have learned from our investigator's report so far.'

Fergus leaned forward. *This must be how a hound feels when the scent of the fox awakens its nostrils.*

'Loadman not being a common name, our man found several references to it here in Carlisle. His main problem was sorting out which brother was which.'

'Mr Loadman could be either.'

'Exactly. However, knowing your Mr Loadman, Adam, was a bare-knuckler, and that his brother was a goods carrier, he managed to separate them. Also, with Walter being incarcerated in gaol it then became easier to track down the fighter, because he could assume all Loadman references during Walter's imprisonment had to be for Adam.'

'Please continue.'

'It transpires Adam Loadman was treated last December for a cracked rib at the infirmary. They patched him up and sent him on his way.'

'That's clever. I hadn't thought of enquiring along those lines.'

'That's what we pay our man for. He lives partly in society and partly in the city's underworld. There's not much he can't find out about, except perhaps the inside of a nunnery.'

Fergus laughed. He was beginning to feel optimistic about finding the bare-knuckler.

'While our investigator is a clever – perhaps one could say canny – gentleman, we can't say the same about Loadman.'

'Why?'

'When he was treated at the infirmary he had to give an address. The Wigton Road, near Bower Street.'

'Where's that?'

'The other side of the west railway tracks. We have a decision to make. Do we send the investigator or shall we go ourselves?'

'Definitely go ourselves. When can we go?'

'I thought you'd say that. I've cancelled the meetings with my clerk this afternoon.'

'We can leave right away?'

'Yes, but it's a rough area. We'll leave the cab waiting, even though we'll have to pay extra.'

It took a while for the two men to find a cabby who would take them west of the railway line and be prepared to wait in that location. On the journey, Fergus was apprehensive for their safety, there being a number of dubious people who viewed their carriage with interest as they passed, but the thought of learning anything about Loadman was too great a pull for him to turn back.

The cab pulled up outside a small brick house in a row of terraces that had seen better days. Although the houses were not that old, they had never been maintained. Several had broken windows patched up with brown paper, the windowsills needed attention and there was rubbish in the street. There was a miasma consisting of stale cabbage, human waste, and general detritus. The whole area was not one anyone would want to linger in during daylight hours, and certainly not in darkness.

After they had alighted from the cab, the driver locked the carriage doors and returned to his driving seat.

'The cabby isn't pleased,' said Fergus.

'I'm not paying him until we get back, otherwise, despite his assurances, he'll not be here upon our return.'

Fergus knocked on the door, noticing the doorstep was filthy. A woman of indeterminate age answered. Her voice seemed too young for her body and Fergus thought perhaps life experiences had aged her prematurely.

Seeing the two men, she drew back as if in fear. 'What?' she asked.

'We're sorry to trouble you, but we're from Trenchard & Son Solicitors in the city, making enquiries regarding a criminal. A man who has abducted a child under false pretences.'

The woman took her time, studying the two men for a minute. Fergus thought they looked the part, so that should reassure her.

'A bairn, you say?'

'Yes.'

'Do I know this bairn?'

'His name is Rory Rooke.'

The woman shook her head and Fergus's expectations fell.

Mr Trenchard pressed on, 'It's not the boy we're asking about, it's the man. His name is Adam Loadman.'

As soon as the name was uttered, the woman began swearing and uttering curses on Loadman's head, in such a manner that Fergus took two steps back.

'I knows him all right,' she said. 'Owes me money he does.' She wiped her nose with one end of her shawl and sniffed loudly.

Fergus was unable to hold back. 'Where is he?' he asked, stepping forward again.

'No idea.'

'He abducted a young boy by pretending to be his father, so if you can tell us anything that might help find this boy, we would be most grateful.'

'Loadman a father? He's a fighting man. Let's hope the lad can defend himself.'

Fergus's jaw tightened. He felt sick. Several times he'd imagined Loadman taking his fists to Rory. He didn't think it would take much for a man who appeared to delight in kicking dogs to escalate to lashing out at a boy.

'All I can tell you is he lived here for six months,' the woman went on. 'Always paying the rent on time, which was just as well, because I had some bloody sheets to deal with, what with him being a bare-knuckler and all that.'

'What's his fighting name?' asked Mr Trenchard.

'I never asked. I didn't want to know. He came and went at all hours, but he was paying the rent. What he got up to illegally outside my house was his business, as long as he was paying on time.'

'You said he owes you money?'

'Aye, he does. Paid regular until about April, so, as you can imagine, I took him to task o'er it. He didn't like that, I can tell you. Anyway, he took off mid-May time. Said he'd a money-payer coming up down south and he'd see me straight when he came back.'

'He took off?' asked Fergus.

'Left his belongings and never came back.'

'Do you still have his chattels?' asked Mr Trenchard.

'You're a joker, aren't you? I sold the lot. Lock, stock and barrel. Mind, I didn't get much. Mostly clothes, and a top hat in a box. It was a good one, though. Brushed beaver.'

'Did he have many visitors or bring anyone into his room?'

The woman stiffened. 'Bring anyone in? You mean women? This is a respectable establishment, there's nowt queer or agin the law goes on here.'

Fergus wanted to laugh. Her house might have been within the law, but it was obvious the surroundings provided a safe haven for the Carlisle criminal fraternity.

'The only visitor he had was his brother, afore Christmastide. Told me it was his brother, but he needn't have bothered. Like him, but scrawnier and smaller. You could tell straight away which was the bare-knuckler of the two.'

Satisfied the woman could tell them nothing further, Mr Trenchard thanked her and took some coins from his pocket.

'Here, take this for your trouble.'

The woman stared at the coins. 'You say it's a wee laddie he's gone off with?'

'Yes, a boy,' said Mr Trenchard, continuing to hold out the money. 'Rory Rooke.'

She pushed his hand away. 'I can't take your money, not as regarding finding a wee laddie.'

Mr Trenchard made a strange noise in his throat, which Fergus interpreted as surprise. He took some coins out of his own pocket. 'I'd like to add these to the payment. You're obviously an honest woman. Take the payment. You've been most helpful.'

The woman hesitated.

'Take it,' Fergus insisted. 'Give it to charity, if it makes you feel better.' He added the coins to the ones still resting in Mr Trenchard's outstretched hand. 'Take it and spend it.'

'All right. There's some wee kiddies need shoes. I hate to see 'em with their bare feet.'

They took their leave, much to the cabby's relief, and drove off at speed.

In the cab, Mr Trenchard said, 'That was illuminating.'

'You mean about "the money-payer coming up down south"?'

'Yes. For my money our bare-knuckler hatched a plan, and "down south" likely refers to Whitehaven.'

'But how did he know to go to Whitehaven?'

CHAPTER TWENTY-NINE

In the governor's office at the gaol, the first item Fergus noticed was a framed sign reading "REPENT YE OF YOUR SINS OR PREPARE TO BURN IN HELL". The letters were printed in thick black gothic script. The frame's mitre joints overlapped, forming a cross in each corner. The sign was positioned on the wall above the governor's head, so whoever was speaking to him couldn't fail to receive the message.

It was obvious from the governor's demeanour he had little time for solicitors and other visitors. He admitted he couldn't remember much about Loadman and had to check in the gaol's admittance book. However, understandably due to the inconvenience at the time, he did remember going out to fetch Mr Trenchard in the snow in February. His answers to their questions were brief, often monosyllabic, and he kept glancing over at a pile of papers on his desk, as if he were wishing to get on. Fergus guessed their visit was upsetting the prison's routine, and the governor was concerned about the possibility of unwelcome news from outside that might unsettle the inmates. Nevertheless, he was giving up his office for their interview.

Walter Loadman's horse-stealing partner in crime was brought in and introduced as Will Stead. The governor took his leave saying he had business to attend to. The prisoner was thin, grubby and wearing patched prison clothes – the sort of man you didn't choose to get too close to because you knew his smell would be offensive. The way he kept staring round the room, Fergus had the impression it was the first time he'd seen the inside of the governor's office. There wasn't much to see – a table, several chests with narrow drawers, a few boxes and a barred window, which kept attracting Will Stead's attention. Compared to a cell where the window was too high to allow the prisoner to see out, Fergus assumed the room was a pleasant, if torturous, change.

Will tipped his chin at Mr Trenchard in recognition, then stared at Fergus. 'Who's he?'

'This is Mr Shackleton,' Mr Trenchard said. 'He's here to ask about Walter Loadman. I can see you recognise me from the trial last January.'

'Walter's been dead a while. You ken that. What do you want?'

'Were you aware Walter had a son?'

Will Stead nodded. 'Aye. He mentioned him just the once, a couple of years back, when we were on our way back from Kendal. He pointed to the road and said, "That's the road to Whitehaven. I've a son there." Turns out straight after he'd registered the birth in Lancaster, the mother took off with the bairn. He wouldn't say why, which made me wonder if he'd set on her when in drink, or summat like that. Then the lad's nan wrote to Walter's mammy six months after he was born, saying they'd moved to Whitehaven. She thought he had a right to know, since he was the boy's da. I guess she wanted them to get back together and get married, for the bairn's sake. Anyway, he told me that's when his ma said, "The lad'll be better off without you. Leave him be, and it'll be cheaper for you." I asked if he'd ever seen the lad and he said not since he was a few weeks old.'

'That's all?'

'That's what his brother said when I told *him* the same.'

'His brother?' asked Fergus.

'Aye, Walter's brother, Adam, came and asked me the same questions. He got quite shirty when I said that was all I knew. He wanted to know about the boy's mother, said he knew her a long time ago. I said he should have talked to his brother about it while he had the chance.'

'What did he say to that?' asked Mr Trenchard.

'Just that it was a long time ago and time had moved on.'

'He's claimed Rory, Walter's son, as his own and taken off with him.'

'Claimed? What's that all about?'

'He's arrived saying he's Rory's father, taken him and disappeared.'

'What about this Amy, his mammy?'

'She passed away last year.'

'So the lad's an orphan? It's a good job then that his uncle's found him and taken him on.'

'We have reason to fear the boy is in danger,' said Fergus. He was feeling buoyant. The visit had been worthwhile, even if they'd learned nothing more than the trigger that had sent Loadman to Whitehaven.

'Walter wasn't cut out to be a wrong 'un,' Will told them. 'He fell in with the likes of me and my pals. I've laid in my cell many a night thinking if he'd been his own man, he'd not have got into horse-stealing, and he'd still be alive today.'

'Anything you can tell us to help catch up with Adam Loadman will help us rescue the boy,' said Mr Trenchard.

'There's not much. Walter was a goods carrier here in Carlisle, but trade got bad with the railway and the like. He wasn't suited to living one step in front of the law. For a start, you could tell when he was lying, and what good is that for a thief? But his brother, the Cumbrian Clouter, he's different. I'll wager he owes brass all over the county. Walter used to talk about his brother's bare-knuckle bouts and how he was doing, but when I finally met Adam in here, I could see straight away he was a low-life chancer. The kind of man that gets drunk and sings lewd songs.'

Takes one to know one, thought Fergus.

'They were noticeably different, and from what I could gather from Walter, they didn't spend much time together.'

'The Cumbrian Clouter is the name Adam Loadman uses to fight?' asked Mr Trenchard.

'Aye. I'd heard all about him, but never met him. I thought maybe he'd come to the trial, but he didn't. Too many police in one place for him to feel comfortable, I guess.' Will Stead laughed.

Fergus thought it probably a true presumption.

'Why do you think he's taken the boy?' asked Mr Trenchard.

'If he's took off with the boy, then it'll be for brass. What's the legal term?' He looked at Mr Trenchard.

'Pecuniary advantage.'

'That'll do,' said Stead. 'I don't understand it, but I like the sound of it.' Seeing Mr Trenchard take out his watch, he asked, 'Will you be sending summat in for my trouble?'

Mr Trenchard nodded, as if he'd been expecting the request. 'If the governor allows it, I'll send in some beef pies for you in the week.'

On the way back to the office, Mr Trenchard said, 'Did you notice the colour of Will Stead's skin?'

'Yes, his complexion is strange.'

'It's being locked up all day does that. The prisoners go a funny colour because they don't get enough daylight. You can spot men recently released from prison by that blue tinge. The first ones I saw were in Lancaster, released from the castle prison.'

'I'll know next time I see someone with that complexion.'

'Now, all we need to do is find the Cumbrian Clouter's next bare-knuckle meeting, and I am hopeful we'll find Rory. I'll file a report with the Carlisle police, but it's unlikely they'll do much, since he's obviously left the area and, owing money, he'll be thought unlikely to return. If we locate him, that's different. They'll prosecute, I've no doubt about that. But I will stress this is about a child more or less kidnapped. That might shift them into doing something.'

'If you can set the investigator back to work, I'll see what we can do in Whitehaven.' Fergus was thinking of Sergeant Adams at the Indian King, who knew a thing or two about bare-knuckle fights.

After settling the investigator's account with Mr Trenchard's clerk and bidding the solicitor farewell, Fergus cancelled his second night at the Crown and Mitre and exchanged his ticket for a late-afternoon train back to Whitehaven. He would surprise Becky by arriving back a day earlier than she was expecting. There was nothing more he could do in Carlisle. He was, however, as confident as Mr Trenchard that knowing Loadman's fighting name would lead them to Rory.

It had been a frustrating day and he hoped he might catch up on some sleep, but he couldn't settle at the hotel. He started wondering what he would do when he caught up with Loadman. Handing him over to the police was not the answer, he was sure of that. Loadman would receive a prison sentence, only to be released with the potential to turn up in later years. He had to be dealt with, and in such a way that he would be kept away from Rory forever.

The next day, an idea came to him as the train pulled into Maryport, and for several miles after that he sported a self-satisfied grin as he pondered Loadman's fate. But then, the nearer the train got to Whitehaven, the more he thought about his debt, and how if the Macintosh & Warrilow contract didn't come through, he could be ruined.

CHAPTER THIRTY

It was impossible for Fergus to surprise Becky, since Charlie was the perfect guard dog. He yapped at strangers, but Fergus was always greeted with rapturous barking and copious tail-wagging.

Becky came out of the bedroom. 'You're back early.' She ran into Fergus's arms and, with her head nestled into his chest, said, 'I heard Charlie and thought it's his "welcoming Fergus home" bark, but you're supposed to be in Carlisle. I'm more than pleased to have you back.'

'I have much to tell you...'

Fergus related the information they'd received about Loadman's lodgings, their visit to the prison and Will Stead's information. He held back the lurid details of where the lodgings were, the description of Loadman as a 'wrong 'un' and his fighting name. Telling Becky their Rory had been taken by someone who went by the name of the Cumbrian Clouter was something she didn't need to know – it would provide her imagination with all sorts of scenarios involving Rory and the man's fists.

'We must go and see Ma and tell her.'

When they arrived at the Indian King, and while Becky was in full flow telling her mother all about what had been uncovered in Carlisle, Fergus made his way to Sergeant Adams. He checked Becky wasn't paying him any attention, then sat down with his back to the bar so no collier could read his lips.

'Sergeant Adams, I need you to find someone for me in the bare-knuckle fraternity. Our abductor is known as the Cumbrian Clouter, and if we find him, then I think we will find Rory. Can you help me?'

Sergeant Adams sucked on his clay pipe. 'Aye, I ken folks'll recognise that name. Why don't you go to the constable?'

'Because I have my own plans for when I find him.'

Sergeant Adams raised his eyebrows, and in a whisper said, 'I've folk can see to him for you. Duff him up good and proper.'

Fergus shook his head. 'Thank you, but no. My own plans don't involve violence, or anything that could land me in gaol.'

Sergeant Adams took hold of Fergus's sleeve. 'There's several big fights coming up. Your man'll be sniffing around them, I'm sure of that. He probably needs the betting brass, especially if he's the young'un to feed and clothe.'

'Where?'

'It changes each year, so the police don't get wind of it in time to bring in special forces. Carlisle, Kendal. Sometimes Carnforth, or as far south as Lancaster, Preston or Chorley.'

'When will you know?'

'A day – maybe two days before. I'll do what I can, I'm owed some favours.'

'Thank you, Sergeant,' Fergus said. 'Bear in mind, I don't want his nickname repeated in front of Becky or Dolly. Such a nickname will only cause them pain.'

He was relieved when he stood up to see Becky and Dolly, heads close together, still in avid conversation. He went into the kitchen and sat in the old armchair that had been Becky's father's favourite. To one side of the hearth was Rory's jacks bag. He loosened the drawstring and emptied the contents into his palm. Placing the jacks in his pocket, he passed the little round ball from palm to palm, until he misjudged the distance and it slipped from his fingers onto the fireside rug. He scooped it up and put it back in the bag with the metal jacks, before tightening the drawstring and putting it in his pocket.

* * *

'You're wearing your pearl.'

He's noticed. Becky couldn't remember having felt so carefree since before Rory was taken. 'We're celebrating.'

Fergus put his head to one side. 'Have I forgotten something?'

She knew he would ask what they were celebrating. 'No, it's that we haven't had anything to be happy about since Rory left, and now I feel the tide has turned; we can dare to hope Rory will be returned to us. I believe you when you say we're going to have him home again soon.' She did believe Fergus, and she was so happy he was home again himself.

He kissed her forehead then sought her lips. 'You're right, we shall be of good cheer tonight.'

Becky laughed, but despite her optimism about Rory, there was another cloud floating in her blue sky. She was being tormented more and more by intrusive thoughts on the same subject: she couldn't believe she wasn't expecting. It didn't help to see Mary so happy with her new son. She wasn't jealous. She didn't want Mary's baby – she wanted her own. That was one reason she hated Fergus going away, and why she'd been so pleased to see him return earlier than expected.

The next morning, after a night of closeness, Becky was cross with herself for having allowed the previous evening's floating cloud to disturb her thoughts. A bairn wasn't everything, and besides, they had years ahead of them for a family. It wasn't the first time she'd reprimanded herself in such a manner, but she hoped it would be the last.

CHAPTER THIRTY-ONE

Dicken waved an envelope. 'We've a letter from Glasgow.'

Fergus felt a rush of excitement. 'I'll take that. I need you to call on Bill – ask him to come here right away.'

'Why?'

'You'll know soon enough. Off you go. Tell him we've heard from Glasgow.'

For the next twenty minutes, Fergus sat with the letter lying on his desk. A host of positive and negative scenarios ran through his mind.

When Dicken returned with Bill, his partner's first words were, 'What do they say?'

'I don't know, I haven't opened it.'

Bill laughed. 'Aren't you renowned for being impulsive?'

'I thought you may like to open it. I don't think I can. Either way, this is the calm before the storm.' He held out a paper knife.

Bill slit the envelope and read the contents straight-faced. Then he grinned. 'They want a quotation.'

'Let me see...' Fergus read the letter then, laughing loudly, banged his fists up and down on his desk, as if making a drum roll.

'What's happening?' asked Dicken.

'We've received a request for a quotation,' said Fergus, 'and if terms are agreed, we're taking a steamship to Mauritius.'

'I'll be captaining the *SS Ketton,*' added Bill.

'We've a new ship. A steamship.'

'Mauritius? A new ship? I don't know anything about any of this!' Dicken was regarding them both as if he thought they were talking off the tops of their heads.

'There was no need for you to know until everything was finalised with the ship,' said Fergus. 'No time for dusting the counter now, Dicken. And I don't need to remind you this is confidential information which, should any word of it leak from your lips, will lead to instant dismissal. Do you understand? I will inform you when we want the world to know.'

Dicken's Adam's apple bobbed up and down. 'Yes, I understand. I won't say anything.'

'To anyone. Now we have work to do. Not least the *pro forma* we shall be working on today. I shall need you to work late – we must have this ready for the early post-boat tomorrow. I want our response to be at Macintosh & Warrilow's office first thing Monday morning.'

Bill cleared his throat. 'If you don't need me, I've papers to file with the harbour master.' He grimaced. 'I've also a wife to inform I may be leaving her with a new baby for six months.'

'She'll not take it in good spirit, we both know that, but it could be the making of the business. Stress the importance of that and the security it could bring for all our families.'

After Bill had left, Fergus asked Dicken to sit with him. 'We need to set out the quotation.'

'The usual?'

'Yes. Terms of Trade – part-payment up front, part-payment upon loading. Then the sixty-day payment of the balance upon presentation of acceptance goods-received notes.'

'It's a long way. What will we be bringing back? Sugar? Tea?'

'Assorted goods.' Fergus wasn't prepared to divulge all their plans to Dicken yet. 'Now, on to the actual specifics.'

They spent the next hour working on the collection, insurance and loading details.

'Don't forget to add "if accepted, this is deemed to be contractually binding and queries appertaining to this Order must be raised within 72 hours of receipt." Attach the usual Terms and Conditions.'

'When is the *Ketton* departing, if they accept?'

'July.' Fergus's thoughts turned to Rory. *Will we have him back by then?*

* * *

The following morning, Sunday, when Fergus opened the warehouse, he noted Dicken had left the office area neat and tidy. He had expected no less, even though he knew it would have entailed him staying until late into the evening. The *pro forma* had been laid out for signature. He read it through before signing the neat copy.

They had only received a request for a quotation. This wasn't the same as a firm order, where they could anticipate the first part-payment from Macintosh & Warrilow. He took down the accounts book and went through their income figures again. It was definite now that future outgoings were going to stretch things beyond the Louisa Line's funds. He had known all along he would have to make a capital input from his personal finances to pay for the steamship, and this would have to come from his dividend income and his salaries from the Louisa Line and Shackleton & Company. A few weeks ago he had been a rich man; now he was out on a limb financially. He picked up a 2lb brass weight he used as a paperweight and turned it over in his hands, considering his situation. Then he took up the quotation, put it in an envelope and made his way to the post-boat office. It was only eight o'clock; he was in plenty of time.

* * *

At noon on Monday Fergus was summoned to the Indian King; Sergeant Adams wanted to speak with him.

Rory. It's going to be about Rory.

There were no spare seats, but Sergeant Adams lifted Molly and put her on his lap to make room.

'You wanted me,' Fergus said. 'You've news?'

'Aye. I called in a few favours from my soldiering days and the big bare-knuckle bouts are going to be at Carnforth again this year.'

'When?'

'The day after tomorrow, Wednesday.'

'Are you sure?'

'Aye, I've a marra helping organise it and, as you'd expect, he's well tapped into it all.'

'Did your mate say anything about Loadman?'

'The Clouter's known, but not much liked. My marra sometimes puts brass down on him, 'cos he says the man's underhand and fights dirty and wins.'

When Fergus returned home at one, Becky reached out and touched his arm. 'Are you all right? You've gone a peculiar grey colour.'

'I've a headache. But it's nothing,' he lied.

'You look proper poorly. Has something happened?'

Fergus told her Sergeant Adams's news.

'With the Glasgow excitement and now this, I'm not surprised you've started with those bad heads again. That's the third in a week. You need some of Dr Fincham's tonic. A spoonful of that will see you right, and we can talk about what to do.'

'Didn't we decide the tonic was only to be taken in emergencies?'

'By the paleness of your skin and that pained expression you get in your eyes, I think you qualify for emergency treatment.'

When Fergus had taken Dr Fincham's tonic, slept for an hour, and eaten, he felt more himself and could think with greater clarity.

'You'll tell the police what you know?' asked Becky.

'I want to find Rory myself first. I'm going to Lancaster tomorrow and Carnforth for the fight.'

'You'll not go on your own, will you?'

'I plan to.'

'You must take someone with you. What about Bill?'

'He'll be halfway to Dublin with Sven on Wednesday.'

'Why don't you take Sven with you? He'll stand you in good stead if there's trouble. Does he have to go to Dublin?'

Fergus rubbed his hands together slowly. 'The second mate could take over for once, I suppose.' He checked his pocket watch. 'It's only half past two, I'll message him and Bill.'

An hour later, Sven was at Coates Lane and he and Fergus were making plans to leave for Lancaster the next day.

'I have a suggestion to make, Mr Shackleton, sir. You need to fit in. Going dressed as a gentleman you'll stand out. I can find suitable clothing if you'll wear it.'

'That's a good idea,' said Becky. 'You can travel as a gentleman.'

Fergus nodded. 'I'll leave the choice to you. We're about the same size. I have a smaller muscular build, but it won't matter, as better too large than too small.'

'The clothes will be clean, but not of the quality you're used to.'

'I'll be guided by you. I have never been to one of these bare-knuckle fights.'

'Neither have I, but I've heard others talk. I'll sound out some of the crew.'

CHAPTER THIRTY-TWO

The train to Lancaster, known to be faster than the coach, was not without its trials and tribulations – not least due to Fergus's fellow passengers and the smoke from the locomotive. An elderly gentleman fell asleep opposite them, arms crossed over his chest, and was soon snoring loudly. A mother and daughter, who had surrounded themselves with cloth bundles fastened with bulbous knots, gossiped in a spiteful way about their acquaintances and discussed the latest fashions. Despite the noise, Sven's eyelids drooped and his head fell forward. Fergus tried to read, but the jolting of the carriage and the incessant chatter, together with the clatter of the train and the snoring gentleman, made concentration impossible. After half an hour he took the example of the elderly gentleman and Sven, and closed his eyes.

Arriving in Lancaster and stepping onto the platform, they were swarmed by porters holding trolleys like ladders on wheels. The platform was crowded with a group of militia, each in full uniform, carrying rifles and sporting large rucksacks. Fergus's eye was caught by a woman carrying a large bonnet box alongside a liveried porter. Balanced on top of her travelling trunk was a ginger cat peering out of a wicker basket, the front of which was fastened by leather straps and silver buckles. The cat was meowing loudly and pitifully. No wonder, Fergus thought, all the hubbub going on.

The Wellington Arms in Common Garden Street, near the New Market, wouldn't have been Fergus's first choice of accommodation. Despite a handwritten sign saying 'Clean aired beds', the place reeked of stale ale and damp. It was no palace, but it was adequate. He'd booked two rooms for two nights and a table for supper that evening.

Although tired after their journey, Fergus suggested they acquaint themselves with their surroundings. It was late afternoon and the town's market stalls were packing up for the day. They strode up King Street until they reached Castle Hill and the castle precincts, where they stopped by a sign advertising 'Best Mild and India Ales'.

'The John of Gaunt. Let's go in here,' said Fergus. 'I'm still worried we won't be in the right place tomorrow.'

'I'll away to the dockside taverns after dusk,' Sven said. 'The dockers will be in by then. They'll know. Best I go alone. If I've got you with me, they'll likely think you're a policeman, and I'll get nowhere.'

* * *

Sven was right, the dockers did have all the details about the fight, and it was still to be held at Carnforth. Early the next afternoon they took a carriage most of the way, then joined a crowd of men progressing as one to the outskirts of the town.

'If it's so easy for us to find our way to an illegal bare-knuckle contest which appears to be an open secret, where are the police?' Fergus asked.

'How many men do you think are here with us?'

He looked around. 'Several hundred.'

'Aye, well, add to that the hundreds coming from other directions and you've a crowd the police don't have enough men to control.'

'So they stand by and watch from afar?'

'More or less. The fights may be illegal, but the bouts are properly umpired and overseen. I'm told the organisers have their own peace-keepers who will step in if needed.'

'Organisers?'

'The public house landlords, the wealthy merchants – even the fighters themselves. Sometimes, if they can get away with it, the landowners. They club together and put up the fighting prize money. And then the real brass is in the on-site betting.'

'You're knowledgeable for someone who's never been before.'

'Until last night I knew as much as you, but I'm pretty much an expert now. Cost me a few ales, but worth it – in particular a mariner who started talking about New Orleans and the Civil War. He and I compared our memories of the place and were firm friends by the end of the evening. Not least because it was my purse that was open.'

'I'll reimburse you for the ale.'

'No need, I'm glad to help get Rory back.' Sven paused. 'You're prepared for them not being at the fight, aren't you?'

Fergus nodded. 'I have thought about that. Where did you say the next one's going to be?'

'Crosby racecourse, according to my informants.'

'Liverpool. When?'

'No date as yet, but within the next month.'

'Even if he's not here, perhaps we can pick up some information.'

Keeping to the crowd's pace, Fergus could see why Sven had suggested he change his clothes. In his normal attire he would have stood out like a red rose amongst white lilies. As it was, he blended in, and even more so because Sven had insisted he blacken his hands and smear some dust in his eye creases.

'It'll make you more like a common mariner,' Sven had said.

The breeches, scratchy and tight, chafed his thighs, and the linen shirt sleeves were overlong. He'd rolled them up and stood to attention for Sven's inspection before they left the hotel.

'No braces?' Fergus had asked.

'You're a mariner, not a ploughman. You'll do. The dusk light'll be dim enough for you to pass amongst the crowd, and when it's dark, and the flares are lit, there'll be no speck of the "toff" about you. We'll move with the crowd as bystanders.'

Despite Sven's efforts to blend him visually into their setting, Fergus felt different. He was in the midst of a sea of flat-capped men spurred on by the thought of the entertainment to come. They were jostling with each other, calling out, clapping their neighbours on the back. They were jubilant, their voices overloud and their movements exaggerated. The scraps of conversation Fergus caught were centred on previous fights and who was going to win that evening. Names and places were bandied about: Longmire of Troutbeck, Jem Mace, Paddy O'Sullivan, Grasmere, Crosby. Yet despite listening hard, he heard no mention of the Cumbrian Clouter.

Men's sweat, fuelled by anticipation, excitement and, he thought, the illegality of it all, filled Fergus's nostrils. He was doing his best not to catch anyone's eye. The last thing he wanted was to have to speak and betray his educated background. When he was pushed up against his neighbours, he had to resist the impulse to apologise. These were men accustomed to moving in crowds, to bumping up against each other, to feeling elbows shoved into the small of their backs and other men's shoes finding their footings on their toes. He was rubbing shoulders with shepherds, innkeepers, coopers, colliers, mariners and all manner of working men of every age. The danger to him was not so much physical; it was more the danger of being seen as different or, as Sven had suggested, being thought a policeman.

After half an hour watching out for hard-baked divots that could trip a grown man and bring him to his knees, they arrived at a gathering in a field. A central arena had been roped off, and fighters were gathered to one side. It was then Fergus realised there was not going to be only one fight, but several.

An official took a sack and pulled out two wooden stakes, studied them, then called out the names. Two men wearing braces stepped forward from the fighters' group. They spoke to each other and shook hands, and then one left the ring.

'What's that about?' asked Sven.

A man standing next to them leaned forward and said, 'Sometimes they won't fight if it's obvious they're going to lose, but my guess is they're from the same county. Two Cumbrians most like. Men from the same county won't fight agin each other.'

Another wooden stake was withdrawn from the sack and a third man stepped forward. He was wearing white tights with drawers over them, making him look more like an acrobat to Fergus than a fighter.

This time there seemed to be no problem. The official rang a bell and, when silence fell, he said, 'This evening's prize fights have twelve pugilist participants – six lightweights and six heavyweights. The fights will consist of a series of knockout bouts, until one man is left standing in each category. The winners will collect prize money of £30 apiece.'

'That's over six months of a ship's master's pay,' said Sven.

The official carried on, 'The next bell, at six o'clock, will mark the commencement of the first bout.' He named the contestants and introduced the referee.

As well as men who were obviously taking bets, there were also young boys flitting in and out of the crowd, having to dodge elbows and overstuffed bellies. Each boy had a bag slung across his chest collecting money and some were giving out slips of paper. Fergus could see straight away that Rory couldn't move quickly enough to be one of those

'There must be a thousand people here,' Sven said. 'We'll never find Rory or Loadman in this crowd. He's not waiting to fight, either. We've come on a wild goose chase.'

'We're standing in the same space, Sven, seeing the same people. We'll have to split up.'

'I've a better idea. It came to me seeing these boys. Take hold of the next one that comes along.'

Several minutes passed before Fergus was able to catch hold of a young lad's arm. The boy struggled and Fergus, tightening his hold and leaning down, said, 'Do you want to make half a crown?'

The lad stopped his wriggling and paid attention.

'We're searching for a boy name of Rory Rooke. We think he's a bottle boy.'

The boy frowned and pulled on his arm. 'Ain't no Rory Rooke as I ken.'

Sven leaned down to his level. 'What about Rory Loadman?'

Fergus hadn't thought of that.

The boy scratched his head. 'You mean the cripple with the Clouter?'

'Yes, that's him,' said Fergus, feeling suddenly alive. 'There's half a crown if you bring him to me or take me to him.'

The boy thought for a moment then peered over his

shoulder. 'I'm on a stint,' he said. 'Best I can do is tek a gander after my boss's been in the ring.'

'When will that be?

'Depends on when his stake gets pulled out o' the sack.'

'Which one is he?' asked Sven, squinting across at the fighters.

The boy pointed. 'That one in the striped drawers.'

'The red stripes?'

'Aye. Any road, I won't be able to bring the lad to you, but I can likely tek you to 'im. Half a crown, you say?'

'Aye, but you can't tell a soul.'

'Is he in trouble?'

'No.'

'You sure? This is all reet queer.'

'Sure as swearing on my nan's grave,' said Sven.

The boy ran off.

'We can only keep our eyes peeled and wait,' said Fergus.

'You think the boy'll come back?'

'For half a crown? Of course he will. It's a fortune for him.'

* * *

The ringing of the bell and an excited roar from the crowd brought Fergus and Sven's attention back to the ring. The two fighters were circling each other. After a short engagement, although they were both lightweights, it was soon apparent one was fleshier than his opponent, whilst the other was nimbler on his feet. Several blows were struck before the men stepped back from each other and the fight's pace relaxed. A few in the crowd opened up a slow handclap that was quickly taken up by others.

The nimbler one then shot a fist forward, catching his opponent on his right cheek and knocking his head back. His opponent retaliated with an upward punch but, due to a slight stumble on his part, the blow landed with the reduced force of a slap. This gave the other man the opportunity to lash out a debilitating blow. The recipient fell to the ground, nursing what could only have been a broken nose. The referee stepped forward and ended the fight, to a roar of disappointment from the crowd.

The official took the winner's wooden stake and put it in a two-handled basket, while the loser picked up his own stake and left the arena.

Words of discontent filled Fergus's ears. 'That was nae worth comin' doon the way,' and 'O'er too quick,' and 'Ill-matched.' While bets were being settled between neighbours and friends, and winners congratulated, Fergus was suddenly transfixed. Across from him and slightly to the left was a young boy. He glanced away, then back at the lad, and in a quiet, controlled voice, said to Sven, 'Don't react quickly, but is that Rory across from us, by the man in the bowler hat?'

Sven narrowed his eyes and peered. 'No, see how he's walking. There's no limp. It's a trick of the light, and understandable in this crowd.'

The bell rang for the next two competitors. This time they were heavyweights and one of them was wearing the red-striped drawers. Each came forward with a young lad holding cloths and a ginger beer bottle – the kind that had a marble for a stopper. Fergus remembered what Sergeant Adams had said about Loadman probably wanting Rory to be his bottle boy. This fight held greater interest for both Sven and Fergus, as one of the boys was the one they'd given the task of finding Rory.

Throughout the ten rounds, Fergus tried to imagine what it was like for a young boy to have to stand on the sidelines, so close, watching two men beat each other. The smell of the blood and sweat must be overpowering. Then the cloths – having to hold bloodied rags. It was no place for anyone, and for their Rory, it was unthinkable.

It was then Fergus gave serious thought to how the past three weeks might have changed his ward – the cheery lad with the toy soldiers, who liked to paint ships on slates and who loved his dog more than anything in the world; a boy who read *Aesop's Fables* and who had rarely been spoken to roughly. What were they going to learn when – if – the lad led them to Rory? Besides physical hardship, the least Fergus anticipated was a loss of innocence along with unwanted experiences.

By the eleventh round, the boy's fighter was all over his opponent, so it was no surprise when the fight came to an end halfway through the twelfth. Fergus checked his watch. It had taken less than half an hour.

CHAPTER THIRTY-THREE

While Fergus and Sven were still making their way to Carnforth, Becky was at Coates Lane, setting the table and warming the kettle on the range. It wouldn't take a minute to bring it up to boiling. She'd sent a note to Elizabeth inviting her and Hector for afternoon tea. When they arrived five minutes after the hour, Becky remembered Elizabeth telling her, "Always give your hostess five minutes' grace, dear" She was living up to her instruction.

'My dear, this little house is charming,' said Elizabeth, holding out a small package for Becky, along with her wrap.

After they were seated in the little parlour, the Shackletons' first topic was Rory and the new developments, and Elizabeth said, 'He's such a lovely boy. So amusing. Before we left for Carlisle, he said to me one day, "Since oranges are called oranges, why aren't lemons called yellows?"' To Becky's astonishment, tears welled up in Elizabeth's eyes. 'Excuse me,' she went on. 'I'm a little overwhelmed by it all. It's been such a shock since we came back to the news.'

'For all of us,' said Becky. 'We still can't believe it.'

Hector, also sporting a sad face, said, 'Why don't you open your parcel, Becky?'

'It's a little something I bought in Maryport the other day,' Elizabeth explained, sounding more her normal, stoical self.

Becky took off the wrapper to find a baby's shawl beautifully knitted with a seashell pattern in each corner. 'It's lovely, and so soft,' she said, running her fingers over it.

'I'm sure you will require one soon,' said Elizabeth. 'The woman who made it crotchets all manner of things. Matinée jackets and the sweetest little nightgowns. It was hard to make a choice.'

Hector laughed. 'So difficult that my dear wife bought enough for triplets.'

'Hush, Hector, you'll spoil my future surprises.'

Elizabeth was looking at Becky intently. Had she been expecting, this would have been the moment to share the news. Since she wasn't, she took the kettle from the range and invited her in-laws to sample her ginger almond biscuits.

'My mama made very good gingers,' said Hector, adding another to the two already on his plate.

'How do mine fare?' asked Becky, thinking he must like them or he wouldn't have helped himself to another. She moved the plate of buttered tea bread closer to him.

'Excellent, excellent.'

Becky felt herself colour up at the unexpected praise.

'You've heard about the steamship?' Hector asked.

Elizabeth stirred her tea. 'We took a steamer from Rye

to Boulogne. It was quite an experience. Hector didn't want to board and I had to practically push him on, but after a short while he found it most congenial. Didn't you, dear?'

Hector nodded. 'I must say my boy's got his sights on expansion. I hope he can keep all his irons hot in the fire. I don't know how he's funding it. He's probably mortgaged up to the hilt.'

Without realising it, Hector had planted a seed in Becky's mind. *How exactly is he funding it? He wouldn't do anything to put our home at risk, would he?*

After they'd gone and Becky was clearing the crockery away, she wondered if Fergus and Sven had found Rory and, if so, whether he were in good health. She knelt down and, looking right in Charlie's eyes, said, 'Rory might be coming home.'

The dog's ears pricked up when she said Rory's name; he raised his head and looked towards the door. Seeing there was no one there, he settled down in his basket again.

'I understand, Charlie, I really do. We all miss him dreadfully.'

* * *

In Carnforth, after another two bouts had taken place with no sign of the boy they'd charged with finding Rory, Fergus was seriously beginning to think either Rory wasn't at the fight, or their boy didn't need half a crown. It was gone eight o'clock already. The sky had that end-of-day, pre-dusk greyness to it. Women were coming round selling ale and hot pies, while others traded only in hard liquors, like gin and whiskey. They were teased by some of the men, but they'd obviously heard it all before and were ready with quick ripostes, jaunty grins and sharp elbows.

At nine o'clock, Fergus felt a sharp tug to his sleeve. 'Mister, that lad you want? I've found him.'

Fergus wanted to cheer and lift the boy up in the air, but he knew he must maintain a calm presence.

'Can you take him to us?' Sven said.

'You'll pay me, won't you, mister?'

Fergus took a shilling from his pocket. 'The rest when you find us Rory.'

'Is he alone?' asked Sven.

The boy shook his head. 'He's with his da. The Clouter.'

Fergus heard Sven curse softly in Norwegian.

'What are they doing?' he asked.

'The Clouter's with their horse, yon side of paddock.' He pointed to the north-side of the arena. 'He's probably counting his brass.'

'And Rory?'

'He's seeing to the horse.'

'Is there any chance you can ask Rory to go with you to do something? To separate them?'

The boy frowned. 'You sure this ain't trouble?'

'Sure, I'm sure,' said Sven.

'And it's an extra shilling if you can bring him to us.'

Fergus could see the extra shilling was tempting, but the boy was nervous, and probably rightly so.

'You're not doing anything wrong,' Fergus said. 'I swear to you.' He took the money out of his pocket so the boy could see it. 'Take us close enough to see Rory, but not so near he can see us. How's that?'

The boy set off and, as they pushed their way through the crowd, it seemed he was giving thought to Fergus's suggestion, as he said, 'There is something I could show him. We've got a rabbit. I don't have to tell him it's a dead one, do I?'

'No, you don't,' said Fergus, thinking the boy was a genius. All boys like rabbits.

They reached the periphery of the crowd and the boy stopped. 'Over there, there's some horses. See the last one on the right?'

It wasn't yet dark, and Fergus and Sven could make out a boy attending to a horse and a man sitting next to him on the ground. It was difficult to see if it really was Rory and Loadman.

Is the boy pulling a fast one? The boy appeared to guess Fergus's thoughts. 'I'll call and, when we come back, you'll see by the way he walks that it's Rory.'

'You're a good lad.'

Sven put a hand on Fergus's shoulder to draw him to one side. 'We must exercise caution. We don't want this lad getting into trouble.'

'I'll not go near enough so the Clouter can see me properly,' the boy said. 'What are you going to do with Rory?'

'We're going to take him home where he'll be safe,' said Fergus.

The boy thought for a moment then nodded, before saying, with unexpected maturity, 'That's a proper thing.

He don't belong here, and that Clouter can be as free with his fists outside the ring as inside. For me, I'm going to be a pugilist, a famous one. Da's getting me lessons in Islington.'

With that, he ran off towards the horses. As he neared, he shouted, 'Hey, you, come over here. I've a rabbit for you to play with.'

The boy, a few feet away from the horse, spoke to the man who nodded. As soon as he set one foot in front of the other, Fergus could see it was Rory. It was all he could do not to rush forward, grab him and run, but he held himself back. As Rory emerged from the gloom, had it not been for his leg and the way he moved, Fergus wouldn't have recognised him.

'Oh, my God, Fergus. Poor Rory,' said Sven.

Fergus couldn't reply. He was struck dumb watching the boy he knew so well, but who was now a stranger, coming towards them.

'It's him, but Loadman's shaved his head,' said Sven. 'And he's lost weight.'

As Rory drew nearer, Fergus saw recognition dawn. He quickly put his finger over his lips, while Sven said, 'Don't run, Rory. Keep moving at a steady pace. Follow this young lad, and don't turn back. We'll be right behind you. We're here to bring you home.'

When they were in the thick of the crowd again, Fergus thanked the boy and gave him his money. As he shot off into the crowd, Rory called out, 'Hey, you were going to show me your rabbit.'

Fergus placed his hand on Rory's back to propel him

forwards. 'When we're back in Whitehaven you can have a pet rabbit all for yourself. That's a promise.'

Despite being told not to, Rory glanced behind. 'And my da? Is he coming too?'

'Do you want to stay with him?'

'No. No, I don't. He's not a nice man.' Rory, his eyes flickering, stood with hunched shoulders. 'Is that policeman with you? He said I had to go with my da.'

Fergus was about to tell Rory about Loadman being his uncle, then thought better of it. Instead, he took his jacks bag from his pocket. 'There's no policeman. Here you are – I brought these for you.'

Rory took the bag. 'I've missed them.'

'You remember Sven, don't you?'

'Aye, from the ships. He's my first mate.'

'He's going to take you home to Whitehaven.'

Rory, so small in the crowd of grown men, nodded. He kept turning his head as if disorientated, and as he did so, Fergus saw three large boils standing proud on the back of his neck. There was a damp earthy smell emanating from him, and Fergus wondered how long it had been since he'd been able to wash.

To Sven, Fergus said, 'Away with you. Take the boy and go straight to the hotel.' He handed Sven a small pouch. 'There's enough here for a carriage. Feed him and, if need be, enlist one of the maids to help you bathe him, and sit with him while he sleeps. See if you can get her to come up with new clean clothes for him. I'll be with you as soon as I can.'

'You're not coming with us?'

Fergus shook his head. ‘I’ve business to attend to.’

‘Mr Shackleton, the man’s a prize fighter. It’s best we both leave.’

Fergus shook his head. ‘He’ll not kill me with a thousand witnesses on hand. I’ll watch and wait. I have a plan.’

‘You’ll inform the police?’

‘There are a dozen or so police here. I may be mistaken, but I think the last thing they want is to be told a missing boy has been found in their midst, and would they please arrest the kidnapper, who happens to earn his living as a bare-knuckle fighter.’

‘You’re probably right,’ said Sven.

CHAPTER THIRTY-FOUR

Twenty minutes passed before Fergus saw Loadman express any irritation. Fergus studied him as he moved his head from side to side, scanning the crowd. He was exactly as people had described him – a malevolent bare-knuckle fighter – and Fergus understood immediately how he'd managed to intimidate Becky and Dolly. But Fergus had the advantage, because Loadman did not know him.

When Loadman moved, Fergus followed. He was in no hurry to alert the man to the fact that Rory had been whisked away, but it was when Loadman started asking people if they'd seen Rory that he knew he must act. If a general hue and cry was set up, it would make things most awkward. Ignoring the voice in his head that said he could still get away without challenging Loadman, Fergus stepped out, barring his way.

'You'll be searching for Rory?' he asked.

Loadman blinked, then, staring hard at Fergus, said, 'What the devil is it to you? Where is he?'

'I can tell you he's safe and in good hands.'

Loadman scowled. 'Who are you?'

'Let's say I'm an interested party from Whitehaven.'

Loadman scratched his head and checked Fergus up and down. 'You're that Shackleton toff, aren't you? You're the shipper he talked about. I can tell you, you'll not get far with him. Kidnapping a lad from his da. Where've you got him?'

Fergus leaned forward, conscious a few people close by were beginning to take an interest in their conversation. 'We both know that isn't true, don't we?'

Loadman's head shot up. 'What's that you're saying?'

'I'm saying you're not his father – you're his uncle, and you took him under false pretences.'

'Rubbish,' said Loadman, beginning to sidle towards the edge of the crowd.

Fergus wondered if he was going to make a run for it, but thought it unlikely he'd leave his horse behind, since it was probably all he possessed.

'It was your bad luck that Mr Trenchard was at the races in Whitehaven. The name Loadman was mentioned in relation to Rory and the whole story discovered.'

Loadman stuck his chin out, trying to out-stare him. 'His da, his uncle – so what? It's all a question of blood.'

'That may have been the case when you first arrived, but you lied to the head constable, so actually it's all a question of abduction of a minor, assuming a false identity, and using false documentation. What do you think? Five years? Eight?'

Loadman swore and spat on the ground.

'You're in a difficult position,' Fergus said, 'but I can make it easier for you.'

Loadman let out a further string of oaths, then said, 'I want that lad back.'

'But you don't really, do you? You thought you could make money from him, either by working him on the fighting circuit, or by extracting money from us. I'll wager you've been thinking of returning him, but he's a good-natured boy, doesn't complain. He'll do as he's asked, because he thinks you're his father.'

'I'll admit the lad's got a good head on his shoulders for a cripple.'

Fergus wondered why having an accident to a leg should affect anyone's intelligence, but Loadman wasn't the man to discuss this with, and it was neither the time nor the place.

'The devil of it is you can't keep him now,' he said, 'even if you really do want him. You're a wanted man. What you need is to disappear. Which is it to be? Carlisle Gaol or Melbourne? Lancaster Gaol or Auckland?'

Fergus paused as Loadman, jaw clenched, chest thrust out, continued his attempt to stare him out.

'You're a wanted man and it's your good luck I found you before the police did.'

'I don't have the brass to take off.'

'I can help you with that. You disappear, and I'll wait until I return to Whitehaven to inform the police I've found Rory. You can be in Liverpool by tomorrow evening.'

'What do you mean, help me?'

'I'll give you fifty pounds to leave the country.'

Loadman tried to smother a smirk. 'The lad means that much to you?'

Fergus said nothing. He'd thought buying the man off would be straightforward, but it wasn't turning out that way. He was as slippery as a freshly caught eel in an aged fisherman's hands.

'A hundred,' Loadman said.

'Sixty,' said Fergus. 'That's eighteen months standard pay for a captain on one of my ships.'

'Guineas?' Loadman was now smiling openly and broadly.

'Don't push your luck. I've made my offer. Take it, or leave it.'

'How will you know I'll not take the money and run off to London with it?'

'Because I'll pass over the money at the dockside in Liverpool tomorrow. And if I were you, I'd rather be free in the colonies, enjoying a good living, than spending the rest of my life wary of being arrested at any moment, always having to wear a scarf to cover my tattoo. Prisoners don't take to men who've treated a child badly – I'm sure you know that. You'd not get an easy ride in gaol, because you'd be at the bottom of the ranks. I don't need to remind you your brother died in Carlisle Gaol. Not all those that go in come out.'

Fergus knew he'd offered the man a lucky second start in life, and most people would think he should turn him in, to be dealt with by the courts. But he couldn't stand the thought of him being anywhere near Rory as he was growing up, especially as he could be released in five years. Rory would then be sixteen, which was an impressionable age.

'I'll be outside the gates to the Prince's Dock in Liverpool the day after tomorrow, Friday, at noon, with the payment.'

'How will I get there?'

'You've got a horse you're not going to be needing, haven't you? I'm sure you'll find a cash buyer somewhere in the crowd. Then you'll have enough to travel in style and time to put some luggage together. Until Friday, then.'

Fergus pushed his way through the crowd towards one of the waiting carriages. He wondered if he'd been successful. There remained a sadness about him. It wasn't like him to behave in such an underhand, threatening manner and he wasn't proud of himself.

At the hotel in Lancaster, Fergus found Rory fed, bathed and asleep, with Sven sitting beside him. New clothes were laid out on a chair. In sleep he was peaceful.

'How is he?' asked Fergus.

'He's been quiet. Seems stunned.'

'It will be the shock.'

'There's something I need to tell you,' Sven said.

'What's that?'

'He has bruising to his arms. Also, those boils are nasty. They need seeing to as soon as he gets home.'

Fergus was horrified. 'You mean he's been beaten?'

'No, I don't think so. I'm no expert, but I'd say the bruises are from being grasped too tightly on the upper arms.'

'Did you ask him about them?'

'No. I thought it best not to draw attention to them.'

'We must get him safely back to Whitehaven. You can escort him and I'll follow on.'

'What about Loadman? Did you speak with him?'

'Yes.'

'What did he say?'

'I confronted him and then he disappeared.' *There, I've told the first white lie.*

'He got away? Will he cause trouble?'

'I doubt it, not now. He knows he's a wanted man, that his deceit has been uncovered, and that the police are looking for him. I would come with you and Rory, but I have business in Liverpool tomorrow.'

Sven cast him a sideways glance 'Business?'

'Yes, which is why I'm asking you to escort Rory back to the Indian King. Dolly and Becky will take care of him and he'll be reunited with Charlie. Then when he's more settled, we can explain about his father.'

'And if he asks on the way back?'

'You can say it's still being sorted out and that he's safe. Something like that. Dolly and Becky can say the same. I expect to be back in Whitehaven late the day after tomorrow.'

Sven was no fool and he had intelligence enough to realise further questioning wasn't going to reveal anything he wasn't supposed to know, and that he might learn information he didn't want to be a party to. As far as Fergus was concerned, all anyone would learn was that Rory had been found and the man posing as his father had run off. He would say the same to the head constable since, whatever happened on Friday, he wouldn't be telling a lie. Technically he was aiding and abetting a criminal to escape capture, but he was certain he could get away with it. He was honest enough to admit to himself he would be lying if he said he was acting solely for Rory's sake – he was acting for his own and Becky's, too.

The next day, Rory had to be woken from a deep sleep at eight o'clock. He remained subdued but was able to manage a small portion of sausage and dumplings for breakfast. His former appetite seemed to have deserted him. Fergus went ahead to the station and bought tickets for the ten o'clock train. He was anxious Loadman might guess they'd stayed in Lancaster and be looking for them. His less emotional inner voice told him Rory's uncle, knowing the game was up and he was a wanted man, wouldn't attempt to take his nephew a second time, but he wasn't taking any chances.

The idea came to him that as a precaution they should ask one of the serving girls at the hotel to escort Rory to the station, while he and Sven followed separately a short distance behind. Although there was no disguising Rory's distinctive gait, in new clothes and with a cap on his head hiding his shorn locks, he wouldn't be instantly recognisable.

Although the way from the hotel to the station was only short, it was a nerve-wracking one for Fergus, and he was relieved when the train pulled out with Sven and Rory aboard. He paid the serving girl and sent her on her way.

CHAPTER THIRTY-FIVE

Becky was in the kitchen at the Indian King pulling glass cloths down from the drying rack attached to the ceiling. She checked Charlie was settled, then took the cloths through to the bar. Dolly was negotiating with a man who'd brought in some rabbits that he'd thrown on the counter. Becky shied away; she hated it when the rabbit man called.

The door opened and Jeremiah Todhunter entered.

'I'm sorry to bother you,' he told Becky. 'I was hoping to find Fergus. I called at Coates Lane first, but no one was there.'

'He's away. Is it urgent?' Becky thought it must be important for him to have taken the trouble to seek Fergus out in the Indian King.

Mr Todhunter took out a letter from his pocket. 'It's news he needs to be aware of. When is he back?'

'I'm not sure. Perhaps tomorrow. Is it about the *Ketton*? Has she failed her inspection?'

'She's passed A1, but it is about her. Can I leave this for him?'

'Yes. Is it bad news?'

'I don't know. It might be.' *He's not going to tell me and that's probably because he thinks I have nothing to do with the business.*

She took the letter. 'I'll see he gets it the minute he's back.'

Becky felt flat for the rest of the day. Charlie seemed to sense her mood, since he didn't pester her for a walk, as he usually did. He was content to lie in his home-from-home basket by the Indian King's range. That was until early evening, when he heard Sven's voice. His ears pricked up, then he stood up, started whining, ran to the door and set his paws to scrabble at it for Becky to open.

Then Becky heard her mother say, 'Come here, poor lad. We've missed you so much.'

Becky leapt up and opened the kitchen door. All the flatness of the day flew away when she saw Rory standing next to Sven. Charlie followed her, barking and running amok, his tail whisking back and forth. Rory broke free from Dolly's grasp and bent down to pick up his dog. Tears of happiness dropped onto his cheeks.

'Charlie, it's me, Rory. Have you been a good lad while I've been gone?'

'Oh, yes, he has,' said Becky. 'An exceedingly good lad. Although he's missed you terribly. As we all have.'

Charlie licked Rory's cheeks, gathering up the tears, his tail waving about erratically.

'Can you put him down so I can hug you, too?' asked Becky. Although she was smiling and laughing, she was crying inside. Their Rory was a shadow of his former self.

Apart from the short hair, he'd lost so much weight in the three weeks he'd had been away, he now had sharp cheekbones. The bright eyes she remembered seemed cloudy, and although he was excited at seeing Charlie, his smile was faded. She later described him to Mary as 'washed out'.

'What happened?' she asked Sven. 'Where's Fergus?'

'I think Rory would like a biscuit or two,' Sven said. 'We've had a long journey.' Dolly took the hint and asked one of the barmen to take Rory into the kitchen and find him a biscuit and a glass of milk. When he turned away, she flinched on seeing his boils had broken out again.

While Rory was out of the way, Sven briefly outlined what had happened.

'Fergus never said anything about business in Liverpool,' said Becky.

'He'll be back on Saturday,' said Sven.

While Dolly went to check on Rory with the barman, there being a lull in the conversation, Sergeant Adams took the opportunity to speak out.

'S'cuse me for interrupting. We're all happy – the lad's safe and Mr Shackleton accounted for – so can an old soldier get his refill?'

Becky leapt up. 'I'm so sorry, Sergeant Adams. What with all the excitement and commotion…'

'Don't worry, lass. It's a joy to me to have witnessed this happy scene.'

Satisfied all was well with Sergeant Adams, and that Fergus had come to no harm, Becky went into the kitchen.

'Rory, shall we stay here tonight, or would you like to come with me to Coates Lane?'

Rory, head on one side, considered her suggestion, then said, 'I'd like to stay here, if you can stay here, too. And Charlie.'

Later, when Rory was asleep, after Charlie had been given special permission to settle down next to him, Becky stood at the end of his bed. He was so much smaller than she remembered. She welled up and thought she might have stayed there sobbing with relief all evening, if Dolly hadn't sought her out and taken her downstairs for some supper.

Becky and Dolly discussed Rory late into the night.

'He's got a haunted look about him, and those bruises upset me,' said Dolly.

'Aye, but we'll see him to rights. Ourselves, Charlie and the rabbit.'

'The rabbit?'

'He told me Fergus promised him a pet rabbit.'

'That's a surprise.'

'There's no reason he would lie.'

'Where'll it go? Charlie'll make a meal of it in no time.'

'I've no idea. We'll have to find somewhere. A promise is a promise.'

As Dolly was putting away the last dishes in readiness for the morning, she said, 'It's convenient Fergus is able to fit in some business in Liverpool. That's worked out for the good.'

'Aye,' said Becky. 'He likes to know what's going on there. He sometimes reads the Liverpool papers. I wonder what's happened about the *Ketton* for Mr Todhunter to want to see Fergus so urgently.'

'What about the letter he gave you? You could steam it open.'

'I could, but I won't.'

* * *

There was an impatient queue in the Liverpool bank on Dale Street on Thursday afternoon. After presenting the banker's draft he'd carried with him from Whitehaven, on the chance they'd find Loadman and his plan would succeed, Fergus was escorted to a small anteroom, by a clerk before being attended to by the manager.

'Mr Shackleton, this is most irregular. May I enquire what the funds are for?'

'You may ask,' he replied, wrinkling his nose at the man. It wasn't the bank's business to ask how he spent his money.

'And?'

'I have business to attend to,' said Fergus.

'What business may that be?'

'I am a well-known shipper in Whitehaven and I have shipping business to attend to.'

The manager kept checking the draft.

'Is something amiss?' Fergus was beginning to feel uncomfortable. Were he unable to withdraw the necessary funds, all would be lost, and Loadman was the sort of man to hold a grudge.

'There's nothing wrong with the draft itself. It's with yourself.'

'Me? What are you talking about? I'm Fergus Shackleton.'

'So you insist, but we don't know you are who you say you are.'

'This is ridiculous. You can match my signature with the original on the draft. That will provide sufficient proof, surely?'

'In circumstances such as this, we require further identification. Do you have any papers? Perhaps the letter heading of your shipping company, or something similar?'

Fergus shook his head. He had nothing of that kind. Then he thought of his pocket watch. 'I can show you my watch. It has my name engraved on it.' He made to take it out, but the manager stopped him.

'I'm afraid that will not suffice, either. You could have stolen the watch along with the draft.'

Fergus tried to control his frustration, and the growing anxiety that he was not going to be able to withdraw the necessary funds. There wasn't enough time to return to Whitehaven for money and come back.

'Do I look like a thief?' he asked.

'That's not for me to say.' The manager made as if to hand back the draft.

'There must be some way we can conclude this satisfactorily,' Fergus said, through clenched teeth.

'Only by independent verification.'

'By that you mean only by someone identifying me?'

'Yes. That would suffice.'

'I'm in Liverpool. I have no idea if there is anyone from Whitehaven here who knows me.'

'That is awkward,' said the manager, pushing the draft across the desk.

Fergus pushed it back. 'Can you not understand that my business is in Whitehaven?'

The manager steepled his fingers and looked over them.

'It's unfortunate you do not have an office here. Don't you have an agent who could vouch for you?'

'We have one, but he has never met me. We correspond by letter. However, there is another Whitehaven company.'

'Which is that?'

'Brocklebank's. They have offices here, and if I'm in luck there may well be someone who can vouch for me. We can send a messenger with a note. I would go myself, but I'm a stranger here. A boy will be quicker.'

The manager stood. 'I can send one of our boys, but it will have to be at your expense.'

'I understand. Now find me paper and a pen.'

* * *

It was over half an hour before the boy returned with a message to say Mr Probert of Brocklebank's offices would be arriving within the quarter.

Fergus's heart sank. He didn't know a Mr Probert from Brocklebank's or anywhere else. He could only hope Mr Probert knew *him* and was not just coming out of curiosity.

After the boy had withdrawn, Fergus could not contain himself and began pacing the room. He was alone. The manager and the draft had disappeared. A familiar throb in his left temple announced the start of a headache and he had no linctus. He looked out of the window onto the busy street and watched the people going about their daily business. None of them could be as desperate as he was feeling. At that moment he thought he was probably the most anxious person in the city.

Hearing voices, he turned around. The door opened and a man he didn't know entered with the manager. He approached Fergus with an outstretched hand.

'Mr Shackleton, you don't know me, but I recognise you.'

Fergus shook the man's hand, then put his hand to his head. His headache was taking hold. 'That is excellent news for my ears today, sir. How do you know me?'

'Last year you gave a lecture at the Seamen's Haven and I attended.'

Fergus was grinning stupidly, but he didn't care. 'I only gave one lecture there and that was on *David Copperfield*. My aunt asked me to speak because the warden was called away.'

'An excellent lecture it was, too.' Mr Probert turned to the manager. 'I can vouch that this is indeed Mr Fergus Shackleton of Shackleton & Company Shipping in Whitehaven.'

'And the Louisa Line,' added Fergus. For one dreadful moment, he thought the clerk was going to ask Mr Probert to prove who *he* was, but it seemed that was not necessary; he only needed Mr Probert to sign a form vouching for Fergus's identity.

After the formalities of identification had been seen to, Fergus asked Mr Probert if he would like to join him for an ale later.

'I'm afraid I can't today. We're very busy, with three ships coming in and the harbour master's papers to complete, but I thank you.'

'Then when you're next in Whitehaven, you will call at the offices?'

'I will be delighted.'

As soon as Mr Probert had left, the manager began spouting apologies and gabbling about keeping to rules. Fergus made no comment. He could not trust himself to be civil.

'We offer a financial advice opportunity should you be withdrawing to make a deposit elsewhere,' the manager droned on. 'I'm sure the bank can match any other bonds or investments you're thinking of making.'

'Thank you, but I'm withdrawing to pay for a service.'

The manager began counting out the notes. 'Shall you be comfortable carrying this amount of cash, Mr Shackleton?'

Fergus sighed. All he wanted was to withdraw his money and find a bed for the night.

'I have a pouch about my person where I can secrete it.'

'We brought you in here so that the withdrawal would not be done in the public eye.'

'You brought me in here so you could interrogate me.'

'I can only apologise again –' the manager spluttered.

Fergus cut him off. 'Enough. I shall be on my way.'

Although he found comfortable lodgings and enjoyed an interesting and informative early evening stroll along some of the docks, followed by a pleasant dinner of hot shoulder of mutton and locally brewed ale, Fergus couldn't relax enough to sleep. He'd brought *Wuthering Heights* to read, as recommended by Becky, but the cold moorland setting only served to feed his general unease. His thoughts kept drifting to whether Loadman would keep their appointment. He would give him until two o'clock.

No one need ever hear a whisper about their arrangement. Sven might speculate, but he would never know for sure that Fergus hadn't set up a *bona fide* business meeting before leaving Whitehaven. If Loadman kept the appointment and boarded a ship, he would disappear, leaving only his name on a ship's manifest. If he failed to appear it would be a hard pill to swallow, but so be it; Fergus was mentally prepared for that eventuality.

CHAPTER THIRTY-SIX

The day dawned fair, and Fergus was in position at the Prince's Dock as a nearby clock struck a quarter to twelve. He felt for the leather pouch inside his shirt. It was a nervous action, betraying his anxiety. He knew it was still there because he could feel the pouch's buckle resting against his side.

The dock was awash with mariners and emigrants – the seamen appearing completely at home, the emigrants being herded, wide-eyed, towards their ships. For a while he watched sailors playing cards on the top of a barrel. To their left, a man was cutting hair, and a small queue of long-haired sailors had formed.

The clock struck noon, and Fergus's anxiety intensified. When the first quarter struck, and the barber was on his fifth customer, he began to wonder if Loadman was watching him from afar, enjoying his anxiety. He wouldn't put it past him to spy on him and then sneak away.

The men playing cards were becoming livelier. An argument attracted Fergus's attention. Then he heard Loadman's voice.

'I wager you thought I wouldn't come.'

Fergus turned to find Loadman behind him. He was dressed smartly, had shaved off his moustache, and was carrying a new suitcase and a worn leather bag.

'I never doubted it,' Fergus said. 'Shall we attend to the business?'

'I've had time to think,' said Loadman. 'I'm leaving my friends and my possessions.'

Fergus wanted to laugh, remembering the landlady in Carlisle who'd told them she'd sold his possessions in lieu of rent.

'And I had to sell my horse to get here, and buy this case and the new clothes.'

'I'm thinking you're getting away lightly.'

Fergus had expected this and had told himself Loadman was not getting a penny more. The man would do his best to ruffle his feathers, of that he was certain, but he wouldn't lose his temper or show any emotion. He waited.

'I think it only right you pay a little extra for depriving me of my friends,' Loadman insisted.

Here was a man who had plucked a child from a happy existence for his own benefit, now claiming *he* would be deprived of friendship. Despite his promise to himself, Fergus had to fight for self-control.

'That is a burden you will have to bear,' he said. 'I'm sure you'll make new friends wherever you go.'

'I'm thinking another fifty pounds.'

'No,' said Fergus.

Loadman brought his face closer. 'Come on, you can afford it.'

'No.'

'What about making it guineas?'

Again, Fergus said, 'No.'

'Then I'll stay.'

'All right, your choice.' Fergus turned and began walking away, counting his steps in his head. *One, two, three, four, five, six...*

He'll let me do twenty, then he'll call me back.

Seven, eight, nine, ten, eleven...

He was itching to turn round, but he knew it was the last thing he should do. The voice in his head said, 'Go on, quicken your pace.' He widened his step.

Twelve, thirteen, fourteen, fifteen, sixteen, seventeen –.

He heard steps behind him and Loadman calling out, 'Stop!'

Always one to take a gamble, and since he'd given Loadman twenty, Fergus carried on.

Eighteen, nineteen, twenty.

'Stop, damn you!'

Fergus paused mid-stride.

'All right, I'll go,' Loadman said.

Fergus turned. He felt lucky enough to try another wager. 'Right, then we go to the shipping office and buy your ticket.'

'What about the money?'

'You get the money at the top of the gangway. I stay on the quay and watch the ship depart.'

'What?'

Fergus repeated the terms and pointed to a shipper's office. 'There. We can buy you a ticket and you can be gone on the next boat out.'

'Where to?'

'I'm feeling generous. You can choose.'

By half past one, Fergus had purchased a ticket for Melbourne and they were in a waiting room which was little more than a holding-area shed. Fergus had paid with his own money, because he didn't want Loadman to locate his money-pouch. The ticket-seller had shown no surprise that someone would saunter in and buy a ticket with immediate departure for such a faraway place. Fergus guessed it happened all the time, with people running away from something, or someone, in their lives.

There was an hour to wait before boarding, and although this was going to be an hour too many for Fergus to spend in Loadman's company, he had no choice. He took out his book and began reading. Loadman attempted several times to engage him in conversation but, failing, took to reading the newspaper an earlier passenger had left on a seat.

The hour turned into an hour and a half and it was with great relief that Fergus heard the Melbourne passengers called. They deposited his luggage with a crewman then made their way to the gangway, where a small queue had formed, and waited in line. Eventually, moving far too slowly for Fergus's liking, they arrived at the top. He handed over Loadman's ticket.

Loadman leaned in close and said, 'I could have been Rory's father, you know, if Amy hadn't run off with my brother. She was mine and he took her.'

Fergus was taken aback. *That's why there was such bad blood between the brothers.* He ignored the comment and produced the money, handing it over to Loadman.

'How can I be sure it's all there?' Loadman asked, fingering the pouch.

Fergus shrugged. 'You can check, but everyone will see what you're doing and what you've got.'

Loadman appeared to consider this, then, weighing the pouch in his hand, said, 'Feels about right.'

'It's all there because, unlike you, I am an honest man.' A man he assumed was first mate was passing. Fergus stopped him and handed him a pound note, saying, 'This keeps him on board and sees he doesn't jump ship in Madeira.'

'Aye,' said the first mate, 'only crew released to set foot on land there.' He took the money with a dead-pan face, folded it, then pocketed it. 'Since you're not travelling with us, sir,' he said, 'I must ask you to leave. However, you're welcome to watch the ship depart in about an hour.'

Fergus thanked him. *I have to see it leave with him on board.*

He found a spot on the quay near some old barrels and untidy ropes, where he could watch the gangway. He hadn't eaten since breakfast and he should have been hungry, but he wasn't. He waited over an hour. The first loosening of the tight spring inside him came when the gangway was closed off. The second loosening came when there was a clear gap between ship and quay. As the distance between vessel and land grew wider, Fergus felt the tightness of his previous despair uncoil more and more. He was still too tense to be euphoric, but he felt a huge surge of joy. It had cost him dear financially, at a time when he was short of money, but he was of the solid opinion every single penny could not have been better invested to secure Rory's future.

CHAPTER THIRTY-SEVEN

Back in Whitehaven, Fergus reported to the head constable. He was shown in immediately and Mr Mastin rose from his desk to greet him and shake his hand.

'The news is all over the town that Rory is back. I've been waiting for you for the details. As I said when you told me of the latest developments, and let me say again, I would never have let him go if I had known.'

Shutting the stable door after the horse has bolted.

Fergus gave Mr Mastin a tight smile. 'Rory is subdued and shocked, but steady in his mind. He'll recover.'

'That is a relief. And Loadman?'

Omitting most of the detail, Fergus related how they'd found Rory and decided not to detain Loadman, fearing for their own and Rory's safety.

'I instructed Sven to take Rory back to Lancaster and I followed a short time afterwards. I thought it prudent to watch from a distance and make sure enough time had elapsed for them to get away. Then I spoke with Loadman and he ran off.'

'You did not think to alert the police?'

'There were only a few policemen on the periphery of a crowd that must have numbered a thousand or more. I may have made the wrong decision, but to me Rory's safety was my priority.'

Mr Mastin sucked in his cheeks. 'I understand your wish not to draw attention to yourselves and the boy and, with a crowd that size, the local police would most certainly have been reluctant to act. A pity, though. I suppose he must have hunted for the lad and, not finding him, would be cautious of his own position as an abductor. You didn't return until today?'

'I had business to attend to in Liverpool.'

'That is unfortunate, causing a delay in tracking Loadman down. However, I expect he is long gone.'

'I would think so too.'

'I will report to Carlisle since this case is listed there, but to be honest, Mr Shackleton, with the boy safe and cared for, this missing fighter will not be high on their immediate concerns. You see, a man like that is not worth tracking down, when it's more than likely he'll come to their notice through some new misdemeanour, or else will appear at another fighting event, and can be tracked from there. I think we can be certain he won't be reporting the disappearance of his so-called son.'

'You're saying as far as the police are concerned, here and in Carlisle, he will be found eventually and be dealt with?'

'I know it's not ideal, but the lad is safe and in good health. That's surely the main thing. Perhaps keep an eye on the boy, although I don't think you'll hear from Loadman again.'

Fergus shook his head. 'Neither do I. Do you want to speak with Rory?'

Mr Mastin cast a glance at the pile of files and papers on his desk. 'I'll call by the Indian King later to check. No need to interview him formally.'

It was clear to Fergus that the head constable was anxious to file the case away. Partly, he guessed, due to his own involvement in authorising Rory's abduction, albeit unknowingly and within the confines of the law.

As he went home to see Becky, Fergus mulled over the meeting. *That couldn't have gone any better. I didn't lie – all I did was not divulge the whole truth.*

Fergus found Becky alone at Coates Lane. They embraced and, closing his eyes, he took a deep breath and drew in her familiar perfume. Her face was towards the light, where the distinctive colour of her eyes, with their unusual grey, was even more pronounced than usual.

He brushed back a lock of hair from where it had fallen over her face. 'I missed you,' he said.

'I missed you, too.' She stepped back. 'Are you all right? Let me look at you.'

'Don't worry – nothing has befallen me. Where's Rory?'

'Ma thought it best for him to stay where it's lively and he has a lot of company. He's well enough, but when I first saw him, I couldn't believe the change in such a short time.'

'Sven and I felt the same. Is he still listless?'

'Charlie brings him out of his shell, but there are times

when he seems to retreat into his own thoughts. What happened? Tell me all while I make us a pot of coffee.'

After he'd given her a broad outline of events, she asked, 'How was your business in Liverpool?'

'It was a question of settling an account and signing some paperwork.' He was relieved when she made no further enquiry.

She handed him a letter. 'This came for you. Mr Todhunter dropped it off.'

Fergus opened it up and frowned.

'What's the matter? You've gone pale. It's about the *Ketton*, isn't it? Is there something wrong with her?'

'The other buyer has put in a higher offer.'

'And we can't match it?'

'No.'

'Is there nothing we can do?'

'Not unless I mortgage our home. Both the company and myself are stretched to the limit.' He couldn't tell Becky that the money he'd given to Loadman had tipped the balance between having enough and being short – that he'd withdrawn money that would have secured the *Ketton* for them.

He sat down and put his head between his hands. 'That's it then. We could have scraped by with the contract from Macintosh & Warrilow, but I have no funds left to increase our offer.'

Becky put her hand on his shoulder. 'After all the work and effort you and Bill have put in.'

'Bill's wife will be pleased she's not going to be losing him for six months.'

'She may yet lose him,' said Becky.

'I don't see how.'

'We can mortgage this house.'

Fergus gave a short laugh. 'No, I don't want to do that.'

'Neither do I, but we could do it. You'll hear any day from Glasgow. We can begin negotiations for the *Ketton* and drag them out a bit, until we hear for definite. Then, if we get the contract, we'll go ahead.'

'You realise, under those circumstances, if the *Ketton* were to go down with all hands there would be no profits. We and our investors would lose our money. We would lose everything bar the insurance, and that wouldn't be enough for us to carry on. Father would disown me, because I would have to sell my Shackleton & Company shares to pay off my creditors, which would mean twenty-five percent of Shackletons being owned by outsiders. Added to all that, I would lose all Aunt Louisa's inheritance.'

'If that happens, then I'll set up a haberdashery business.'

'You're not joking, are you?'

'No, I'm not. What if our ship comes in?'

'Then we'll make a lot of money.'

'Put in an offer tomorrow. I've not come from money, and I can go back to not having any. Can you?'

Fergus thought. 'Yes, if I have you by my side during the day and to warm our bed at night.'

* * *

The following afternoon, Becky had an appointment to see Dr Fincham that she'd kept from Fergus.

He greeted her and beckoned her to take a seat. 'What brings you to see me today?' he said kindly.

Becky was suddenly embarrassed. She'd spent all morning rehearsing what she was going to say before she left home. It was quite straightforward, but now she was sitting opposite the doctor, she was unexpectedly tongue-tied.

Dr Fincham smiled encouragingly. 'I can assure you that in my profession, at my age, there is nothing I have not heard before.'

Becky nodded.

'Are you in pain?' he asked.

She shook her head. 'There's probably nothing wrong with me, but I just had to come.'

Dr Fincham dipped his pen and reached for a piece of paper. 'There's something that's keeping you awake at night?'

'Yes. Other people's expectations of me.'

'And those expectations are?'

'That by now I should be...' Becky trailed off. She felt silly. She'd allowed senseless early morning worries to continue during the day.

'Perhaps I can help you. Are we talking about a child?'

'Yes,' said Becky, relieved that the correct subject had been raised. 'My mother and Fergus's parents are anxious for a grandchild, and other people make jokes. They all want me to be expecting. They buy me baby clothes, and talk about how my life will change when I'm a mother.'

'And Fergus?'

'People don't talk to Fergus about it like they do to me. It's when I'm on my own.'

Dr Fincham put his pen back in its holder and moved

the piece of paper to one side. 'My dear Becky, this is a personal matter between you and Fergus, and I can appreciate the distress other people's comments are causing you. I doubt they realise that by expressing their hopes they are causing you embarrassment.'

'What if I can't have bairns?'

His eyes twinkled. I have no fears there is anything amiss. You are young, recently married, both you and Fergus are healthy. You have given me no reason to think there will be a problem.'

'There is nothing wrong with me that I know of. I do want children and so does Fergus. I'm sure of that.'

'You will appreciate that on the ships, childbirth was not a concern of mine. However, in Mauritius I tended many of the young wives and delivered their babies, so I am not without experience. I can tell you that, contrary to what many people think, pregnancies do not always occur within a few months of marriage. It can take a while, even a year or more, and not all first pregnancies come to term. This can cause distress, but it's nature's way.'

'So, there's no need to worry?'

'Certainly not. In fact, I would have been surprised had you told me today that you were expecting a baby. Does that put your mind at rest?'

'Aye,' said Becky. 'It does.'

'Do you want a child so soon? Would you not like time with Fergus and Rory, without the distraction of an infant?'

'I feel it's expected. That it's my role.'

'Is it the role *you* want, or what other people are deciding for you?'

Becky was thinking about the two matinée jackets she'd already made in anticipation. 'A bairn is what's expected of me.'

'My advice is not to worry. I have no doubts that in due course a baby will appear. Until then, you must try your best to ignore people's comments and innuendos.'

Becky left the surgery and strolled down to the harbour to watch the crews loading and unloading the ships. A barrel organ was playing and some children were dancing to it, watched by their mothers. Dr Fincham was right – the starting of their family was no one else's business. She felt better since he'd explained it could take some time, although she hadn't been as truthful as she might have been. The comments upset her because she *did* want a baby – but did she want a child to give meaning to her existence as a wife? To give herself something to do?

A pair of gulls close by began fighting over a damp bread crust and the harshness of their cawing broke into her thoughts. Of one thing she was certain: although she wasn't sure exactly what she wanted, Fergus made her happy, and wasn't that the best thing in the world?

* * *

Early on Monday, Fergus asked Dicken, 'Can you find me a rabbit? A white one.'

'All the butchers sell rabbits, but I don't remember ever seeing a white one hanging up. Do they taste different?'

'Not a dead one. A live one. I promised Rory.'

'Oh, that kind of rabbit. There's sometimes a man in the market has live ones. Does it have to be white?'

'Perhaps not.'

‘Where are you going to keep it?’

‘I don’t know. My promise was made in the heat of the moment, and now I think about it, neither the Indian King, nor Coates Lane have anywhere suitable.’

Dicken held out several letters. ‘There’s post for you.’

Fergus sat at his desk and flicked through them until he came to one from Glasgow. He put the others to one side, picked up his paper knife and hesitated. *In a moment I may be facing a promising future, or all the work of the last few months will come to nothing.*

He opened the letter and read.

‘*19th June 1861*

Dear Mr Shackleton, Sir,

We are in receipt of your communication of the 9th inst and reply herewith.

We are pleased to reply that your quotation, terms and conditions are acceptable. We enclose a signed pro forma and further details. Should the third week of July be acceptable to you for collection from Glasgow, we look forward to receiving your Letter of Acknowledgement. Further details can be discussed in the near future.

Yours Truly,

Guthrie Macintosh
Macintosh & Warrilow,
Weston Works,
Cook St.,
Glasgow’

For a full two minutes, Fergus sat and stared at the letter, while his brain did somersaults in his head. Then he broke out one of his widest smiles. *It's going to be a busy day. I've a ship to purchase, a contract to finalise and enquiries to make regarding a mortgage – although if Macintosh & Warrilow make their first instalment on time, the latter should prove unnecessary.*

'Dicken, whatever you're doing, put it away. I have to go out, and I want you to draw up a Letter of Acknowledgement to this.' He handed over the letter. 'I'll sign it when I've seen to my business.'

* * *

After Fergus had seen Jeremiah Todhunter, who confirmed their offer on the *SS Ketton* had been accepted, Fergus rushed home to see Becky.

'We have a future,' he shouted, as soon as he was in the house.

'They want you to go to Mauritius?'

'Indeed they do,' he said, putting his arms around her waist and swinging her around.

'Stop, you're making me dizzy! When will you collect? And will the money come in time?'

'The third week of July, which means the first payment will come at the end of this month.'

'In time for us not to mortgage our house?'

'All being well. We'll have the loans and my capital invested, but the horizon looks a lot less choppy now.'

'That just leaves us with one very small problem.'

'What's that?

'Rory's rabbit. He keeps talking about it.'

'I've every intention of getting him one,' Fergus said, 'but where to put it?'

'I've been thinking. There's room for a hutch and small run at Queen Street. Why don't you have a quiet word with your ma? If the staff are prepared to see to it while Rory's at sea, that will be ideal. And they will have plenty of leftovers to feed it with.'

'She'll have a fit.'

'I don't think she will. She was so upset about Rory, she sobbed when she was here. And she's been making a fuss of him since he came back. I suspect there's a budding friendship there.'

'That's a surprise.'

'You would have noticed if you weren't so busy.'

Fergus shrugged.

'You need to explain to Rory that he's not going to Mauritius with the *Ketton*,' Becky went on. 'He knows all about it.'

'He's too young, and besides, Nicholas says he needs feeding up. Rory told him Loadman only gave him one proper meal a day. Lack of funds, I suppose.'

'Do you think Loadman will reappear?'

'No, I don't. He's a wanted man.'

On the train to Whitehaven, Fergus had reaffirmed to himself he would never tell anyone, including Becky, how he'd paid off Loadman and stood on the dock and watched the ship head off down the Mersey. No one – not even on his deathbed. It was his secret, and some secrets were best taken to the grave.

* * *

The next day, Fergus signed the Letter of Acknowledgement and sent Dicken off with it for the post-boat. The previous evening, he'd asked Rory if he would take on the task of checking off a delivery from Cockermouth at the warehouse, thinking it was better to keep him busy than have him dwelling on the previous three weeks.

When Rory arrived to begin work, Fergus thought he seemed more his old self, but the new sadness in his eyes remained. Charlie's company would be a big help in teasing out the old Rory.

'Are you happy to be back in Whitehaven?' he asked.

'Aye, it's my home.' There was a pause, and then Rory said, 'Mrs Dolly told me that man wasn't my real da. Is that right?'

'Yes. He was your father's brother. Your uncle.'

'Mrs Becky said that, too. Will he come back for me again?'

'No. I can promise you that.'

'Like you promised me the rabbit?'

Fergus didn't know what to say. The two promises rested on such different foundations. Perhaps an eleven-year-old saw things simply as 'a promise is a promise'.

'When you're older, you'll understand everything that's happened.'

'If he were my uncle, where is my da?'

Fergus had been expecting this question. The family had all agreed to wait until Rory asked, thinking it better he asked for himself than be fed information before he was ready. As the moment had arrived, Fergus thought it best to tell the truth, but slowly.

'I'm sorry to say that your father passed away.'

'Like Nan and Mammy?'

'Yes.'

'I won't ever see him?'

'No.'

'Then will I be your ward again?'

'I hope so. I've asked Mr Needham to sort that out for us.'

Rory thought things through. 'What did my da die of?'

'He was poorly, like your mother.'

'Where did he die?'

'In Carlisle.' *Please don't ask where.*

'I really am an orphan?'

'Yes, you are, but there are plenty of people who care for you and want the best for you. You are not alone in this world.'

'That man didn't care for me, like you and Mrs Dolly and Miss Becky. I've got my boils back.'

'Was he unkind to you?'

'Sometimes he shouted at me and held me tightly, and he smacked me a couple of times when he said I was bad, but I don't think he knew how to look after a lad. One time he wanted me to drink beer, and another time some gin.'

'And did you?'

Rory shook his head. 'Mrs Dolly always told me I must never drink anything from the bar, because it will make me proper poorly. Or smoke a cigar or a pipe.'

'She's taught you well.'

'I might try a pipe when I'm fifteen and indentured like the other apprentices. Anyway, I've been thinking, seeing as how you and Miss Becky are married, shouldn't I be calling Becky Mrs Becky?'

When Fergus related their conversation to Becky, he said, 'And that was that. Nothing more was said about his father or Loadman. Perhaps he's closed that chapter of his life.'

'Perhaps, but it's not the end of the book. He'll have to be told the truth one day.'

THE DEPARTURE

The third week of July, 1861

Word spread rapidly through the town that the Louisa Line's *SS Ketton* was leaving for Glasgow and Mauritius and, as a result, a huge crowd gathered on the quay to see her off. The rope factory brass band, in uniform, was playing enthusiastically. Dicken was giving out commemorative handbills. When he'd first seen them, he'd declared them a waste of money. However, when Fergus suggested he might like to ask his new friend, Miss Evangelina from Croxall's Stationery and Bookshop, to help, he'd coloured up before declaring perhaps they were a good idea, after all.

The quay was thronged with relatives, friends, and townsfolk, all watching the last-minute preparations being made on board. Ropes were inspected and the last batch of fresh supplies from Frisby's loaded. The crew waved and called to their loved ones. Mary, eyes red-rimmed, was standing next to her mother, holding William, the new baby. Earlier in the week she'd confided in Becky that she had a terrible feeling she was never going to see Bill again. Becky had done her best to comfort her, but they both knew it would be an eventful voyage, with so many miles to be covered.

A special area had been roped off for the private investors and influential townspeople. Drinks were being served within it, and staff from Queen Street moved smoothly amongst the guests, offering delicate pastries on silver salvers.

Elizabeth sought out Rory, who was standing beside Becky. 'I've heard you're disappointed not to be going with them,' she told him. 'But you will another time when you're older, I'm sure. I looked in on your rabbit this morning. I think he likes it at Queen Street. The staff give him a lot of cabbage leaves and Cook tells me he's very fond of basil.'

'It's reet grand of you to have taken him in. Reet grand.'

Elizabeth beamed at Becky, who was thinking, *this time last year I never would have imagined Elizabeth and Rory might become firm friends.*

With Bill having briefly left the ship to stand by Fergus's side, and the band taking an ale break, Fergus gave a short speech wishing all a safe voyage. He thanked the harbour master for allowing them to hold the festivities, which he referred to as 'The *SS Ketton* Farewell Jamboree'. He also took the opportunity to make a brief public mention of the need for a wet dock. Rector Longrigg was then invited to say a prayer to bless the ship and all who sailed in her, which he carried out with much aplomb.

Afterwards, Fergus spoke briefly to Nicholas Fincham, who was laughing and issuing congratulations. As they parted, he saw his father making his way towards him.

'You've done me proud, son. There's more than a bit of my father in you.'

Finding Hector's words unexpectedly comforting, Fergus replied, 'And a lot of you too.'

'Maybe. My father had a saying: "In the shipping business, you're only as good as the thickness of your hull".'

'The *SS Ketton* is a sound ship, Father. Look at her – and she's in the hands of an experienced master, with a tried and tested crew.'

'There was greater meaning to my father's words than the physical strength of the ship, son. He was also talking about the man in charge, the man carrying the responsibility on his shoulders for the ship and her crew. In this case, it's you. You're only as good as the strength of *your* hull.'

Fergus thought for a moment, then said, 'And how strong is *my* hull, Father?'

'Strong enough for the shipping business. I've no doubts on that now. You've proved yourself to me and to others.'

THE END

ACKNOWLEDGEMENTS

Once again, I found much to inspire me in the Cumbrian archives in Whitehaven and I thank the archivists for their help and support. In particular I sourced information concerning discussions on Whitehaven's dry dock, seamen's wages, Isaac Dickinson's diary 1860 – 62, Whittle's ironmongers, the Brigantine 'Kitty' and various law suits.

My thanks also to the University of Glasgow Library for finding and forwarding fascinating information from Mirlees, Watson's & Co's order book regarding the shipping of sugar production parts to Mauritius in 1860 – 62 ref: UGD 118/2/411

Similarly, thanks to the Research Officer at the Liverpool Record Office who confirmed that the last meeting at Crosby race course was in 1876 when I was wondering if I should set the bare-knuckle fighting near Liverpool or in Carnforth.

Special thanks to my beta readers for providing valuable feedback: Carrie Armitage, Mike Bird, Jeremy Gibbs, Pat Langridge, Carol Meads, and Dr Christopher Roberts. Thank you all. Each one of you has contributed to, and improved, this novel.

When I was staying in Whitehaven during the summer of 2023, Jackey Savage not only personally made me feel welcome, but went the extra mile by researching the address in Queen St where I was staying. Her online Streets of Whitehaven Through Time - learning about those who lived behind the doors, is to be highly recommended.

Margaret Mcgee kindly pointed out an incorrect spelling of Cumbrian dialogue in an earlier book which I have corrected in this novel. This is much appreciated.

Michael Moon Books of Lowther St, Whitehaven have been supportive and informative and my library on Whitehaven and shipping in general grows as a result.

Once again, I thank my excellent production team: My editor Helena Fairfax, My proofreader Julia Gibbs, and my publisher Sarah Houldcroft of Goldcrest Books. They all encourage and support me. My cover is designed by Tim Barber of Dissect Designs.

My Romantic Novelist Association author friends in the Belmont Belles and Beaux are a great source of inspiration and provide like-minded friendship. I'd find it hard without you all to call upon when I need assistance. Lizzie Lamb, Sue Moorcroft, Madlyn Morgan, Ros Rendle, and Adrienne Vaughan to name, but a few.

Thanks to the family of course, and to Jim, my husband, who lives it all with me on a daily basis.

ABOUT THE AUTHOR

Lorna was born and brought up in the UK. Her forebears on her mother's side fled the Irish famine in the 19th century to settle in Parton, near Whitehaven in Cumberland. In the mid-1850s they emigrated to Vancouver Island, Canada, to open up the new coal mines. Coal was also important to Lorna's father's side of the family as they were involved in the coal-trading business with Coote and Warren, covering East Anglia and the north London suburbs.

After teaching the piano and raising a family, Lorna exhibited and lectured on antique Chinese textiles in the UK, New York, China and Hong Kong. Following on from that she studied and taught at the School of Oriental and African Studies (SOAS) in London gaining a doctorate in Chinese history. She now writes historical fiction full time and lives in Stamford in a very old house with stone walls and lots of beams. Just the place for a historian. She is very fond of rabbits.

Contact Lorna

www.lornahunting.com

X: @lornahunting

Facebook: @huntinglorna

Instagram: lornahunting

Threads: @lornahunting

Blue Sky: @lornahunting

If you've read and enjoyed this book, please leave a review on Amazon or Goodreads.

ALSO BY LORNA HUNTING

All books available from Amazon

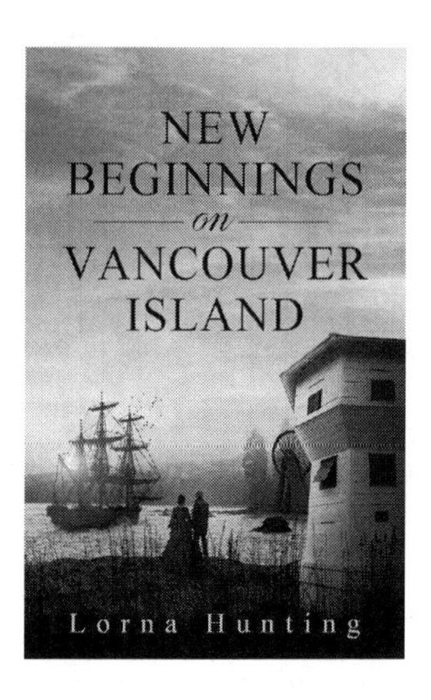

The year is 1854 and Stag Liddell, a young collier from Liverpool, signs up to work in Vancouver Island's new coal mines. Whilst waiting for his ship to Canada, he meets ambitious school teacher Kate McAvoy who is also making the trip.

As the ship nears its destination, Stag and Kate's relationship begins to blossom, but damning information comes to light and a pact made years before comes into play.

Will their budding romance survive these devastating revelations? And will they both achieve their dreams in this new land?

5* Reviews for *New Beginnings on Vancouver Island*

'This is not merely a fascinating "good read" it is also a wonderful learning experience of 19th Century life and culture in Cumbria of the time; the hazardous sea-faring travelling to the "New World" with its dangers round the Cape, it's harsh on board traditions and class divisions; culminating in the uncertain life expectations for new people joining earlier settlers on Vancouver Island, all hoping to extend their often tenuous hold on life itself. Altogether an excellent and well researched historical novel which leaves us wanting more!'

'A great debut novel. In depth characters to hold one's imagination and visualise how tough travel would have been. Obviously much research has gone into this with very readable results. Look forward to the next one.'

'This book... is a cross between a history book and a novel. It is particularly well-written and the author clearly has a love for the subject matter. With an explosive start, the reader is drawn on. I enjoyed the relationships within the story, although these almost played a supporting role to the historical facts. I look forward to the next book by this author.'

'This is a well-researched story with a compelling plot which above all is a good read. Some parts are predictable, but others are not, and the trauma of such a long voyage round Cape Horn is thought provoking in its detail. This was real travel, and not for the faint hearted. Most enjoyable.'

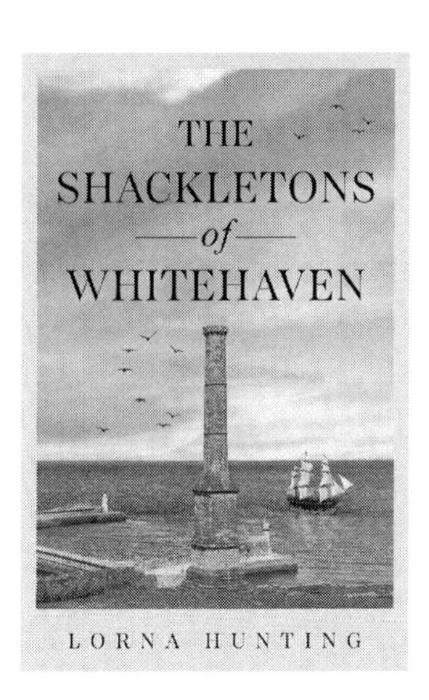

Will book-loving Fergus Shackleton find success in business and love despite his overbearing father, Hector?

By forging his own path is Fergus going to turn into his father, the very person he is trying to escape?

Is chasing success going to change Fergus so much that his girlfriend, Becky, is forced to doubt their future together?

Will the price of success be a broken heart?

5* Review for *The Shackletons of Whitehaven*

'The characters were relatable, the setting vivid, and the plot highly engaging. The book is beautifully written and as I was drawn into the story I found I couldn't put it down. I highly recommend this book and can't wait to read more by this author! Five stars!

Grace Williams, a young English missionary, arrives in Colville, Vancouver, in 1857 to find the community neither wants nor seems to need her. When her superior, Reverend Palmer, disappears into the snowy woods, on a foolhardy mission to seek converts amongst the Salish First Nations people, Grace is left behind to oversee their mission. There are no half-measures in this place where they do things differently, and she is forced to find self-confidence and rise to the challenge.

Grace is grateful to Sam Gray, a widower, and Long Ben Sloane, the sawmill manager, who befriend and aid her in her mission to improve people's lives and find acceptance. In this wild outpost, the two men become an invaluable support, but only one will win her heart...

Printed in Great Britain
by Amazon